ROAR

Cecelia Ahern is one of the biggest selling authors to emerge in the past fifteen years. Her novels have been translated into thirty-five languages and have sold more than twenty-five million copies in over fifty countries. Two of her books have been adapted as films and she has created several TV series.

She and her books have won numerous awards, including the Irish Book Award for Popular Fiction for *The Year I Met You* in 2014. *PS, I Love You* was awarded two Platinum Awards at the 2018 Specsavers Bestsellers Awards, for UK and Ireland.

Cecelia lives in Dublin.

Roar is also available on audio, read by Aisling Bea, Adjoa Andoh and Lara Sawalha.

🐦 @Cecelia_Ahern
📷 @official_CeceliaAhern
www.cecelia-ahern.com

Also by Cecelia Ahern

PS, I Love You
Where Rainbows End
If You Could See Me Now
A Place Called Here
Thanks for the Memories
The Gift
The Book of Tomorrow
The Time of My Life
One Hundred Names
How to Fall in Love
The Year I Met You
The Marble Collector
Lyrebird

Young Adult novels
Flawed
Perfect

ROAR

CECELIA AHERN

HarperCollins*Publishers*

HarperCollins*Publishers*
1 London Bridge Street
London SE1 9GF

www.harpercollins.co.uk

First published by HarperCollins*Publishers* 2018
This edition published 2019
2

Copyright © Cecelia Ahern 2018

Cecelia Ahern asserts the moral right to
be identified as the author of this work

A catalogue record for this book
is available from the British Library

ISBN: 978-0-00-828353-7
Export A format: 978-0-00-828354-4

Typeset in Sabon LT Std by Palimpsest Book Production Limited,
Falkirk, Stirlingshire

Printed and bound in Great Britain by CPI Group (UK) Ltd, Croydon CR0 4YY

For all the women who . . .

I am woman, hear me roar, in numbers too big to ignore.
Helen Reddy and Ray Burton

Contents

1

The Woman Who Slowly Disappeared

1

There's a gentle knock on the door before it opens. Nurse Rada steps inside and closes the door behind her.

'I'm here,' the woman says, quietly.

Rada scans the room, following the sound of her voice.

'I'm here, I'm here, I'm here, I'm here,' the woman repeats softly, until Rada stops searching.

Her eye level is too high and it's focused too much to the left, more in line with the bird poo on the window that has eroded over the past three days with the rain.

The woman sighs gently from her seat on the window ledge that overlooks the college campus. She entered this university hospital feeling so hopeful that she could be healed, but instead, after six months, she feels like a lab rat, poked and prodded at by scientists and doctors in increasingly desperate efforts to understand her condition.

She has been diagnosed with a rare complex genetic disorder that causes the chromosomes in her body to fade away. They are not self-destructing or breaking down, they are not even mutating – her organ functions all appear perfectly normal; all tests indicate that everything is fine and healthy. To put it simply, she's disappearing, but she's still here.

Her disappearing was gradual at first. Barely noticeable. There was a lot of, 'Oh, I didn't see you there,' a lot of misjudging her edges, bumping against her shoulders, stepping on her toes, but it didn't ring any alarm bells. Not at first.

She faded in equal measure. It wasn't a missing hand or a missing toe or suddenly a missing ear, it was a gradual equal fade; she diminished. She became a shimmer, like a heat haze on a highway. She was a faint outline with a wobbly centre. If you strained your eye, you could just about make out she was there, depending on the background and the surroundings. She quickly figured out that the more cluttered and busily decorated the room was, the easier it was for her to be seen. She was practically invisible in front of a plain wall. She sought out patterned wallpaper as her canvas, decorative chair fabrics to sit on; that way, her figure blurred the patterns, gave people cause to squint and take a second look. Even when practically invisible, she was still fighting to be seen.

Scientists and doctors have examined her for months, journalists have interviewed her, photographers have done their best to light and capture her, but none of them were necessarily trying to help her recover. In fact, as caring and sweet as some of them have been, the worse her predicament has grown, the more excited they've become. She's fading away and nobody, not even the world's best experts, knows why.

'A letter arrived for you,' Rada says, stealing her from her thoughts. 'I think you'll want to read this one straight away.'

Curiosity piqued, the woman abandons her thoughts. 'I'm here, I'm here, I'm here, I'm here,' she says quietly, as she has been instructed to do. Rada follows the sound of her voice, crisp envelope in her extended hand. She holds it out to the air.

'Thank you,' the woman says, taking the envelope from her and studying it. Though it's a sophisticated shade of dusty pink, it reminds her of a child's birthday party invitation and she feels the same lift of excitement. Rada is eager, which makes the woman curious. Receiving mail is not unusual – she receives dozens of letters every week from all around the world; experts selling themselves, sycophants wanting to befriend her, religious fundamentalists wishing to banish her, sleazy men pleading to indulge every kind of corrupt desire on a woman they can feel but can't see. Though she'll admit this envelope does feel different to the rest, with her name written grandly in calligraphy.

'I recognize the envelope,' Rada replies, excited, sitting beside her.

She is careful in opening the expensive envelope. It has a luxurious feel, and there's something deeply promising and comforting about it. She slides the handwritten notecard from the envelope.

'Professor Elizabeth Montgomery,' they read in unison.

'I knew it. This is it!' Rada says, reaching for the woman's hand that holds the note, and squeezing.

2

'I'm here, I'm here, I'm here, I'm here, I'm here,' the woman repeats, as the medical team assist her with her move to the new facility that will be her home for who knows how long. Rada and the few nurses she has grown close to accompany her from her bedroom to the awaiting limousine that Professor Elizabeth Montgomery has sent for her. Not all the consultants have gathered to say goodbye; the absences are a protest against her leaving after all of their work and dedication to her cause.

'I'm in,' she says quietly, and the door closes.

3

There is no physical pain in disappearing. Emotionally, it's another matter.

The emotional feeling of vanishing began in her early fifties, but she only became aware of the physical dissipation three years ago. The process was slow but steady. She would hear,

'I didn't see you there,' or 'I didn't hear you sneak in,' or a colleague would stop a conversation to fill her in on the beginning of a story that she'd already heard because she'd been there the entire time. She became tired of reminding them she was there from the start, and the frequency of those comments worried her. She started wearing brighter clothes, she highlighted her hair, she spoke more loudly, airing her opinions, she stomped as she walked; anything to stand out from the crowd. She wanted to physically take hold of people's cheeks and turn them in her direction, to force eye contact. She wanted to yell, *Look at me!*

On the worst days she would go home feeling completely overwhelmed and desperate. She would look in the mirror just to make sure she was still there, to keep reminding herself of that fact; she even took to carrying a pocket mirror for those moments on the subway when she was sure she had vanished.

She grew up in Boston then moved to New York City. She'd thought that a city of eight million people would be an ideal place to find friendship, love, relationships, start a life. And for a long time she was right, but in recent years she'd learned that the more people there were, the lonelier she felt. Because her loneliness was amplified. She's on leave now, but before that she worked for a global financial services company with 150,000 employees spread over 156 countries. Her office building on Park Avenue had almost three thousand employees and yet as the years went by she increasingly felt overlooked and unseen.

At thirty-eight she entered premature menopause. It was intense, sweat saturating the bed, often to the point she'd have to change the sheets twice a night. Inside, she felt an explosive anger and frustration. She wanted to be alone during those years. Certain fabrics irritated her skin and flared her hot flushes, which in turn flared her temper. In two years she gained twenty pounds. She purchased new clothes but nothing felt right or fit right. She was uncomfortable in her own skin, felt insecure at male-dominated meetings that she'd previously felt at home in. It seemed to her that every man in the room knew, that everyone could see the sudden whoosh as her neck reddened and her face perspired, as her clothes stuck to her skin in the middle of a presentation or on a business lunch. She didn't want anybody to look at her during that period. She didn't want anyone to see her.

When out at night she would see the beautiful young bodies in tiny dresses and ridiculously high-heeled shoes, writhing to songs that she knew and could sing along to because she still lived on this planet even though it was no longer tailored to her, while men her own age paid more attention to the young women on the dance floor than to her.

Even now, she is still a valid person with something to offer the world, yet she doesn't feel it.

'Diminishing Woman' and 'Disappearing Woman' the newspaper reports have labelled her; at fifty-eight years old she has made headlines worldwide. Specialists have flown in from around the world to probe her body and mind, only to go away again, unable to come to any conclusions. Despite this, many papers have been written, awards bestowed, plaudits given to the masters of their specialized fields.

It has been six months since her last fade. She is merely a shimmer now, and she is exhausted. She knows that they can't fix her; she watches each specialist arrive with enthusiasm, examine her with excitement, and then leave weary. Each time she witnesses the loss of their hope, it erodes her own.

4

As she approaches Provincetown, Cape Cod, her new destination, uncertainty and fear make way for hope at the sight before her. Professor Elizabeth Montgomery waits at the door of her practice; once an abandoned lighthouse, it now stands as a grand beacon of hope.

The driver opens the door. The woman steps out.

'I'm here, I'm here, I'm here, I'm here,' the woman says, making her way up the path to meet her.

'What on earth are you saying?' Professor Montgomery asks, frowning.

'I was told to say that, at the hospital,' she says, quietly. 'So people know where I am.'

'No, no, no, you don't speak like that here,' the professor says, her tone brusque.

The woman feels scolded at first, and upset she has put

a foot wrong in her first minute upon arriving, but then she realizes that Professor Montgomery has looked her directly in the eye, has wrapped a welcoming cashmere blanket around her shoulders and is walking her up the steps to the lighthouse while the driver takes the bags. It is the first eye contact she has had with somebody, other than the campus cat, for quite some time.

'Welcome to the Montgomery Lighthouse Advance for Women,' Professor Montgomery begins, leading her into the building. 'It's a little wordy, and narcissistic, but it has stuck. At the beginning we called it the "Montgomery *Retreat* for Women" but I soon changed that. To retreat seems negative; the act of moving away from something difficult, dangerous or disagreeable. Flinch, recoil, shrink, disengage. No. Not here. Here we do the opposite. We advance. We move forward, we make progress, we lift up, we grow.'

Yes, yes, yes, this is what she needs. No going back, no looking back.

Dr Montgomery leads her to the check-in area. The lighthouse, while beautiful, feels eerily empty.

'Tiana, this is our new guest.'

Tiana looks her straight in the eye, and hands her a room key. 'You're very welcome.'

'Thank you,' the woman whispers. 'How did she see me?' she asks.

Dr Montgomery squeezes her shoulder comfortingly. 'Much to do. Let's begin, shall we?'

Their first session takes place in a room overlooking Race

Point beach. Hearing the crash of the waves, smelling the salty air, the scented candles, the call of the gulls, away from the typical sterile hospital environment that had served as her fortress, the woman allows herself to relax.

Professor Elizabeth Montgomery, sixty-six years old, oozing with brains and qualifications, six children, one divorce, two marriages, and the most glamorous woman she has ever seen in the flesh, sits in a straw chair softened by overflowing cushions, and pours peppermint tea into clashing teacups.

'My theory,' Professor Montgomery says, folding her legs close to her body, 'is that you made yourself disappear.'

'*I* did this?' the woman asks, hearing her voice rise, feeling the flash of her anger as her brief moment is broken.

Professor Montgomery smiles that beautiful smile. 'I don't place the blame solely on you. You can share it with *society*. I blame the adulation and sexualization of young women. I blame the focus on beauty and appearance, the pressure to conform to others' expectations in a way that men are not required to.'

Her voice is hypnotizing. It is gentle. It is firm. It is without anger. Or judgement. Or bitterness. Or sadness. It just is. Because everything just is.

The woman has goosebumps on her skin. She sits up, her heart pounding. This is something she hasn't heard before. The first new theory in many months and it stirs her physically and emotionally.

'As you can imagine, many of my male counterparts don't

agree with me,' she says wryly, sipping on her tea. 'It's a difficult pill to swallow. For them. So I started doing my own thing. You are not the first disappearing woman that I've met.' The woman gapes. 'I tested and analysed women, just as those experts did with you, but it took me some time to realize how to correctly treat your condition. It took growing older myself to truly understand.

'I have studied and written about this extensively; as women age, they are written out of the world, no longer visible on television or film, in fashion magazines, and only ever on daytime TV to advertise the breakdown of bodily functions and ailments, or promote potions and lotions to help battle ageing as though it were something that must be fought. Sound familiar?'

The woman nods.

She continues: 'Older women are represented on television as envious witches who spoil the prospects of the man or younger woman, or as humans who are reactive to others, powerless to direct their own lives; moreover, once they reach fifty-five, their television demographic ceases to exist. It is as if they are not here. Confronted with this, I have discovered women can internalize these "realities". My teachings have been disparaged as feminist rants but I am not ranting, I am merely observing.' She sips her peppermint tea and watches the woman who slowly disappeared, slowly come to terms with what she is hearing.

'You've seen women like me before?' the woman asks, still stunned.

'Tiana, at the desk, was exactly as you were when she arrived two years ago.'

She allows that to sink in.

'Who did you see when you entered?' the Professor asks.

'Tiana,' the woman replies.

'Who else?'

'You.'

'Who else?'

'Nobody.'

'Look again.'

5

The woman stands and walks to the window. The sea, the sand, a garden. She pauses. She sees a shimmer on a swing on the porch, and nearby a wobbly figure with long black hair looks out to sea. There's an almost iridescent figure on her knees in the garden, planting flowers. The more she looks, the more women she sees at various stages of diminishment. Like stars appearing in the night sky, the more she trains her eye, the more they appear. Women are everywhere. She had walked right past them all on her arrival.

'Women need to see women too,' Professor Montgomery says. 'If we don't see each other, if we don't see ourselves, how can we expect anybody else to?'

The woman is overcome.

'Society told you that you weren't important, that you didn't exist, and you listened. You let the message seep into your pores, eat you from the inside out. You told yourself you weren't important, and you believed yourself.'

The woman nods in surprise.

'So what must you do?' Professor Montgomery wraps her hands around the cup, warming herself, her eyes boring into the woman's, as though communicating with another, deeper part of her, sending signals, relaying information.

'I have to trust that I'll reappear again,' the woman says, but her voice comes out husky, as if she hasn't spoken for years. She clears her throat.

'More than that,' Professor Montgomery urges.

'I have to believe in myself.'

'Society always tells us to believe in ourselves,' she says, dismissively. 'Words are easy, phrases are cheap. What specifically must you believe in?'

She thinks, then realizes that this is about more than getting the answers right. What does she want to believe?

'That I'm important, that I'm needed, relevant, useful, valid . . .' She looks down at her cup. 'Sexy.' She breathes in and out through her nose, slowly, her confidence building. 'That I'm worthy. That there is potential, possibility, that I can still take on new challenges. That I can contribute. That I'm interesting. That I'm not finished yet. That people know *I'm here*.' Her voice cracks on her final words.

Professor Montgomery places her cup down on the glass table and reaches for the woman's hands. 'I know you're here. I see you.'

Roar

In that moment the woman knows for certain that she'll come back. That there is a way. To begin with, she is focusing on her heart. After that, everything else will follow.

2

The Woman Who Was Kept on the Shelf

It began shortly after their first date, when she was twenty-six years old, when everything was gleaming, sparkling new. She'd left work early to drive to her new lover, excited to see him, counting down the hours until their next moment together, and she'd found Ronald at home in his living room, hammering away at the wall.

'What are you doing?' She'd laughed at the intensity of his expression, the grease, the grime and determination of her newly DIY boyfriend. He was even more attractive to her now.

'I'm building you a shelf.' He'd barely paused to look at her before returning to hammering a nail in.

'A shelf?!'

He continued hammering, then checked the shelf for balance.

'Is this your way of telling me you want me to move in?' she laughed, heart thudding. 'I think you're supposed to give me a drawer, not a shelf.'

'Yes, of course I want you to move in. Immediately. And I want you to leave your job and sit on this shelf so that everyone can see you, so that they can admire you, see what I see: the most beautiful woman in the world. You won't have to lift a finger. You won't have to do anything. Just sit on this shelf and be loved.'

Her heart had swelled, her eyes filled. By the next day she was sitting on that shelf. Five feet above the floor, in the right-hand alcove of the living room, beside the fireplace. That was where she met Ronald's family and friends for the first time. They stood around her, drinks in hand, marvelling at the wonder of the new love of Ronald's life. They sat at the dinner table in the adjoining dining room, and though she couldn't see everybody she could hear them, she could join in. She felt suspended above them – adored, cherished, respected by his friends, worshipped by his mother, envied by his ex-girlfriends. Ronald would look up at her proudly, that beautiful beam on his face that said it all. *Mine.* She sparkled with youth and desire, beside his trophy cabinet, which commemorated the football victories from his youth and his more recent golf successes. Above them was a brown trout mounted on the wall on a wooden plate with a brass plaque, the largest trout he'd ever caught, while out with his brother and father. He'd moved the trout to build the shelf, and so it was with even more respect that the men in his life viewed her. When her family and friends came to visit her they could leave feeling assured that she was safe, cocooned, idolized and, more importantly, loved.

She was the most important thing in the world to him. Everything revolved around her and her position in the home, in his life. He pandered to her, he fussed around her. He wanted her on that shelf all of the time. The only moment that came close to the feeling of being so important in his world was Dusting Day. On Dusting Day, he went through all his trophies, polishing and shining them, and of course, he'd lift her from the shelf and lay her down and they would make love. Shiny and polished, renewed with sparkle and vigour, she would climb back up to the shelf again.

They married, she quit her job, nursed her children, cuddled them, spent sleepless nights caring for them on the shelf, then watched them sleep, gurgle and grow on the rug and playpen beneath her. Ronald liked for her to be alone on the shelf, he employed childcare so that she could have her space, so that she could stay in the place he built for her, so that he wouldn't lose a part of her to the children, or that their special relationship wouldn't be altered. She had heard of couples who were torn apart after having families, husbands who felt left out when babies arrived. She didn't want that to happen, she wanted to be there for him, to still feel adored. The shelf was her place. She cared deeply for everyone from there, and because of her position in the home, everyone always looked up to her. It was only later, when the children had grown up and left the house, twenty years after the day she first climbed onto the shelf, that the loneliness took hold of her.

With the suddenness of an alarm bell, in fact.

It was the angle of the TV that started it. She couldn't see what Ronald was watching. It had never bothered her before because she was always content to see the faces of her children watching television rather than the TV itself. But the couch was now empty, the room quiet, and she needed distraction, escapism. Company. Ronald bought a new television, a flat screen that went on the wall, which meant it couldn't be tilted, and it was suddenly out of her view, just as her children were. And then there were the gatherings Ronald organized without inviting her or telling her, that would go on around her, involving people she had never met, and some women she wasn't sure of, right there in her own home – under her very nose, as it were.

She watched from above as his life carried on beneath her, as though she wasn't in the room, as though she wasn't a part of his life. Wearing a smile to hide her confusion, she would try to cling on, she would try to join in, but they couldn't hear her up there on the shelf and they'd grown tired of looking up, of raising their voices. They'd moved on. Ronald would forget to top up her drink, to check on her, to introduce her. It was as though he'd forgotten that she was there. And then he built the extension; it took him months, but once he was finished and the kitchen extended out to the back garden, suddenly all the gatherings and dinners moved out there. The TV room that had been the formal room, the centre of their home, was now a small, comfortable den. It had lost its grandeur. She'd reached the point where she felt she wasn't a part of his life any more.

And now it's Saturday night, and she's been alone all day while he's been out golfing, while the children are busy getting on with their own lives.

'Ronald,' she says.

He's on the couch, watching something that she can't see. He makes a sound in response but doesn't look up at her.

'Something doesn't feel right up here.' She hears the tremble in her voice, feels the tightness in her chest. *When you put me up here, it was for everybody to see me, to be the centre of everything, but now . . . now everything is carrying on without me, out of sight. I feel so disconnected.* She can't say it, the words won't come. Even thinking this way scares her. She likes her shelf, she is comfortable on her shelf, the shelf is her place, it's where she has always been, it is where she should always stay. He put her there to remove all the concerns and responsibilities of life from her, *for* her.

'Do you want another pillow?' he asks. He chooses a pillow beside him and throws it to her. She catches it and looks at it and then at Ronald in surprise, heart pounding, things inside her hurting. He stands up then.

'I can buy you a new one, a bigger one,' he says, silencing the television with the remote control.

'I don't want a new pillow,' she says quietly, taken aback by her response. Usually she loves such things.

It's as though he doesn't hear her, or perhaps he does and he ignores her. She can't figure it out.

'I'm going out for a few hours, I'll see you later.'

She stares at the closed door, listens to the car engine start up, in utter shock. It's been building up slowly over the years, but this is her moment of realization. All the little signs come together and hit her now, almost knocking her from her perch. He'd placed her on this shelf, a cherished woman whom he adored and wanted to protect and showcase, and now that everyone has seen her, has admired her, has congratulated *him* on his achievements, there's nothing left. Now she's just part of the furniture, a shelf adornment like the rest of his trophies, tucked away in an old comfortable den. She can't even remember the last Dusting Day; how long has it been since he took her down to polish her?

She is stiff. She realizes this for the first time. Her body needs to move. She needs to stretch. She needs room to grow. She's spent so many years sitting up here representing an extension of Ronald, of his achievements, that she no longer has any idea what she represents to herself. She can't blame Ronald for this; she willingly climbed up onto this shelf. She was selfish in lapping up the attention, the praise, the envy and the admiration. She liked being new, being celebrated, being his. But she was foolish. Not foolish to think it was a beautiful thing, but foolish to think it should be the only thing.

As her mind whirs, the pillow that she has been hugging for comfort falls from her hands and lands softly on the floor. It makes a soft *pfft* on the plush carpet. She gazes at it on the floor and as she does, another realization dawns.

She can get off the shelf. She can step down. She'd always had the ability to do that, of course, but somehow it seemed her place, the natural place to be, and why would anybody leave their place to become displaced? Her breath quickens at the dangerous new thought, dust catches in her throat and she coughs, hearing a wheeze in her chest for the first time.

She has no place gathering dust. She lowers herself down. One foot on the armchair beneath, where Ronald used to sit holding her feet in his hands while he watched TV – until the new flat screen was installed. She reaches out to the wall to steady herself. The brown trout is the only thing she can grasp. Her stockinged foot slips on the armrest of the chair. Her hand flies out in panic, searching for something to cling to, and grips the open mouth of the trout. Under her weight, the trout swings on the wall. It has only been hanging on by one nail all these years. So precarious. Something of such importance, you'd have thought her husband would've secured it better. She smiles at the thought. The trout swings off the nail and as she places faith in the armchair, falling into it, she watches the trout fall from the wall and land on the cabinet beneath. It smashes the glass cabinet, home to the football and golf trophies. Crash, smash, it all comes tumbling down. Then there's silence.

She giggles nervously, breaking the silence.

Then she slowly lowers one foot to the floor. And then

21

the other. She stands up, feels her stiff joints crack. The floor she has watched for so long, that is so familiar to her eye, feels unfamiliar beneath her feet. She wriggles her toes in the plush carpet, plants her feet in its fibres, truly roots herself in this new surface beneath her. She looks around the room and it seems so alien to her now that her view is different.

And suddenly she feels compelled to do something with her new life.

When Ronald returns from the pub he finds her with a golf club in hand, his best driver. His football and golf trophies lie on the floor, covered in broken glass. The brown trout looks up at him from the mess with its dead eyes.

'It was too dusty up there,' she says, breathless, as she swings again at the wooden shelf.

It feels so good, she takes another swing.

The wooden shelf splinters, bits fly everywhere. She ducks. He cowers.

As Ronald slowly peels his arms away from his face, she can't help but laugh at his shocked expression.

'My mother used to keep all her fancy handbags in dust-covers. She stored them in her wardrobe, saving them for special occasions, but they stayed there until the day she died. All those beautiful cherished things, never seeing the light of day, because even the rare special occasions in her life weren't deemed exceptional enough. She was always waiting for something more extravagant to come along, instead of wearing them on her arm to brighten her every day. She would tell me I didn't appreciate things enough, that I should cherish my possessions more, but if she was here now I would tell her that she'd got it all wrong. She should have appreciated the everyday things that she had, realized their value, made the most of them. But she didn't; she locked the potential away.'

Ronald's mouth opens and closes without any words coming out. He looks like his framed trout that has smashed to the floor.

'So,' she swings at the wall again and declares firmly, 'I'm staying down here.'

And that was that.

3

The Woman Who Grew Wings

The doctor said it was hormonal. Like the random hairs that had sprouted from her chin after the birth of her babies, over time the bones of her back had begun to protrude from her skin, stretching out from her spine like branches of a tree. She has chosen not to go for the X-ray her doctor suggested, nor has she heeded his bone density and osteoporosis warnings. It isn't a weakening she feels in her body, it is a growing strength, spreading from her spine and arching across her shoulders. In the privacy of their own home, her husband traces the line of her bones on her back, and when she is alone she strips naked and stands before the mirror to study her changing body. Sideways on, she can see the shape that is emerging beneath the flesh at her shoulders. When she ventures outside, she is thankful for the hijab that falls loosely over her shoulders, hiding this mysterious growth.

She would feel fearful of these changes in her body were it not for the immense strength swelling within her.

She has not been in this country long, and the other mothers at the school watch her even though they pretend otherwise. The daily gathering at the school gate that intimidates her. She finds herself holding her breath and increasing her pace as the gates come into sight; lowering her chin and averting her eyes, she squeezes her children's hands tighter as she delivers them to their classrooms. The people in this nice town think of themselves as polite and educated, so there are rarely any comments made, but they make their feelings known through the atmosphere they create. Silence can be as threatening as words. Conscious of sidelong stares and uneasy silences, she pushes through the tension while the town quietly makes plans and draws up regulations that will make it more difficult for a woman like her to be in a place like this, for a woman who looks like her to dress as she does in a place like this. Their precious school gates. The gates protect their children and these mother-clusters are the guardians of those children. If only they knew how much they have in common with her.

Even if it's not those mothers who are pushing through paperwork to make life difficult for her and her family, it is people like them. And the men they share their beds with at night. Perhaps, after their rounds of tennis and pots of tea, they shower and go to their offices to implement rules, stop refugees and immigrants from entering their country; these good people, these cappuccino-drinking, tennis-playing, coffee-morning fundraisers who care more about book weeks and bake sales than human decency. So well-read they start to see red when the alien invasions in their fiction start to manifest themselves in real life.

She feels her son watching her as they walk; their son of war, as her family called him, born into war, in a life consumed by pain on all levels: economically, socially, emotionally. Her anxious boy, always so uptight, always trying to look ahead and sense what terrible thing can happen next, what terrifying, degrading thing his fellow humans can surprise him with, the jack-in-the-box cruelty of life. He is always readying himself, rarely able to relax and revel in the joys of being a child. She smiles at him, trying to forget her woes, trying not to send those negative messages through her hand to his.

It's the same story every weekday morning, and again at collection time; her anxiety gets the better of her and her son of war senses it. Then again at the supermarket when she is on the receiving end of an insulting comment, or when her highly qualified engineer husband is trying to politely convince someone he is capable of so much more than sweeping streets and every other menial job he scrapes by with. She heard a rumour once that the mosques in Canada do not face Mecca, that they are a few degrees off. Distressing, to say the least; but she can go further than that, she has a theory that the world's axis is off too. If she could, she would fly up into space and fix the axis of the world, so that it would spin fairly.

Her husband is grateful for everything they get, which only fuels her fury. Why should they be so grateful for the things they work so hard for, as if they were pigeons pecking at crumbs tossed on the ground by passers-by?

She rounds the corner with her little girl and boy and the school is in sight. She readies herself, but her back is throbbing. It has been aching all night, despite her husband's gentle massages; she'd waited until he'd fallen asleep then moved to the floor so as not to disturb him. Though it throbs and aches constantly, there are times when the pain levels escalate. She's noticed it grows more intense whenever the fury rises within her, when things get her so angry she has to fight the urge to reach out and rattle the world, give it a good shake.

At her husband's insistence, she'd gone to the doctor about the changes in her back. It had been such a waste of money for so little insight that she refused to go for a follow-up appointment. They need to save what little money they have for emergencies. Besides, the throbbing and aching reminds her of how she'd felt during her two pregnancies; it's not the pain of deterioration but of life blooming inside her. Only this time the new life her body is sustaining is her own.

She straightens up, but her back feels heavy and she's forced to hunch over again. The school gate is in sight now, surrounded by clusters of mothers, standing around talking. There are some kind eyes, of course there are; she gets one hello, one good morning. Some eyes don't register her at all, they rush past, preoccupied with keeping to their stressful schedule, lost in thought, making plans, trying to catch up with themselves. Those people don't offend her. It is the others. The cluster. The tennis bags on their backs, the white skirts stretched over their plump bottoms and gym leggings, flesh squished at the seams, squeezed so tight it is trying to find a way out. That group.

One notices her. Lips barely move as she speaks. The discrimination ventriloquist. Another set of eyeballs. And then another. Some more ventriloquism, less talented this time. The whispers to each other, the stares. This is the daily reality of her picked-over life; she's observed in everything she does. She's not from here, she could never change that, she doesn't want to be like them, she doesn't want to be part of their cluster, and they distrust her for that.

She is late this morning and she is angry with herself. Not because her children will be a few minutes late, but because she is arriving during the most dangerous minutes. The mothers, having delivered their children to their classes, now mill around the gates, heads together, making plans, organizing collections, playdates, parties that her children will not be included in. She can see no way of getting to the school without walking by them, but they are a large group and the path is narrow and so she would either have to squeeze by the wall, walking single file with her children, or by the cars, brushing up against the dirty SUVs. Or through them. She could go through them. All of those things would mean drawing their attention, possibly having to talk.

She is angry with herself for hesitating, for the growing

fear inside her at a small cluster of silly women. She didn't flee from a war-torn country, leave everything and everyone she loves behind, for this. She didn't sit on that overcrowded inflatable boat with nothing from their old lives except the clothes on their backs, while seawater sloshed at their feet threateningly, and her children trembled under her grasp. In the darkness. In silence. Hoping for the coastline to appear. To endure that and then to sit in a container, in the dark, with no air, and not enough food, the stench of their waste in a bucket in the corner, and the fear in her heart – not for the first time – that she had sealed her children's fate, that she had dug their graves with this decision. She didn't go through all that so that she could be stopped in her tracks by these women.

The throbbing in her back intensifies. It spreads from her lower spine all the way to her shoulders. Shooting pain, that aches but also brings a strange relief. Like contractions during labour, coming and going but building in intensity all the time, powerful waves of super strength.

As she nears the women, they stop talking and turn to her. They are blocking the path, she will have to ask them to move aside. It is childish, but it is real. The pain in her back is so intense it prevents her from speaking. She feels the blood rushing to her head, her heartbeat loud in her ears. She feels her skin straining on her back, tightening. She feels as though she will be torn open, just as when her babies were born. And it is because of this she knows that life is coming. She lifts her chin, she straightens up, she looks the women directly in the eye, not afraid, not intimidated. She feels immense power, immense freedom, something these women don't understand – and how could they? Their freedom has never been threatened, they have no experience of how effective war is in turning men, women and children to ghosts, in turning the mind into a prison cell, and liberty to a taunting fantasy.

The skin on her back is taut now and she can feel the fabric of her black abaya stretching and stretching. Then there's a ripping sound and she feels air on her back.

'Mama!' her son says, looking up at her wide-eyed. 'What's happening?'

Always anxious about what's next. She delivered him to freedom but he is still in custody, she sees it in him every day. Not so much her daughter, who is younger and adapted more easily, though both will forever see all life through the gauze of truth.

The abaya rips completely and she feels a violent surge from behind, as she's pulled upward. Her feet leave the ground with the force of it, then land again. She takes the children with her.

Her son looks fearful, her daughter giggles. The women with the tennis bags look at her in shock. Beyond them she sees a lone woman, hurrying away from the school, who stops and smiles, hands to her mouth in surprise and delight.

'Oh, Mama!' her little girl whispers, letting go of her hand and circling her. 'You grew wings! Big beautiful wings!'

The woman looks over her shoulder and there they are:

majestic porcelain-white feathers, over a thousand of them in each wing, she has a seven-foot wingspan. By tensing and untensing her back muscles she discovers that she can control her wings, that all this time her body was working in preparation for flight. Her primary wings are at the tips of her fingertips. Her daughter squeals with delight, her son clings to her tightly, wary of the women staring at them.

She relaxes her muscles, folds her wings closer to her body and wraps them around her children, cocooning them. She lowers her head and huddles with them – it is just the three of them, wrapped in white warm feathery delight. Her daughter giggles. She looks at her son and he smiles shyly, surrendering to this miracle. Safety. The elusive treasure.

She slowly opens her wings again, to their full grand span, and she lifts her chin in the air, feeling like an eagle on top of the highest mountain. Proud, reclaimed.

The women still block the path, too shocked to move.

The woman smiles. Her mother once told her, the only way to the end is to go through. Her mother was wrong; she can always rise above.

'Hold on tight, my babies.'

She feels their trusting grips tighten around her hands; they cannot be torn apart.

Her wingspan is enormous.

Those little hands gripping hers are all the motivation she needs. Everything was always for them. Always has been, always will be. A better life. A happy life. A safe life. Everything they are entitled to.

She closes her eyes, breathes in, feels her power.

Taking her children with her, she lifts upwards to the sky, and she soars.

4

The Woman Who Was Fed by a Duck

She sits on the bench in the park every weekday at lunchtime, the same bench, the same park, beside the lake. The wooden bench is cold beneath her. She curses, stands, pulls her coat down lower over her rear end and sits again, the padding protecting her a little more. She unwraps her ham-and-cheese baguette and spreads the tinfoil open over her lap. A squished tomato oozes beneath the bread, causing it to become soggy. This tips her over the edge.

'Fucking shitty motherfucking tomato.'

She could tolerate her intolerable colleagues at work. She could tolerate the disgusting man on the bus beside her this morning who picked his nose for the entire trip and rolled his snot on the balls of his fingers as if she couldn't see him. But the tomato. The fucking tomato is the icing on the cake. She'd only wanted cheese and ham and this unwanted addition has turned her bread to mush, leaving the cheese squished and stuck to the bread as though it's all one gooey substance.

'Bastard tomato,' she grumbles, throwing the entire baguette on the ground. The ducks can have it.

Every lunch hour she visits the city park. Her office is nearby. Stocks, trading, asshole colleagues. This bench is the quietest, it is set away from everybody else. She comes here to feed the ducks and as she does she mumbles about the people who piss her off. She vents her frustrations over her fuckwit boss, her delusional colleagues, the turbulent stock markets. Feeding the ducks is her punchbag.

Most of her colleagues go to the gym on their lunch breaks, run off their issues for forty-five minutes and return to their desks cocksure and smelling of active shower gel and deodorant, and throbbing with testosterone. She prefers the fresh air, the peace, no matter what the weather. She needs to grumble and rant, and with every piece of bread she throws, a problem is eliminated and a little of the frustration ebbs away. Only, she's not too sure it works – sometimes she finds herself getting worked up into a seething frenzy as her head fills with all the things she should have said – valid points and arguments she should have made back in the office.

She stares at the lump of soggy bread roll she has thrown on the ground. A few ducks fight over it, peck at it, but ultimately it falls well short of the all-out battle she'd thought it would spawn, which only goes to prove how unappetizing the baguette is.

'You should have broken it up into pieces,' a male voice interrupts her thoughts. She looks up and around with surprise. There's nobody there.

'Who said that?'

'Me.'

Her eyes fall upon a mallard, standing away from the other ducks that are pecking at the bread roll, and each other.

'Hi,' it says. 'I'm guessing by the look on your face that you can hear me.'

Her mouth falls open. She's speechless.

He laughs. 'Okay, nice talking,' he says, then waddles off towards the lake.

'Wait! Come back!' She snaps out of her shock. 'I'll give you some bread!'

'Nah, thanks,' he says, but he waddles towards her. 'You shouldn't feed ducks bread, you know. Aside from the fact that uneaten bread causes changes to the chemical and bacteriological content of the water, which in turn increases the risks of avian disease, it's bad nutrition. The recommended food for ducks is defrosted frozen peas, corn or oats. That kind of thing.'

She stares at him, completely lost for words.

'Don't be offended, it's sweet of you, all right, but white bread is the worst, it has no nutritional value whatsoever. Ever heard of angel wing?'

She shakes her head.

'Didn't think so. It's caused by an imbalance of nutrients

in a duck's diet. It causes a deformity in ducks' wings, can hamper our flight or stop us altogether, which is, you know, crappy.'

'Gosh, I'm so sorry. I had no idea.'

'That's okay.' He studies her. He can't help himself. 'Mind if I sit with you?'

'Sure.'

He flies up to the bench. 'Work getting you down again?'

'How did you know?'

'You're here every day. Fucking Colin. Fucking Peter. Fucking world markets. Fucking Slimming World. Bastard tomatoes.'

'You hear all that?'

'Hear it? We feel it. Every time we hear you coming, we armour up. You fire those pieces of bread at us like grenades.'

'Sorry,' she replies, biting her lip.

'That's okay. We figure it does you some good, even if it takes a duck eye out here and there.'

'Thanks for understanding.'

'We're all human, after all,' he says.

She looks at him, baffled.

'That was a little bit of bird humour for you,' he chuckles. 'But seriously, everybody needs to have a place where they can let loose. Where they feel safe.' He has a faraway look.

She studies him. 'Do you?'

'Yeah sure, there's this great river region in Senegal where I go for the winter. There's a sweet little pintail that I meet up with. We watch the sunrise and sunset, we hang out by the river. That's my place.'

'It sounds beautiful.'

'It is.'

They sit together in silence.

'How about we reverse it?' he asks suddenly.

'You want me to fly to Senegal? I'm not sure I'm your pintail's type.'

The duck laughs. 'Let's reverse the feeding.'

She giggles. 'Are you going to throw bread at me?'

'In a way. A little food for thought.'

'Okay.'

'It's not my place to say it, which is why I never said it before, but you seem more open to it today, being able to hear me speak and all. You seem angry. Very stressed, frustrated. I get the impression you don't like your job very much.'

'I like my job. And if there was nobody in the office, I'd love my job.'

'Hey, look, who are you talking to? If I was the only duck in this pond, life would be much easier, let me tell you, but I pass the time watching people and I've noticed you. You're not very good with people.'

'Or ducks, by the sounds of it,' she says, trying not to take offence. She'd always thought she was a good people person. She stayed out of everybody's way, never asked questions, never got into conflict with anyone . . .

'You'll be better with ducks after this. As for the people: you should tell Colin he needs to trust your instincts. Tell him you were right about the Damon Holmes account. The account taking that turn for the worse had nothing to do with you and everything to do with the earthquake in Japan.'

She nods.

'Tell Paul to stop interrupting you in meetings. Tell Jonathan you don't enjoy the dirty emails, that donkeys don't do it for you. Tell Christine in Slimming World that you'd appreciate it if she stopped telling people your husband was her first boyfriend. She may have taken his virginity but you took his heart. And tell your husband you don't like tomatoes; he's adding them to the baguette because he senses you're stressed. It's his way of making things more special for you. He doesn't know that your bread is soggy by lunchtime, or how much the sogginess bothers you.'

The woman nods, taking it all in.

'Stop hiding here and making things worse. Deal with it head-on. Calmly. Stand up for yourself. Talk to people. Be an adult. Then come here and just enjoy feeding the ducks.'

She smiles. 'Oats, corn and peas.'

'That'll do just fine.'

'Thank you, duck. Thank you for the advice.'

'Sure,' he says, flying down from the bench to the ground and waddling into the lake. 'Good luck,' he adds, swimming to the centre and narrowly avoiding the piece of bread that flies from another direction, towards his head.

The woman stands, feels dizzy, and quickly sits down again. Something the duck said hit a nerve.

Stop hiding. Talk to people.

She's heard those words before, but not in a long time. As a child the words seemed to pass everybody's lips; from her mother at children's parties, from her father when he took her anywhere, from teachers, from every adult whose path she crossed until she made it her intention at a very young age not to cross people's paths. After that, the only time she'd heard the words as an adult was from her then-boyfriend, soon to be her ex-boyfriend, though his exact words had been, *Stop hiding. Talk to me.*

She had always been a hider and she never wanted to talk. As a child she was afraid to speak up because she knew she wasn't allowed to tell them the things that she wanted to say. They wanted her to be normal and act normal, but nothing really was normal, and she couldn't tell them that. If she couldn't say what was real then there was nothing else to say, and avoidance became the name of the game. There was only one person who had ever truly understood her, never uttering those words, even in her childhood. Her eyes filled up at the thought of him: Granddad.

Her parents' marriage had been a volatile one. She was an only child and whenever things fired up at home, her granddad would come to collect her and they'd go for a drive. They'd have chats, little ones, innocent ones. She felt safe in his company because she was safe in his company. She loved the smell of his woollen cardigans, and the way he removed his full set of teeth and chattered them in her face to make her laugh. She loved the feel of his fat wrinkled hands when her small hand got lost in his grip, and the smell of pipe smoke from his wax jacket. She loved being away from her house, even more being *taken* away. She always felt that he was rescuing her, showing up at the right time as if by magic. Only now did it occur to her that most likely he came because her mother had summoned him; a surprising revelation to have after so many years of viewing the same events with the same pair of eyes.

When she was with Granddad, he'd helped her to forget the things she was afraid of. It wasn't so much that he didn't shine a light on the darkened corners of her mind, more a case of making her forget such a thing as darkness existed.

He didn't push her to explain anything. He already knew. He didn't tell her to stop hiding because he helped her escape, and that escape in childhood had become her hiding place as an adult.

He used to take her to feed the ducks.

When the yelling started, and the banging, the insults and the tears, he would arrive, she'd hear the honk of his car horn, and she would run down the stairs and out the door, holding her breath like a soldier racing from a battlefield, ducking grenades, never looking back. She would hop into the car and there would be peace. Silence in her surroundings and in her mind.

They'd feed the ducks together and he'd make her feel safe.

He sounded very much like the duck she'd spoken with.

So now she sits on the bench in the park by the lake,

stunned, remembering him, smelling him, hearing him, feeling him all over again. She cries through her smile, and smiles through her tears, and then, feeling lighter, she stands and walks back to her office.

The Woman Who Found Bite Marks on Her Skin

She noticed the mark on her skin on her first day back at work after nine months' maternity leave. It had been a stressful morning. She had packed and repacked her work tote the previous night like an anxious child before her first day of school, and still, despite the endless planning, the thinking and rethinking, the freshly puréed food in pots packed away in the freezer and one in the fridge for the next day, the lunches prepared, schoolbags ready, diaper bag packed, changes of clothes in case of after-school sports grass stains, potty-training failures and explosive diarrhoea due to new formula, the school uniform washed and ironed, afterschool tracksuit ready for activities – still, after all that organization, the constant run-throughs of what-if scenarios, they ended up late.

She couldn't sleep with all the thinking, planning, organizing, preparing, fallback-plan-making; everything was going through her mind and on top of that she had to cope with anxiety about her first day back at work. Would she be able to pick up where she'd left off? Would she muddle things up as she had been doing at home – adding bubble solution to the chicken dinner and only realizing when she went outside to blow a tin of chopped tomatoes into the air for her confused children? Would she be able to function? Was she still relevant? Had her portfolios been given away? Would her clients be happy to see her return? What if her replacement had been more efficient, quicker, faster, *better*? What if they were looking for flaws, examining her under the microscope, looking for a reason to get rid of the woman with three kids? There were people who wanted her job, people who could stay longer in the evening, arrive earlier in the morning, change their schedule at a moment's notice. Young men, older men with children, young women, women with no children because they didn't want them, couldn't have them, or who were afraid to risk it all.

She had dropped the six-year-old at school, then the three-year-old at Montessori, then the nine-month-old at daycare. Every single drop-off had broken her heart, each one more than the last. Each child howled as she left him, looked at her with sad searching eyes as if to say, 'Why are you leaving me like this?' Stamping images in her mind of their crumpled-up faces, tormented and accusing. Why was she doing this to them? Nine months at home had been lovely – stressful at times but lovely, with at least one daily psychotic screaming episode that scared her more than the kids, but still, they'd been together and she'd loved them and they had felt loved. So why was she putting them through this? Most of her salary went on childcare. She could get by without working if she really had to, if they economized even further. It wasn't about the money. Well, it was a little, but not completely. She was going back to work because she needed to. She loved her job. She wanted her job. Her husband wanted her to have this job, not just so she could help pay the mortgage but because he loved that other woman that she became when she worked, the one that felt a little more contented, a little more useful, satisfied, relevant, a little less cranky. Though she certainly wasn't feeling that way on her first day back.

She watched her baby in the arms of the stranger whose nametag said 'Emma' and her heart twisted. She hated Emma. She loved Emma. She needed Emma. The baby screamed and she felt her nipples twist and leak. Her silk shirt was already soiled, not by the kids for once but by her own body. She blasted the heating, directed the fan towards her wet boobs, placed a cabbage leaf in each bra cup against her breasts, and searched the radio for anything to take her mind off abandoning her children.

That night as she was inspecting her body after the shower, she noticed the red mark. It was on her right breast, the fleshiest part of her body.

'It's a heat rash,' her husband said.

'It's not.'

'You always get these spots when you take a hot shower.'

'The shower wasn't very hot. I've been out for twenty minutes.'

'It's dry skin, then.'

'It's not. I've just moisturized.'

'Well then, what is it?'

'That's what I'm asking you.'

He pushed his head closer to her breast and squinted.

'Did Dougie bite you? It looks like a bite mark.'

She shook her head. Not that she remembered. But maybe he had. Though he'd barely looked at her when she'd collected him from daycare that evening and had fallen asleep in the car on the way home so she'd had to put him straight to bed. She recalled the struggle while handing him over to Emma at daycare. She didn't remember him biting her, but maybe.

She'd slept well that night after the emotional day, despite a bed-wetting incident, an unscheduled night bottle and a sleepwalker. The two eldest ended up in bed with her husband while she ended up in the spare bedroom with the baby. Still, the best night's sleep one could ask for under the circumstances.

The following day the mark on her chest had turned a purple colour and she found another. She'd noticed it after lunch, when she managed to sit alone in the local restaurant and order food for herself, by herself, actually finishing her cup of tea while it was still hot, then went to the toilet alone for the first time in a very long time. She thought she'd sat down on a pin or a thumbtack but found nothing on her desk chair. In the toilet cubicle, she pulled out her compact mirror and found an even larger red oval-shaped mark on the white flesh of her buttock. She didn't show her husband that one but she was careful with the children, making sure none of them were nipping at her when she wasn't looking.

It was during an overnight business trip to London that she began to grow really concerned. One too many stares at her on the plane – on which she had been able to sit alone, without having to share a seat belt or a seat, or distract her children from kicking the seat in front of them or running up and down the aisles, or screaming at the top of their lungs – caused her to rush to the bathroom as soon as they landed. She discovered that her neck was covered in red marks, which were much larger than the previous ones and definitely bite marks, with tiny tooth incisions clearly visible. She hid her neck beneath her scarf, despite the stifling heat in the car she shared with her male colleagues, and later in the hotel realized the marks had spread all the way down her left arm. While on Skype, talking to the kids, who were too hyper to pay her any attention, she showed her husband the bite marks.

His annoyance and distrust were evident. '*Who* is away with you?'

They argued and she couldn't sleep, feeling rage and hurt, on the one night she had a bed to herself. To top it all off, at 1 a.m. the hotel fire alarm went off and she found herself outside on the street in her gown, in the cold, for thirty minutes until she could return to her room.

When she got home, her baby wouldn't come to her, would only stay in his father's arms and anytime she neared him he screamed as though his legs were being sawed off. Which was what hers felt like. Her husband found her sobbing in the bathroom; when he saw her body, covered in marks in various shades of bruising and swelling, he knew something was seriously wrong. The pain was agonizing.

She went to the doctor the following day. It was a Saturday and she didn't want to – all she wanted was to be with the kids – but gave in when her husband insisted and his mother offered to have the kids for the afternoon. The pain was getting worse by the hour.

The doctor was equally confused but more suspicious. She confirmed that these were bite marks, prescribed painkillers and a lotion, then pushed some pamphlets about domestic abuse into her handbag as she left the surgery, telling her to be in touch if it continued.

Three weeks later, she was unrecognizable. The marks had spread to her face; there was bruising on her cheeks and chin, and the tips of her ears looked as though they'd been nibbled. She hadn't missed any work – she couldn't, not after nine months' maternity leave; she had too much to prove, too much to catch up on. But she was exhausted. She looked ravaged and drained of all colour. The doctor arranged for blood tests. All appeared normal, nothing that could cause or be related to the marks on her skin. She and her husband fumigated the house, they got rid of the carpets and laid timber flooring in case dust mites were the cause of her agitated skin. And every weekday morning she'd say goodbye to her babies, who no longer cried when she left them, which made her feel even worse and caused her to cry all the way into the city, where she'd apply a layer of extra-thick foundation so she could pass for a competent professional in the office. When socializing at the weekend, she would lather on body make-up to cover her bitten legs, and play the super-attentive wife and friend.

Of an evening she would try to keep the baby awake in the car on the way home, sometimes lowering the windows to let the fresh air in, singing loudly, blaring the radio, anything so she could have time with him awake. But no matter what she did his eyelids would flutter, unable to stay open beyond 6:30 p.m. She drove home faster, avoided conversations or phone calls leading up to 5 p.m. She charged from the building to get to her baby as fast as she could, but each time the motion of the car would cause his long lashes to flutter closed.

It wasn't long before she found herself in the hospital, rigged up to wires and machines. Not able to be at home with the kids, or at work, the guilt was overwhelming. They would visit her but it was heartbreaking. Not being able to play with them and hold them as she wanted to hurt her soul. Work tried to accommodate her new 'out of office' temporary arrangement, but she couldn't give herself to them completely. She felt like she was letting everybody down.

Her flesh had been devoured by hundreds of angry bite marks that began as nips but ended in blood-inducing tears of flesh. The physical pain was crippling, but the inability to be everything to everyone at all times was even worse. Since entering hospital her condition had deteriorated; the number of marks on her skin had been growing by the day, and that evening an angry sore had developed on her wrist, right over her pulse, as she looked on in horror.

Blood tests and scans might not have yielded any results thus far, but being alone in the hospital had given her time to think, precious hours alone that she hadn't had time for since becoming a mother. Tied to her bed with wires and tubes, she couldn't move, she couldn't get out without alerting the nurses and making an event of it. She wasn't working and as she had no other human beings to aid and comfort, it was just her, alone in a room, with her thoughts. All the pacing was done in her head and after a time even her mind got tired, stopped, sat down. Drummed its fingers. Waited.

The suffocation passed and her breathing began. With the in-out flow of her breaths, thoughts began to shift. Everything was separated, organized, put into the relevant boxes: the time this happened, the time that happened, the things she said and should have said, and experiences she'd resolved to put behind her or relive in another way. A spring cleaning of her mind, until everything was filed away neatly in her mind and the surface was clear. A clear mind in a clear room.

She looked around. What had put her here?

She felt her wrist to check her pulse and discovered it had calmed. The machine beside her, attached by wire to her forefinger, confirmed this. The caged tiger in her had stopped pacing. As she felt her pulse, with the finger that wasn't hooked up to the pulse oximeter, her fingers brushed her most recent bite mark. She ran the tip of her finger along the jagged teeth marks on her skin, back and forth, gently, slowly, methodically, and she recalled the moment it had appeared.

She'd received a visit that afternoon from her husband and children. They had been excited to visit her, were hyper, jumping around the room, sending toy characters on adventures in, on, around the hospital equipment; Barbie wrapped in her new IV wire dress, Lego Batman in deep distress under a wheel of the bed, a teddy bear leaping on the remote control, trying to come up with a new algorithm for poo land. Her children had snuggled up beside her on the bed, stolen the jelly and custard from the tray, talked and babbled a mile a minute about their exciting and busy lives. She had listened, her heart full, loving the sound of their little voices, their developing words, their confused but practical grammar that she never wanted to fix. Her husband sat in the armchair by her bed, leaving the spotlight on her, her moment with her babies, watching her, trying to hide his concern.

And then their time was up, visiting hour had come to an end and the nurses, who had kindly turned a blind eye to the number of visitors in her room, gave a light knock on the door to warn them. She watched as they bundled up in their coats, woollen hats that squeezed their soft cheeks together, and chubby hands disappeared into mitts. Wet kisses on her cheeks and lips, little arms barely able to wrap around her body; she breathed them in and never wanted them to let go. But she had to.

She ran her fingers over her bite mark.

The familiar feeling had been building up, the feeling that let her know when a new mysterious mark had arrived on her skin. This was the first time she'd identified it, she'd thought before that it was spontaneous, sporadic, without any pattern at all, but now she realized there was a pattern.

She had kissed her husband, his turn to have her attention, and apologized again.

'Stop apologizing,' he'd said gently. 'Just get better.'

She'd apologized to the children too.

'It's not your fault you're sick, Mummy,' a little voice said.

She'd watched them leave, heard their noisy chatter and the beginnings of bickering down the hall and she felt so sorry. Sorry because she was sorry. Sorry because she felt guilty.

Her fingers stopped moving over her wrist. Guilt. When she dropped her baby off at crèche, she felt guilty. When she couldn't collect them from school, she felt guilty. When she couldn't take a day off when they were ill, she felt guilty. She felt guilty about her cluttered house. She felt guilty when she discovered a friend had gone through the most traumatic moment of their lives without telling her and she'd been oblivious to it, she'd missed the tired eyes, the revealing lack of sparkle or words that held back the truth. She felt guilty for forgetting to call her parents, for making a mental note to do it and then allowing herself to be distracted. She felt guilty at work for not being at home, she felt guilty at home for not being at work. She felt guilty for spending too much money on a pair of shoes. She felt guilty for stealing the children's pizza. She felt guilty for falling back on her workouts.

She had stored up so much guilt she felt as though she was guilt incarnate.

She hated that every time she was somewhere she was thinking of where she should be. She hated that she felt she had to explain herself, justify everything, she hated being judged, she hated feeling judged when she knew she wasn't being judged. She hated living in her head.

It was wrong. It was all wrong. She knew these thoughts were irrational, because she liked her career and she was a competent mother with so much love in her heart.

Her fingertips brushed her wrist again. She turned her wrist over and examined her skin. The most recent bite seemed paler. It wasn't gone but it wasn't as angry, as raw and red as it had been. She sat up in the bed, her heart pounding, trying to slow her breathing and her mind again. The numbers on the machine warned her about her heart rate. Nothing good came from her busy mind.

Guilt.

It was the guilt.

The guilt was, quite literally, *eating her alive*.

Her skin had become a patchwork quilt of guilt.

This terrified her, but realizing the root of the mysterious skin disease was enough to bring a flicker of hope. She only ever needed to know what was wrong, and then she could fix it. It was what she told her children when there was some concern eating at them. It was the great unknown that fed the fear.

Excited, she pushed the sleeves of her nightgown up her arms and studied her skin. These marks too were fading; the more violent ones were now less red and raging. And as she studied each one she remembered the moment, the defining moment each one had arrived. The business trip to London. The second night in a row to get a babysitter. The school trip to the museum she hadn't been able to take. Their ten-year wedding anniversary night she'd gotten so drunk she'd vomited on the daffodils in the front garden and ended up sleeping on the bathroom floor. The third no in a row to a friend's dinner invitation.

All of these bite marks were moments, moments she had felt she wasn't enough for the people who needed her.

But she knew that wasn't true. The people who loved her told her so. They told her every day and it was their voices she needed to listen to.

She climbed out of bed, she disconnected the IV from her vein, removed the pulse oximeter from her forefinger. The manic beeping from the machine began. Ignoring it, she calmly took out her bag and started packing.

'What are you doing?' asked Annie, the wonderful nurse who had cared for her during her stay.

'Thank you for all that you've done, Annie. I'm sorry to have wasted your time—' She stopped herself. The guilt again. 'Actually, I'm not sorry. Thank you. I appreciate your kindness and care, but I have to go now. I'm better.'

'You can't leave,' Annie said gently, at her side.

'Look.' The woman held out her arms.

Annie looked at them in surprise. Ran her fingers over the fading bites. She lowered herself to her knees, lifted the hem of the woman's gown and inspected her legs.

'How on earth?'

'I let the guilt get to me,' the woman said. 'I let it eat me up. But I won't any more.'

Or at least, she'd try not to let it. She could do this. She could do it all, because she wanted to and because she had to. Because it was her life, the only one she had, and she was going to live it as best she could, embracing every moment, going to work, being with her family and refusing to apologize to anyone for it, least of all herself.

Annie took in her determination and smiled. 'So why are you rushing home now?'

The woman stopped and thought about it. She was doing it again.

'The marks are fading but they're not gone. If you push it, they may return. I suggest you get back into bed, let yourself get better and then you can go home. Rested.'

Yes, the woman decided. One more night, guilt-free, sleep-filled. And then she would return. Return home. Return to herself. Celebrating everything, guilt-free.

6

The Woman Who Thought Her Mirror Was Broken

'X, R, S, C, B, Y, L, R, T . . .' she says, calling out the letters on the sign before her.

'Okay, you can remove your hand now,' the optician says and so she lowers her hand from her right eye, and looks at him expectantly.

'Your visual acuity is very good,' he says.

'I don't know what that means.'

'It refers to clarity of vision dependent on optical and neural factors; the sharpness of the retinal focus within the eye, the health and functioning of the retina and the sensitivity of the interpretive faculty of the brain.'

'Harry, I used to babysit you. I caught you dancing in the mirror to Rick Astley, singing into your deodorant bottle, with your shirt off.'

He blinks, a flush appearing on his cheeks. He rephrases: 'What it means is that you have 20/20 vision. Perfect eyesight.'

She sighs. 'No, I don't. I told you that. They're my eyes. I should know.'

'Yes,' he shifts in his chair, the professional side of him disappearing and the nervous young boy in his place. 'This is what I don't quite understand. You seem so sure of your ailing eyesight but you're not experiencing any headaches, sore eyes, no blurred vision, you can read perfectly well. There's no issue with your distance sight, in fact you read the bottom line of the eye chart, which many people can't read. I don't understand where your difficulty lies.'

She throws him the same look she had thrown him when she'd found him with his head hanging outside the bathroom window, sneaking a cigarette. He'd shouted to her that his stomach was upset, but she'd used a coin to unlock the door from the outside. If he didn't have an upset stomach before, he had one after. She had been a terrifying babysitter. Despite the fact they were both twenty years older now, her intimidating stare held the same power over him.

He tries to remember he is a grown man now, married, two children. Holiday home in Portugal. Mortgage half-paid. She can't hurt him any more. He straightens his spine.

She breathes in and out. Counts to three silently. He's qualified, an academic, but clearly he's still the stupid teenager whom she caught jerking off into a sock.

'It started happening a few weeks ago,' she explains.

'What did?'

'The problem with my feet.'

He stares at her blankly. 'You're being sarcastic, aren't you?'

'Of course I am. What am I here for?'

'Your eyes.'

'My *eyes*,' she snaps.

The grown-up Harry, the husband and father is gone. He's back to the humiliated teen. The sock memory.

'I can't quite pinpoint it, but I would say it happened about three weeks ago. I woke up the morning after my birthday party and I felt wretched. I could barely recognize myself but I put that down to the tequila slammers, you see, so I let another few days go by before I realized it wasn't just a hangover, there really was something wrong.'

'And what exactly is wrong?'

'They are seeing me wrong.'

He swallows. 'Your eyes are seeing you wrong?'

'They aren't seeing me as they should. They're showing me a different version of me. It's the wrong version. It's *not* me. There's something wrong with them. Perhaps it's not the vision, perhaps I need an X-ray or an MRI. Perhaps it's not the lens – what if it's the pupil or the iris or . . . another part.'

'Let me get this straight . . .' He leans forward, elbows on his knees, long thighs, long arms and fingers, quite attractive really for someone who was such a little pain in the ass. There's the trace of a smile on his lips and this maddens her.

She can see he's trying not to laugh. She shouldn't have come here.

'You're here because you look at yourself in the mirror and see yourself differently?'

'Yes,' she says calmly. 'My eyes are not showing me how I feel. Therefore the message that the eye is sending to me is wrong. Do you understand? I look different, not how I feel at all. I got a bit of a fright at the sight, actually.' She hears the tremble in her voice, so does he, and his smile quickly fades. He softens, looks a bit concerned. She thinks of him cosying up to her with buttered popcorn and monkey fleece pyjamas when he woke up from a bad dream. He wasn't always a shit.

'Don't you think that there might be another explanation?' His voice is gentle.

She thinks hard, he's trying to tell her something. He's being gentle about it and then suddenly – bam – it's all so clear. What an idiot she's been! She throws her head back and laughs.

'Of course! Why didn't I think of it before? It's so obvious! It's not my eyes that are the problem at all.'

He seems relieved that she's not going to fall to pieces on his chair, in his office. He sits up and smiles.

She claps her hands gleefully and stands. 'Thank you so much for your time, Harry, you've been a fantastic help.'

He stands too, awkwardly. 'Have I? I'm glad. You know, I won't charge for this session.'

'Oh, don't be silly,' she reaches for her purse. 'I've taken plenty of money from you – or your family at least – over the years, and both of us know I wasn't worth it.' She laughs, so happy to have this resolved. So pleased it's not an eye problem.

He takes the money awkwardly. She waves away the receipt.

'So . . . what are you going to do, may I ask?'

'Well, if it's not my eyes, Harry, what else could it be?' she says. 'I'm going to get the mirror fixed of course!'

The mirror man, Laurence, stands before the full-length mirror in her bedroom, scratching his head.

'You want me to do what?'

'Fix it, please.'

Silence.

'That is what you do, isn't it? According to the website, you're an artisan glass and mirror company.'

'Well yes, I mainly design custom pieces. But we also do mirror and glass installations and replacements, repair work to the frames, chips in the glass, that kind of thing.'

'Perfect.'

He still looks confused. He'd taken a quick sweeping look at her bedroom as he entered, she's not sure if he noticed that only one person sleeps here, just her, no husband, not any more. Apparently they're almost through the worst of it; her separated friends tell her the light is at the end of the tunnel. She certainly hopes so, she's nearing the end of her tether and thinking her eyes are a problem isn't helping things.

'What's the problem?' she asks.

'The problem is, I don't see a problem with this mirror.'

She laughs. 'Do I pay for that diagnosis?'

He smiles. He has dimples. She suddenly wants to fix her hair. She wishes she'd paid more attention to her appearance before he arrived.

'Well there is a problem, trust me. Can you replace the glass? I'd like to keep the frame. It was my mother's.' She smiles, a bigger one than she'd intended; his smile is contagious. She chews the inside of her cheek to stop herself, but it doesn't work. His just grows. His eyes start to wander over her, goosebumps rise on her skin.

'Is it cracked?' He drags his gaze away from her and studies the mirror, running his hands over the finish. She can't stop watching him.

'No. It's not. But it's broken.'

'How is it broken?' He frowns, scratching his head again.

And so she tells him how she went to the optician but there seems to be no problem with her eyes; so the logical conclusion both she and the optician came to was that the mirror must be broken.

He stares at her, curious; but gently so, not in a judgemental way.

'Maybe you've heard of this problem before?' she asks.

He goes to say something, then stops himself. 'Sure,' he says. 'It's a common problem.'

'Oh good,' she says, relieved. 'If it wasn't the mirror, I wasn't sure who to go to next.'

'Is this the only mirror you use?' he asks.

'Um . . .' It seems a strange sort of question. She's never given it any thought before. 'Yes. Yes, it is.' She has been avoiding mirrors for a while. Since everything in her life went to shit, she couldn't be bothered to look at herself. It was only when she started looking again that she noticed the problem.

He nods. Quick look around her bedroom again. Perhaps he sees now that only one person sleeps in it. Is it that obvious? She wants it to be obvious.

'I'll have to take it with me, back to the studio. I'll have to take out this pane, cut one that will fit just right. And I could freshen up the frame for you too, bring life back to it.'

She's hesitant to let it go.

'I'll keep it safe, don't worry. I know it's important to you.'

The woman sees her mother posing in front of it. Pictures herself as a little girl, sitting on the floor beside her, watching her get ready to go out, wishing she could go with her too, thinking her mother is some exotic creature that she will never resemble. She smells her mother's perfume, the one she saves for her special nights out.

Twirl, Mummy.

And she would. She always did. Swirling pleats. Billowing skirts. Revealing side splits.

She glances in the mirror again. She doesn't see the little girl. She wasn't expecting to see her, was she? She sees a version of herself that she doesn't like. Older. She looks away. She's not herself. Nope. This mirror has to go.

'I could use another mirror, I suppose . . .'

'No, don't do that,' he says. 'This is the one you want.' He rubs the frame lovingly, delicately. 'I'll make this perfect for you.'

She stifles a school-girlish giggle. 'Thank you.'

And before she closes the front door behind him he says, 'Promise me you won't look in any other mirrors until this one is ready?'

'I promise,' she nods. When she closes the door her heart is pounding.

He rings the next day to tell her that he'd like her to come to his studio to pick out a piece of glass. She wonders if it is necessary. She wonders if he is just trying to see her again, hoping that's the case.

'Aren't they all the same?' she asks.

'The same?' he cries in mock outrage. 'We have plane mirrors, spherical mirrors, two-way and one-way mirrors. I don't want to decide until I see what it is you like.'

She pulls up to his business address in her car the following day. She has spent more time on her appearance. She used the bathroom mirror, it seemed a little off too but certainly closer to the version of herself that she was used to, as she applied make-up, feeling giddy, and also like an idiot for getting ahead of herself.

She expected a dirty warehouse or a retail outlet, some-where cold with hard surfaces, soulless, but it's not what she finds. Down a pretty country lane, she travels to a converted barn set off from a thatched cottage. The inside looks like something from a design magazine; a studio filled with the most stunning mirrors she has ever seen.

'I use reclaimed wood for the frames,' he tells her, bringing her on a tour around the studio, lined with mirrors of all shapes and sizes. 'This is the most recent. I'm almost finished, the wood is from a tree root I found while out gathering,' he explains, pointing to the woodland stretching out for acres beyond the barn. 'It doesn't have to be grandiose wood.' He points at a bathroom mirror: 'That was made from reclaimed pallet wood.'

She runs her hands along all of the frames, impressed by his artistry, feeling a little embarrassed that she contacted a man with such a gift to fix a pane.

He developed the barn himself, he says, explaining about windows and light rebounding. She has no idea what exactly he means but it sounds beautiful. And if ever there was a man made for spending his days working with mirrors, it's him. She feels something when she looks at him, something she hasn't felt for a very long time, a lifetime ago, when she was another person. The person she doesn't look like any more.

He comes close to her, places his hands on her two arms and turns her around. The personal touch surprises her.

'Your mirror is over there,' he says, pointing.

She sees her mirror in the corner of the room. He has done exactly what he said he'd do, he brought it back to life. It has been sanded and varnished and she can see it as it was, in her parents' bedroom, by the wardrobe, Daddy's shoes lined up beside it, Mummy's hair curlers plugged into the wall on the ground.

She walks over to it and stands before it, seeing his reflection as he stands behind her. She looks at her reflection. She takes herself in, examines herself.

'You fixed it already,' she says with a smile. She's back. It's her again. She looks rejuvenated, as though she's had a facial or invested in a new expensive moisturizer, which she hasn't. It was the mirror all along, she knew it. 'I thought I was here to choose a pane, you tricked me!' she laughs.

'You're happy?' he asks, his eyes sparkling as the light of dozens of mirrors bounce light around the room and make him look like he's glowing.

'Yes, it's perfect,' she says, examining it again.

She sees a red dot on the glass and reaches out to touch it. Her hand hits the pane, no dot to be felt. Confused, she spins around to look at him in the flesh. 'What kind of mirror did you use?'

'Look at it again,' he says, a strange look on his face.

It feels like a trick. She slowly turns and faces the mirror again. Examines the frame, the glass, everything but her face really, because he's behind her and she's self-conscious and fluttering inside. The red dot is still on the glass and she wonders if it's a test, though she has already reached out to touch it and it's not physically there.

'Have you ever heard of a thing called simultaneous contrast?'

She shakes her head.

'It's a painting term.'

'You paint, too?'

'Just as a hobby. It's a term for when certain colours look different to our eye when placed next to each other. The colours aren't altered, it's just our perception.'

He allows this to sink in.

'Turn around and look at yourself again,' he says gently.

She slowly turns around and really takes herself in this time. Her eyes scan over her older face, her fuller cheeks, the wrinkles around her eyes, her fuller stomach. She pulls her blouse away from her waist self-consciously and as she's doing so she sees the red dot again. Instead of reaching out to the glass, she looks down at her body and finds the sticker on her arm. 'How did that get there?' she asks, peeling it off.

He's grinning.

'You stuck it there,' she says, remembering her surprise at his touch when he spun her around. He'd used that opportunity to place the red sticker on her arm.

'The mirror test. All of us mirror artists do it,' he says, joking.

'The first time I saw the sticker, I thought it was on the mirror,' she says, figuring his test out. 'The second time I realized it was on me.'

He nods.

'It's not the mirror, it's me,' she repeats, and the message hits home. 'It wasn't the mirror that was broken, it was me all this time.'

He nods again. 'Though I wouldn't say you were *broken*. It's all about perception. I didn't want to touch the mirror. It's perfect as it is.'

She turns around and faces the mirror. Studies her face, her body. She's older. She's aged more this year than she feels she has in five years, but this is her now. She's changing, she's ageing, more beautiful in some ways, other ways it's harder to take.

'Well?' he asks. 'You still want to replace it?'

'No. It's perfect, thank you,' she says.

The Woman Who Was Swallowed Up by the Floor and Who Met Lots of Other Women Down There Too

It was all because of the work presentation. She hated presentations, always had since she was at school and the two idiots at the back of her classroom would hiss 'sssss' at her flaming red face. They hurled abuse at everybody but she was an easy target – her face would burn up, blazing red, as soon as she heard the sound of her own voice and felt the layers-peeling power of eyes on her.

With age, the flaming redness had lessened, but her nerves channelled themselves through her body and manifested as a severe knee tremble. She wasn't sure which was worse. The red face that didn't affect her speech or the knee quiver that caused her entire body to vibrate, shuddering as if she was out in the cold, despite her sweaty armpits. Her skirts would shake so that she resembled a cartoon character; she could almost hear the bone-clattering sound, like a bag of bones being shaken. She'd have to hide her hands too, or close her fingers to make fists. It was worse if she had to hold paper because the paper never lied. Always best to place the sheet on the table, hands closed to fists, or wrapped around a pen. Sit if possible, trousers preferable to skirts, and best to wear pants with narrowly tailored legs because the less loose fabric there was to tremble, the better; however the waist needed to be loose to aid deep breathing. Better to be as casual as possible, coffee or tea to be drunk in a take-out cup to avoid cup and saucer rattling in trembling hands.

It wasn't as if she didn't know her stuff. She damn well did. She strode around her apartment as if giving a TED Talk. In her apartment she was the most competent, inspiring deliverer of quarterly sales figures that the world had ever seen. She was Sheryl Sandberg giving her TED Talk, she was Michelle Obama saying *anything*, she was a woman warrior spilling facts and figures, so self-assured in her own home, at night, alone.

The presentation was going fine, perhaps not as inspiring and earth-shattering as the rehearsal the previous night, with fewer insightful glimpses into her personal life and absolutely no humour, unlike the comedic ad-libbing she'd busted out to her ghost audience. It was definitely safer and more to the point, as perfect as she could hope for, apart from her annoying repetition of the phrase 'per se', which she had never used in her life regarding anything, but there it was now, a part of almost every sentence. She was already looking ahead to drinks later with her friends where they would giggle over her critical yet hilarious self-roasting. They'd toast to 'Per Se!' and spend the night using it in every sentence, creating a challenge perhaps, even a drinking game.

'Excuse me, Mr Bartender,' she imagined a friend leaning across the bar, with an arched eyebrow. 'Could I get another Cosmo, per se?'

And they would all dissolve in laughter.

But she had gotten too far ahead of herself in her thoughts, she had gotten too cocky. All had been going well in her presentation until she'd disappeared into a daydream and taken her eye off the ball. She'd left the moment. She was surrounded by her dozen-strong team, those relieved to have finished their part of the presentation, others eager to have their moment in the light, when the door opened and in walked Jasper Godfries. The CEO. The new CEO who'd never sat in a sales meeting before in his life. Her heartbeat hastened. Cue knee tremble, cue shaking fingers. Hot skin, short breath. Her entire body, suddenly in flight mode.

'Sorry to interrupt,' Jasper announces to the surprised room. 'I was stuck on a call with India.'

There are no free chairs because nobody is expecting him. People shift around, making room, and she finds herself standing, facing them all and her new CEO. Knees knocking, heart pounding.

Her colleagues look at the papers in her hand, some with amusement, some in pity, pretending they don't notice how they violently shake. Jasper Godfries' eyes remain on hers. She tries to relax her body, control her breathing, calm her mind, but she can't think clearly. All she can think is *the CEO, the CEO, the CEO*. She hadn't planned for this in any one of her one hundred possible scenario run-throughs all week.

Think, think, she tells herself as all eyes are trained on her.

'Why don't you take it from the top,' her boss, Claire, says.

Fucking Claire.

The voice inside her head shrieks with panic but instead she smiles, 'Thank you, Claire.'

She looks down at her notes, flicks back to page one and everything blurs. She can't see, she can't think, she can only feel. Her anxiety is physical. It's all going on in her body. She feels trembling in her knees, her legs, her fingers. A heart that beats too fast, they must be able to see it vibrating through her blouse. A cramp in her stomach that tightens. Nothing, nothing in her mind.

Claire says something to urge her along. They all turn the pages. They go back to the start. Back to the start. She can't do it. Not all over again. She hadn't prepared to do this twice.

Her throat tightens, stomach loosens. Panic. She feels a bubble of air, slowly, quietly release from her bottom. She's thankful it's quiet but it doesn't take long for the hot, thick smell of her panic to circulate the room. She sees it hit Colin first. She sees how he jerks and moves his hand closer to his nose. He knows it was her. It will soon reach Claire. It does. Her eyes widen and her hand goes to her nose and mouth, subtly.

She looks down at the paper, shaking violently, worse than ever before, and for the first time in twenty-five years she feels the hot red blaze return to her cheeks where it burns, burns, burns her skin.

And she hears the words, 'per se', leave her lips, followed by a nervous giggle. They all look up from their notes to stare at her. Every single surprised, amused, irritated pair of eyes studies her. Judges her. It's an awful, quiet, long, loaded silence, and all she wants to do is run out of the room or wish for the ground to open up and swallow her.

And that's when it happens. A beautiful inviting black hole opens up between her and the boardroom table. Dark and promising, deep, welcoming. She barely thinks about it. She would rather be anywhere but here.

She jumps in.

She falls through darkness and lands in darkness.

'Ow,' she rubs her buttocks. Then she remembers what happened and she covers her face with her hands. 'Oh fuck.'

'You too, huh?'

She looks up and sees a woman beside her, wearing a wedding dress, with a name badge that reads *Anna*. She doesn't want to know what Anna did, she doesn't want to think of anything but analyse her own stupid mistake over and over again.

'Where are we?' the woman asks.

'Cringeville,' Anna moans. 'Oh God, I am such an idiot.' She looks up, face contorted in pain. 'I called him Benjamin. I called him Benjamin,' Anna says, freaking out, looking at the woman as though she can understand the gravitas of her mistake.

'His name isn't Benjamin?' the woman asks.

'No!' Anna barks, causing her to jump. 'It's Peter. *Peter*.'

'Oh, well, that's not even close to Benjamin,' the woman agrees.

'No it's not. Benjamin was my first husband,' she wipes her eyes. 'Right in the middle of my wedding speech, I call my new husband *the wrong name*. The look on his face.'

'Benjamin's face?'

'No! *Peter's* face.'

'Oh.'

Anna closes her eyes, squeezes them shut as if trying to make it all go away.

'Poor you,' the woman cringes for her, feeling slightly better about her own embarrassment. At least her moment hadn't been her wedding day, it had only been in front of the CEO and the people she sees and works with every day of her life. No, it's still bad. She sighs, cringes again.

'What did you do?' Anna asks.

'I panicked and farted during a work presentation in front

of my colleagues and the new CEO that I was trying to impress.'

'Oh.'

Anna's voice shakes and the woman senses she's holding back a laugh.

'It's not funny,' she cringes, covering her flaming cheeks again. Suddenly the ceiling above them opens, there's a blast of bright light, sand trickles down. They guard their eyes. A woman tumbles down with the sand to the floor beside them.

'Oh God,' the woman whimpers. *Yukiko* is written on her name badge.

'What happened?' the woman asks Yukiko, eager to forget her own humiliation and the memory of her colleagues' faces when her fart drifted to the table.

Yukiko looks up, pain on her face. 'I just walked the full length of the hotel's beach with my boob hanging out.' She adjusts her bikini at the memory. 'I was wondering why everyone was smiling at me. I just thought that everyone was so friendly . . . I wished for the ground to open up and swallow me,' she says, looking around.

The ceiling opens again and they hear piano music, smell delicious food.

A woman jumps down and lands on her feet. *Marie*. She immediately starts tugging at her skirt, which is tucked right up into her underwear, revealing the cheeks of her bottom, and she wanders off deeper into the darkness on her own, muttering in French. The three women watching don't even bother to ask.

'So how long do we stay down here?' Yukiko asks.

'Forever, hopefully,' the woman replies, settling down in a dark corner. She thinks about her presentation again, about the expressions on her colleagues' faces, and she shudders.

'I've been here a while. The ceiling opens up to the place you escaped from and you climb back up again. Two women left ahead of me,' Anna explains. 'I guess they knew it was their time to go.'

'Probably when the cringe dies,' the woman adds, hoping it will happen at least in this lifetime.

'Never going to happen,' Yukiko says, sitting down and wrapping her arms round her almost naked body. She relives her moment on the beach. 'My nipple was out and everything . . .' she groans before hiding her face.

Another hole opens further down, and a woman stumbles into the pit. 'Jesus,' she holds her head in her hands. 'You're a bloody eejit, Nora, why don't you ever think before you speak?'

Anna laughs, not at anyone in particular but at the situation. 'Maybe Peter will think my mentioning Benjamin was funny. We joked about me making the mistake, but I never thought it would actually happen. Maybe I should pretend it was a joke.'

A small hole opens above her.

'Or admit the truth,' the woman suggests.

'What happened?' Yukiko asks.

'She confused her husband's name with her ex-husband's name in her wedding speech.'

Yukiko's eyes widen.

The hole above them closes instantly. Anna is not ready to go yet and they all learn how this works. Nobody leaves the cringe hole until they are ready to leave the cringe hole. They could all be here for some time.

'You two aren't helping,' Anna says, covering her face. 'Oh God,' she groans. 'His parents, his brothers, his horrible sister, they'll never let me live this down.'

'But it's not the worst mistake in the world, is it?' the woman asks. 'Peter isn't going to leave you just because you made a genuine mistake. A wedding is an emotional time, you were nervous. It was probably the one name you didn't want to say and it popped out. And in the grand scheme of things it's not as if one of you is ill, or cheated, or argued.'

'Or walked up the aisle with your boob out,' Yukiko adds.

'Or farted in front of the entire congregation,' the woman adds, and Yukiko looks at her with her nose crinkling now that she knows her cringe story.

Anna laughs. 'True.'

'It was just a mistake with a name,' the woman says gently.

'I guess so,' Anna smiles, and relief passes across her face. 'You're right. Thanks, ladies.'

The same hole reopens in the ceiling above them. They hear a toilet flush. A man calling, 'Anna! Anna! Please come out!'

'You're hiding in the bathroom?' the woman asks.

She nods and looks up. 'Time to face the music.'

'Good luck,' the woman wishes her.

'Thanks. You, too.'

She lifts her wedding dress above her knees so she can climb up to the hole, they watch her fix herself and her dress as she stares at the locked bathroom door. As she takes a deep breath and reaches for the lock, the ground closes up and she's out of sight.

Just as Anna disappears, another hole opens and they see a toilet.

'Is that Anna again?' Yukiko asks.

'No. Different toilet,' the woman says, moving closer to peer up.

The smell that drifts down is so awful, they skitter away covering their noses and mouths.

The woman who fell down the hole stands up and looks at the hole that's closing over and then at them all. *Luciana.*

'Oh shit,' the woman grimaces, holding her nose. 'That really stinks.'

'I know,' Luciana cringes. 'And there's a long line of women who just heard me do it and are waiting to get in. It's disgusting. I'm staying down here till the smell goes.'

'You might have to start paying rent,' Yukiko grumbles, holding her nose.

Another hole opens and a woman tumbles down, cursing. She looks at the three women facing her. She paces, chewing on her lip, then finally pauses and looks at them. Her name badge reads Zoe.

'I just asked a mother at the school gates when her baby is due. There is no baby, she's just really fat. Like pregnant fat. I see her every day, it was in front of the other mums.' She moans.

A hole opens up further down and another woman falls to the ground, whimpering, 'I slipped on my way to the bar, walking past his table.'

A voice calls from the dark at the other end of the hole. 'I couldn't stop laughing at the funeral.'

And a further voice from the darkness, hollow, haunted. 'I went in for a hug and we kissed on the lips.'

'Oh please, that is all nothing,' says Marie, the woman who had her dress tucked into her underwear. She has a French accent and she emerges from the darkness smoking a cigarette, like a scene from a predictable spy movie. 'It's not like walking through the entire restaurant with the back of your skirt tucked into your lingerie,' she adds through gritted teeth.

The women listening suck in air.

The ceiling opens and another woman stumbles down, naked, draped in a bed sheet, with a haunted expression. On her bare chest the name badge reads *Sofia*. No one asks her, they don't need to know what situation she just escaped, and she ignores the others, too lost in her head.

A fragile voice from deep in the darkness speaks up, and as the woman's eyes adjust to the gloom, she suddenly sees a body sitting on the floor that she hadn't noticed before. She realizes the woman must have been there since she arrived. The shadowy figure places something on the floor and slides it. It stops at the woman's feet. She picks it up, and reads the name badge. *Guadalupe.*

When Guadalupe speaks her voice is gravelly, deep, as though she's been here for some time, without water. 'Slide it back.'

ID confidentially shared, the woman slides it across the floor and Guadalupe catches it and the name badge disappears into the darkness again. She can't even bring herself to wear it.

'I sent an email to the wrong person. The message was about them, they should never have seen it,' she says, looking at them all with big eyes. 'I keep reliving the moment I pressed send. I wish I could take it back.' Finished sharing, she drags herself back to the dark corner she'd been hiding in.

'How long have you been here?' the woman asks.

'I'm never leaving,' is Guadalupe's croaky reply.

Marie snorts and sucks on her cigarette. The woman decides she will not stay in this hole for such a length of time, she cannot cringe and regret her mistake forever. She has a life to live.

Another hole opens and a glamorous woman tumbles down. She's wearing a beautiful gown for a black-tie event. She looks at them in shock. 'I won.'

'You won?' the woman asks. 'Congratulations. What did you win?'

'An award. The award I've worked for all my life.'

'That's amazing. You don't seem so happy.'

'I fell,' she whispers, still stunned. 'I tripped on the steps on the way up the stage. In front of everyone. *Everyone.*'

'Oooh,' they all say in unison.

'Yowch,' Luciana winces.

The ceiling opens above them again. The woman sees the wood panelling on the boardroom wall, the table, can make out Colin's foot, his striped rainbow-coloured sock. She doesn't want to stay, but she's not ready yet, she panics.

'Hey, take deep breaths,' Zoe offers.

The woman complies and together they do deep breathing.

'In through the nose,' Marie says.

'Out through the mouth,' Yukiko finishes.

The woman looks up through the hole. They're just people, people she knows. She knows her stuff, she is over-prepared, she always over-prepares in case of moments like this. She can do this.

At least she didn't call her husband the wrong name on her wedding day, at least her skirt wasn't tucked into her underwear, at least her boob wasn't hanging out. She didn't ask her overweight colleague if she was pregnant. She didn't misdirect a sensitive email. She messed up her presentation, she embarrassed herself. But it wasn't live on television. It's redeemable.

The remaining women in the hole watch at her, anxious for her next move. Another hole opens and a young woman stumbles down, confused. 'Canada is in America, right?' she pleads and in their faces she knows she's wrong. 'No! Of course it's not. Idiot.' She hits her head and mumbles, 'Worst job interview ever.'

The woman looks back up at the hole. At least she knows her stuff. It could always be worse. Everybody gets nervous sometimes. But the fart . . . she'll have to try to pretend it was someone else. She needs to reconcile this moment and move on.

'You just down or going up?' Marie asks, sucking on the last of her cigarette.

The woman smiles. 'I'm going back up.'

'Well, good luck, I'm never going up there again,' Yukiko says.

'You will, trust me. There's always something worse that could happen,' the woman says.

In the distance she hears a woman fall to the ground with a shriek, 'But the woman looked like a man!'

She takes a deep breath and steps up to the hole.

In an instant, she is standing back where she was, in front of the boardroom table, papers in her hands. While time has passed for her, it's as though she never left the room for her colleagues. All eyes are still on her. The shaking has stopped. The worst has happened. She lived through it. She survived.

'Apologies, guys,' she says firmly. 'Let's start over, shall we? I've outlined South Africa's sales in the graph and as you can see we've witnessed a sharp increase over last quarter's numbers, which I'm pleased with. Still, there's enormous room for growth, which is where the proposal on page two comes in.'

As she turns the page, the women down in the black hole smile up at her, give her the thumbs up, and the surface closes over.

8

The Woman Who Ordered the
Seabass Special

Sarah, the young waitress, walks away from the table of businessmen, her cheeks flaming. She heard the comment about her, from one of the men to another, under his breath. She has spent her life hearing comments such as his. She wishes somebody else could wait on their table but they have been seated in her zone. If she had met them at the door and had been the one to seat them, she would have put them elsewhere, but she was in the kitchen placing an order and now she is forced to deal with this confident crew, at least one of whom finds her lisp amusing. There's always one.

Sarah feels a pair of eyes on her as she takes the order to the chef. She is being watched by a lone woman at a table for one. She enters the kitchen, places the order, tries to compose herself, stop the shaking of her body and the fury she feels inside and then tends to the lone woman.

'Would you like a drink while you're waiting?' Sarah asks the woman.

'A sparkling water please, no lemon, no ice.'

The order stops Sarah in her tracks. The customer too, has a lisp. She wonders if she is being mocked, again, but the woman appears earnest.

While Sarah goes behind the bar to fetch the bottle of sparkling water, she watches the lone woman. She kicks her heels off beneath the small square table, and slowly rolls her ankles, back and forth, side to side. She takes her hair down, shakes it loose so that it falls down her back. She exercises her neck.

It's clear that she's had a long day already, but there are no signs of stress, just physical tensions in her body. She ties her hair back, more casually this time, high off her neck, away from her face.

She takes out a small tube of lotion from her leather handbag, squeezes out a little and massages her hands, slowly, calmly, while staring into space, lost in thought. The waitress watches her, she can't take her eyes off her, there is something hypnotic about her slow, self-assured rhythmic movements. It is as though she has rehearsed them, in this exact order. The lotion disappears into her bag and a lip balm appears, which she rubs over her lips, still lost in a hypnotic gaze. The tube disappears into the bag and the waitress waits for what will come out next. A phone probably.

Maybe a diary. There is a fat briefcase by her feet under the table, an expensive leather one with gold clasps at the locks and some wear and tear. It is used regularly, not just for special occasions, as if it is important and everything in it is too, just like the woman. Sarah can tell by the way the woman is guarding it with her legs, pushing it flat against the wall, making sure it doesn't fall down and that nobody steals it. Legal documents probably, which would be in keeping with the black cloak worn in court by barristers that she removed when she entered and hung over the back of her chair. Barristers speak for a living, something that strikes Sarah as astonishing, because she has avoided speech, and public speaking in particular, for as long as she can remember.

Nineteen years old, Sarah has had a lisp all her life, a tongue that would never obey despite the speech therapy classes she was sent to. A tongue that insists on protruding and touching her front teeth, directing the air-flow forwards whenever she makes an 's' sound, making a 'th' sound instead. This interdental or frontal lisp is supposed to be treatable, this functional speech disorder that it is now, as opposed to the sweet, funny and endearing habit she had as a young child. When those who were entertained by it began telling her to grow out of it, she knew it was time to fix the problem. But it didn't go away, would not go away, and in school she was ridiculed constantly. Now, as an adult who recently started university and this part-time waitressing job, the ridicule is less overt – but the raised eyebrows are still there, the amused eyes, the guys she meets in clubs who lose interest when she speaks.

Her speech therapist said it was her mind, not her tongue that wouldn't obey. One would almost think she wanted to speak like that. But she knew she didn't. Ever since the lisp had stopped being cute, she had learned to only speak when it really mattered. It was astonishing to learn how much speech had not mattered to her. Instead she grew to be good at listening, and a keen observer.

Sarah examines the woman's clothes. Black suit, tailored, expensive – just as the lotion and lip balm brand had been. She guesses the woman has come directly from court; sometimes lawyers make it as far as here for lunch and dinner, but mostly they opt for restaurants closer by. She can't take her eyes off the woman and the way she holds herself. And there was that order of sparkling water with no ice, delivered with such confidence and no apology. Sarah has delivered almost every word from her own mouth with an apology since childhood. Even her name presents a challenge. Sometimes she gives a different name; depending on who's asking, and on her confidence levels. Briana is her favourite alias; she delivers that name with the confidence of a young woman named Briana, and she's often wondered how different life would be, not without a lisp, but with a name she could at least pronounce.

Finally, the customer folds the menu, pushing it closed with her manicured nails. Real nails, clear varnish, natural white tips.

'Are you ready to order?' Sarah asks, approaching the table, placing down the sparkling water, without ice and lemon. She notices the tone of her own voice, she sounds different. She wants to please this woman, she wants this woman to like her, she wants to be this woman's friend. She has an authority Sarah wished she held. She admires that she is unapologetic when she speaks.

'Yes, thank you,' the woman replies pleasantly, looking up.

Sarah hears the lisp again, and her heart skips a beat. It wasn't a joke and she hadn't imagined it the first time.

'Super,' she says, rather breathless. A word she never would have used before now, she is surprised she said it herself.

The large table erupts in laughter, it takes over the space of the small bistro. They weren't laughing at Sarah but she can't help but feel that all laughter is directed at her.

The woman looks at the table of men, reopens the menu, appears to rethink her order and then, as though a decision has been made, she smiles.

'Could you tell the chef that I'd like the seabass special, please, with a side of steamed spinach and celeriac salad.'

The waitress's eyes fill up, goosebumps rise on her skin. She hates asking people if they wanted to know the special. She avoids that word every day, trying to figure out how else to point out the food on the blackboard in the bistro. *And here: our meal of the day.*

'You'll do that, won't you?' the woman asks. But she's not asking, she's telling her, supportively, encouragingly.

Sarah shifts uncomfortably from one foot to the other. 'I'll just write it down here.'

'You should tell him.'

The chef has a temper. He's one to be avoided – that was the first thing she was told when she took this job. He isn't patient, with her or with others, especially not her. There used to be a waiter who had a stammer but he couldn't take the goading, so he left the job, went somewhere speaking wasn't imperative. Nobody in this bistro has time to listen, and it's a trait echoed in the real world. Sarah has been interrupted often by those eager to finish her sentences for her, sometimes to make it easier for her, but often because they've no patience with someone who needed to take their time. She's accustomed to backs being turned on her mid-conversation, or eyes watching her mouth as she speaks. Speech impediments bother people. And sometimes one comment can be enough to shut a person up for ever.

'You can do it,' the woman says.

Sarah nods, takes a deep breath, and walks purposefully to the kitchen with the order in her hand.

The chef isn't shouting, he has his head down, sweating, putting finishing touches to the table of seven's main course dishes.

'Good timing,' he says, sprinkling salt over the last sole on the bone and giving her the nod.

She must have a funny look on her face.

'What's wrong?' he asks.

'I'd like to tell you my next order.'

He frowns. Not enough time for this crap.

'The woman at table four would like . . .' Sarah looks down to read the order in her lightly trembling hand, but she knows it by heart and so looks up again and lifts her chin. 'She would like the seabass special, with a side of steamed spinach and celeriac salad.'

He studies her for a beat. She places the order on the pass, and he looks up at it, reads it as if to confirm. She stands and waits. She's not sure what she's waiting for but it was a groundbreaking moment in her life. What comes after groundbreaking moments?

Normality apparently.

'Grand,' he nods, finally. 'Take these out before they get cold,' he says then, and rings the bell on the counter.

She smiles, lifts the plates and strides out to the restaurant, cheeks flushed, head high, feeling exhilarated as though she has taken her first skydive, soaring from dizzy heights.

'Now tell me,' the woman says to Sarah when she returns to her table with her seabass special. 'What do you recommend for dessert?'

Sarah readies herself. 'I would personally recommend the sweet strawberry posset with raspberry sorbet.'

The lone woman claps her hands together gleefully.

The woman eats slowly, thoughtfully, rhythmic and methodical. Then she slips on her shoes and her black court cloak, and pays, leaving a generous tip.

Sarah floats through her duties for the rest of the day. Something has been unlocked, as though some secret code was transferred from one woman to the next, a magic code that taught her to accept herself and to be unapologetic for the way that she is, to speak when she wants to speak, never to hold back on her words for fear of how people will treat her.

All because of the woman with a lisp who ordered the Seabass Special with Steamed Spinach on the Side, a Sparkling water with no ice, and for seconds a Sweet Strawberry posset with raspberry Sorbet.

9

The Woman Who Ate Photographs

She had been searching for a baby photograph for her son's school project and as soon as she'd opened the first page of the photo album, she was lost in the memories, sucked into a time warp and unable to escape. It was one particular photo that did it. Scott at four months old, his cheeks so enormous he could store food in them for a year, his roly-poly legs up in the air mid-kick, alight with raucous laughter. His eyes on her. Always following her as she moved around like she was the most important thing in his world. She wanted to nibble those cheeks, those legs, kiss him over and over and inhale his sweet baby-powdery smell.

Before she knew what she was doing, the photo was out of the sleeve and in her mouth and she was chewing. She stopped chewing, her eyes widening at the realization of what she was doing. But then in an instant, a tidal wave of emotions, smells and memory enveloped her, wrapping her up in a warm, cosy cocoon of love and nostalgia. She closed her eyes and swallowed.

Her head swirled, she felt like she was on a high. She sat back on the couch and felt that bouncing baby boy in her arms, felt his fingers pull at her lips, claw at her hair, rock back so suddenly that she had to wrap him tighter, support his neck. She smelled his breath so close to her face as he nuzzled her. That smell, the feel of his soft skin, the sounds from his developing voicebox. She felt the fabric of their old velvet couch beneath her legs, the same familiar concerns in her mind, ones she hadn't even thought about for so long. For fifteen minutes she sat alone, caught in her past life. Then suddenly, just like that, it was gone. He was gone from her.

Her eyes pop open, her heart pounding wildly. Immediately she looks to the photo album, licking her lips greedily, trembling fingers hovering excitedly over the photographs as though staring hungrily into a box of chocolates. She chooses her next delicacy carefully. Scott, four days old, just home from hospital. She grabs it, keeps her eye on the door as she pushes it into her mouth, unable to do it fast enough. Chewing photograph paper is difficult. It takes a lot to break down, her jaw aches, the taste makes her retch, but when she reaches the other side, the smells, the sounds, the sights flash into her mind, while the ache in her jaw and the bad taste fade away.

His newborn baby screams. More milk, he never could have enough milk. She's back to midnight and three a.m.

feeds, tiredness not yet hitting her as she's still on her two-week high. Feelings of utter joy, of purpose, of longing.

'Mum,' a voice interrupts her. 'Are you okay?'

Her eyes open. She sees Scott, now fifteen, standing at the door. He is disgusted by most things these days, including her, but now there's concern in his eyes. She must look a state.

'Yes, I'm fine . . .' She sits up and realizes there's a film of sweat on her forehead. She's sticky under her arms. 'I was just looking for that baby photo you asked for.'

His face softens and he enters the room. He sits down beside her but when he reaches for the album, she instinctively clings to it tighter. He looks at her, and tugs at the album. Realizing her idiocy and taken aback by her possessiveness, she finally relents. Her stomach grumbles and her heart pounds as he flicks the pages; she needs more. She needs the hit of nostalgia, the fix that transportation to another place gives her.

'Where are the newborn photos?' he asks, looking at the empty first few pages of the album.

She stifles a burp.

Later that night when everybody is asleep, she sits up, wide awake, feeling an overwhelming longing. She watches her husband, remembering how he was when they met, before the years altered him. She throws off the bedclothes and retreats to the darkened living room with the photo album in her hands. She flicks excitedly to the summer they first met.

Lots of passion, thrilling sex, spine-tingling secret looks and gentle touches. She relives it all, eating one photo after another, and then lies back on the couch to feel everything from the past; the sensuality, the tingle of excitement, the uncertainty, the hope for the future.

Her mother and father. No longer alive. She runs her finger down their faces before lovingly devouring them, reliving every childhood moment with them; birthday parties and holidays, Christmas mornings and first day of school. Days later and she has worked her way through her childhood – stopping when she reaches her teenage years. Too complicated. She doesn't wish to revisit those years. She moves on. The need for more photographs grows, it is constant, and while the feeling of being lost in nostalgia is wonderful, the actual eating of the photographs is a difficult task.

Over time she becomes clever.

She drizzles the photos with olive oil, seasons with salt and pepper and places them on a baking tray in the oven. When they're brittle, she pops them in a blender and sprinkles them over her dinner. While the family sits around the table, she gets lost in her own world, secretly but still in their company, no cause for hiding at night any more. It is exciting because she doesn't know which memory she'll get lost in, she didn't label the sprinkles and so the feelings that hit her, the years and moments she relives, are unexpected. She becomes drawn to the feeling of surprise as well as the high of the actual memory.

She finds new ways to consume her memories; mixing the

blended photos with tea-leaves, allowing them to infuse with the boiling water. It takes time to ensure that the memories aren't diluted, but she gets there, she wants them to be as strong as the moment she lived them. She leaves the tea to steep overnight, she grows accustomed to drinking it cold. She keeps packets of the ground paper in small plastic bags, to carry around with her wherever she goes. It helps her when she's out with her family, for hours on end without access to her albums; she can add the sachets to boiling hot water when the cravings begin. And the cravings are intense. They come in the form of aches behind the eyes, stomach cramps, a trembling from inside as though caused by extreme hunger. What began as a once-a-day habit has grown now that the drinking enables her to indulge in more regular highs.

She feels her husband's concern but she pretends that she doesn't. She realizes she has been distracted lately. She has avoided friends' company, choosing instead to stay home and retreat to her nostalgia. She doesn't plan for it to be a permanent thing, it is just for now, to help her through the day. There have been so many changes. The children are teenagers, they don't need her so much, not in the way they used to. Of course her relationship with her husband has changed, it was bound to over twenty-five years. She is noticing these changes and she supposes she is going through a time of transition, one that requires reflection. Thinking about how things used to be, that warm cosy feeling of being wanted, needed, really yearned for makes her feel safer.

It is the face of her husband that startles her when she returns home one day after a few hours out. She had forgotten her sachet of blended photos that she carried around as seasoning and so couldn't sprinkle it over her salad at lunch as she usually would. Instead of bliss, the salad tasted cold. The tea she drank did nothing for her, the entire lunch was a boring experience, sitting in the café, trapped in the present with nothing to entertain her mind. She returned home feeling like a drug addict who needed a fix, to find her husband sitting at the kitchen table with the empty photo albums before him.

'Where are the photographs?' he asks. No anger in his tone, but perhaps fear.

She makes her way to the kettle, she needs something to settle her for this, perhaps the nice honeymoon photograph of them on the beach that she'd been saving, the one taken in a moment when she felt he could protect her from everything.

'No,' he reaches out and gently stops her from emptying the sachet into her mug. 'Not that stuff now. I don't know what it is, but it makes you far away. Talk to me.'

She sits down beside him, feeling the fight go out of her.

'What have you been doing with the photographs?' he asks again. 'I see you with these books all of the time.' He flicks through the pages. 'All of our memories, they're gone. What did you do to them?' His eyes fill.

'I ate them,' she says quietly, and he looks at her in surprise. 'It's true. I ate them all.'

'I was afraid you'd thrown them out, that you'd burned them,' he says. 'But to hear this I'm relieved, even though it's . . .'

'Weird. I know,' she says. 'It first started when Scott needed a baby photo for school. I took down the photo albums from the attic – why did we store them there, where we can't see them?' she asks and he shakes his head, unsure. 'And I came across the one of him during his first Christmas.'

Her husband laughs, remembering. 'His Christmas pudding costume.'

'Do you remember?' she lights up. 'He was such a little pudding. Rolls on his legs, his arms.'

'That boy wouldn't stop feeding, I thought he'd drink you dry until you disappeared completely,' he remembers and they laugh.

'He just looked so delicious, and I remember that time in our life,' she looks at him, eyes filling. 'It's not so long ago but it's forever ago. And it's gone. And it's never coming back. I couldn't help myself.' She wipes her nose with a tissue. 'Things have moved on too much, things keep changing . . . when I eat them, I'm back there again, being back there, where I know what's happening and going to happen, feels safer than here. I miss those moments.'

'We're still making moments,' he says gently. 'And the past isn't gone. We lived those moments, they are already part of us; we're made of them.'

Something new to digest.

'But we still have new moments to make, I think you've

forgotten that. We're all here, with you, making moments every day, and lately we've lost you. I know the kids feel it too. Here, look at this.'

He takes out his phone and slides the photographs across one by one. She's either not in any of them or, when she is, she's looking elsewhere, looking lost, chasing the past.

She studies her image and her eyes fill with tears. These are not photographs she would want to eat ten years from now. She looks so sad. Her husband reaches out to her.

'We miss you. We want you back.'

He pulls her close, like the evening he first asked her to dance. He presses his lips to hers, like the day they first walked hand in hand on the beach; he runs his fingers through her hair and grips her tight, like the first time they made love. A deep, long kiss, a message, a silent conversation similar to their earlier days, like the time at the first wedding they went to as a couple and watched their friends marry before them, both wishing for the same thing. The kiss that first revealed the shared wish. All the moments she'd consumed recently.

They communicate with each other through this kiss now. A new moment.

It tastes better than any photograph.

10

The Woman Who Forgot Her Name

She's feeling frazzled. Only twenty minutes to get ready for her night out. A Saturday of activities with the children: drama, football, art and then two birthday parties, a complicated drop-off that overlapped with a pick-up and so a deal was brokered with another mother, meaning she became responsible for two more children, one who hit his head getting out of the car by trapping his foot in the seat belt, sending him tumbling to the ground. Drama averted, hospital trip avoided, it was suddenly dinnertime. Leaving the children to eat, she dives in for a quick shower, hoping the babysitter will have arrived by the time she comes out.

The taxi driver shows up early and starts getting impatient because she's not ready. Five minutes later, he's claiming that she's kept him waiting ten minutes, which leads to an argument over whether she's five or ten minutes late. Blood pumping with anger and irritation, she feels that going out for a meal is the last thing she wants to do. More conversations, more mental stimulation, no room to think for herself, no room for nothing. Nothing would be nice.

She enters the restaurant, already sweating despite her shower, having gone from blasting her head with a hair dryer that was too hot, to an overheated taxi, to cold air, to air-conditioned restaurant. Her head is hot from the hair dryer, her coat is on, along with scarf and gloves; she can feel her make-up melting. She's stressed, distracted, faint, not really there. The restaurant manager stares at her expectantly.

'I'm sorry,' she says, pulling her scarf from around her neck, enjoying the feeling of air on her skin. She looks at the manager again. Frowns. She removes her gloves and coat, killing time. Restaurant staff appear to take them from her.

'Thank you.'

She feels less faint now, her skin less clammy, her body temperature comes down, she should be able to think more clearly and yet . . . she looks at the restaurant manager again. She reads his name badge: Max.

'I'm sorry,' she frowns. 'What did you ask me?'

'For your name.' He smiles politely. 'Or the name of the booking.'

Nothing comes to her mind.

Nothing.

'I booked it in my name,' she replies, buying more time. 'Which is . . .'

'For eight p.m.,' she glances at the clock. Despite everything, she is only five minutes late.

'For how many people?' he asks, trying to be helpful.

'Two people.' She is sure of this though she can't remember with whom she is dining. She squeezes her eyes shut. Nope. Nothing. Why can't she remember her name? She thinks hard. She pictures her home. She pictures her house. Her three children. Her job. Her office. Her desk in the corner with the high-heeled shoes beneath that she leaves behind in the evening. They're a trusty black pair of heels, they match most things – not that it matters, nobody ever sees her bottom half, she's always behind the desk fielding calls. Half the time she doesn't even wear shoes. She tries to think of her colleagues, she plays out their conversations in her head, visualizes their day. If she can see them talking to her, then surely she'll remember her name.

'Can you do this? Can you call? Can you be a doll and . . . ?'

She doesn't hear them say her name.

She moves back to her house in her mind. Pictures her three boys. 'Mummy. Mummy. Mummy.' Always Mummy.

'I don't suppose it's booked under Mummy?'

Max laughs. 'I'm afraid not.'

'Maybe you can give me a hint,' she says, leaning over the counter, to look at the bookings. His hand blocks the page. She moves back instantly.

'I'm sorry.'

She thinks of her husband. His handsome face. What does he call her? *Honey. Baby. Sweetie.* Coming up behind her in the morning as she makes school lunch sandwiches. *Hey, sexy.*

She smiles to herself.

'There are three eight p.m. bookings for tables of two,' Max says, trying to help. 'One person has arrived for one table. Perhaps you know him?'

They walk into the restaurant and the lone man stands as soon as he sees her. His face lights up as though he knows her.

Max grins and leaves her to it as a waiter holds out a chair for her. She greets the gentleman with a tight smile, searching for him in her memory bank, everywhere, anywhere, in the darkened corners, beneath the layers. He's at least twenty years older than her, balding, well dressed in a suit, not particularly new or fashionable but safe and clean and neat. She searches his face for clues as she approaches him, clinging tightly to her purse.

'Hello,' she says.

'It's me, Nick,' he says, holding up his hands as if to display the goods.

She laughs nervously. 'Nick, I'm . . .' she stalls.

'Karen, of course,' he finishes. 'Sit down, sit down.'

'Karen,' she says her name, feeling the name in her mouth, rolling it around, seeing if it fits. She's not sure, but then her mind is still filled with nothing, who is she to argue if this man who knows her says that she's Karen?

'I'm sorry I'm a few minutes late,' she begins. 'There was a little confusion with the table.'

'Oh, no need to apologize. I was early. Too eager. Or nervous. It's so good to finally meet you after so long.'

'How long has it been?' she asks, narrowing her eyes, trying to imagine him as a younger man, a man perhaps she knew once upon a time.

'Three months? We would have met sooner of course, but that's my fault. I'm a little nervous to go out since Nancy died.'

'Nancy . . .' she studies him, the grief and loss in his expression. 'Your wife.'

'Nancy was my greatest friend,' he says sadly. His eyes fill. 'This is exactly what my friends told me not to do. I shouldn't talk about her.'

'Talk about her!' she encourages him. 'It's completely understandable,' she says, instinctively reaching across the table to hold his hand in hers.

'Thank you.' He takes a handkerchief from his pocket with his free hand and dabs at his eyes. 'Rule Number One of what not to do on a date,' he smiles miserably. 'First thing I do is talk about my wife.'

She stiffens, freezes, then slowly pulls her hand away from his, along the table like a snake, not wanting to be seen. A date? Her heart hammers. She thinks of her husband. His handsome face. *Hey, sexy.* She wouldn't have an affair on him, would she? Wouldn't she have remembered?

'Nigel,' she says, cutting into his story about his last promise to Nancy on her deathbed.

'Nick,' he says, looking at her, a little coldly.

'Nick, yes, of course, that's what I meant.' She looks at the reception desk where Max is standing, his back to her. She was hoping to get his attention but his head is deep in the reservations book. She thinks of her phone, she can read her messages for her name. She picks up her handbag and Nick watches as she roots in her bag.

'Are you okay?'

No phone. She left it at home or in the taxi. At home. She can suddenly see it. By the sink in her bathroom, beside the scattered make-up and brushes. She hopes the babysitter will call her at the restaurant if there are any problems. Though if the restaurant calls her name, will she know it's for her? This worries her. She looks up at the man across from her claiming to be her date.

'Niall—'

'Nick,' he frowns.

'Nick. Yes. Nick, you are a lovely man, but I don't think that I'm the right woman for you. I mean, I *literally* am not the right woman for you. I don't think that I am Karen.'

'No?'

'No. I'm having a bit of an identity crisis at the moment. Please bear with me. Have we ever actually met in the flesh before?'

'Well no . . . you emailed me a photograph, though you do look much, dare I say, *younger* than the image in the photo, and it's usually the other way around.' He frowns, puzzled.

Max appears, guiding a new arrival through the restaurant.

She's stressed-looking, complaining of traffic delays following an accident. As he approaches, Max's eyes widen; he points to the new arrival and mouths *Karen*.

The woman stands and picks up her handbag. Nick looks at her in surprise.

'You're leaving already?'

'Nick, you are a wonderful man. I hope you find happiness.' She leans in to give him a hug and whispers, 'Don't tell the story about Nancy's deathbed wish.'

'No?'

'No,' she says gently.

His cheeks flush as he looks over her shoulder and it's as though she has disappeared because all he can see is Karen.

'Karen!' he says, shocked. 'You are a vision.'

Karen's stress visibly lessens and she giggles nervously.

The woman who can't remember her name hurries back to the bookings desk with Max.

'So that wasn't my table,' she says nervously, biting her lip.

He laughs. 'You don't say. Well, isn't this fun.' He leans in conspiratorially and surveys the restaurant. 'We have two remaining tables of two. One person is waiting at table five and nobody has arrived yet for table eight. If they don't show up soon, they're going to lose their table.'

'But I could be here.'

'You are here.'

'You know what I mean.'

'I do. Good point.'

'You know you could just tell me the names of the bookings and that would help me,' she says, peering at the bookings again. His hand swiftly blocks the page.

'What's to say you'd remember?'

'I might.'

'You might not. And I think you'll figure it out better this way.' He looks around, a glint in his eye. 'Try her, on table five.'

The woman studies the diner at table five. She's incredibly fashionable, wearing clothes that look like they're from the future but probably will be on Madison Avenue next season. She's chic, everything about her looks expensive, from her haircut to the frame of her glasses.

The woman sighs. 'She doesn't look familiar.'

'You can't even remember your own name, familiarity has gone out the window. Try her,' he says, then ignores her as he greets the next group to arrive.

The woman takes a deep breath and adjusts her outfit. She likes what she is wearing but if she'd had one minute more to get dressed she might have chosen something better. This woman is dressed in black, head to toe, she appears so elegant and the woman who has forgotten her name feels like a clown in her colourful pleated skirt and blouse. She should have kept it simple, she wants to take the necklace from around her neck, but it's too late, the woman is looking at her.

She stops at the table, waiting for the woman to tell her to go away, that she's waiting for somebody else.

'Olivia?' the woman at the table asks, as she approaches.

The woman who has forgotten her name purses her lips and sits down. Olivia doesn't seem familiar to her either. 'Hello.'

'Veronica Pritchard, thank you so much for coming today.'

'You're welcome, Veronica,' the woman says, clearing her throat. Max arrives at the table to fill her glass with water.

The sophisticated woman suddenly seems nervous, a tiny crack in her smooth exterior. The woman who has forgotten her name waits for her to speak.

'I suppose I should tell you why I contacted you.'

'Yes, please.' She gulps some water.

'Well, I was told you are the best, naturally.'

The woman splutters, then puts down her glass, as Max rolls his eyes and walks away.

'I've been working for thirty years in my company, and never, ever have I reached a point like this. To be frank, I thought it was for the weak-minded and I was never weak-minded.'

The woman waits for more.

Veronica clears her throat. Her fingers are weighed down with rings on almost every part of the finger.

'Thirty years of scents. Thirty scents, not including special Christmas editions, I have created without a problem. Some years I had so many options, I had to choose among them. I've now used up all of those options, even though they weren't the best. I have to admit it: I have a block. That is why I contacted you. They say you are the best muse in the country.'

The woman who can't remember her name stares at her. 'Muse?'

'Influencer, whatever it is you call it,' she waves her hand dismissively. 'I've heard them speak of you, quietly in our circles of course, don't worry. I know you like to operate secretly.'

'Secretly. Yes.' The woman feels nervous. She searches her mind. She sees herself sitting at her desk at work, fielding calls, making appointments, but no, not feeling like much of an influencer. Certainly not at home with three boys and a husband. There's too much to do to be going around influencing others.

'Tell me about your scents,' the woman says, reaching for the bread, stuffing it into her mouth so she doesn't need to speak.

'They are luxurious. Expensive. Each transports people to a time and a place of splendour and grandeur, beyond their daily lives, beyond the ordinary.'

'What's wrong with the ordinary?' the woman asks, frowning.

'Excuse me?' Veronica is rattled to be interrupted when she is just getting started.

'Why do you want to go beyond the ordinary?'

'So that people can be transported. So that people can escape. I want my scents to move people. To feel special. Extravagant.'

'I find that the magic of a scent is that it can take you back to a time in your memory, a time of such importance in your life that you're there instantly, magically—' The woman snaps her fingers. 'Nothing else can move you like that. Except maybe a song.'

Veronica ponders this. 'But what separates me from others is the luxury element.'

'I'm not saying make an Irish stew fragrance,' the woman laughs. She thinks, 'When I met my husband I always thought his skin smelled of marshmallows,' she shares. 'Always so sweet and soft. And then the same with my children. We made milky sweet-smelling babies. Whenever I see marshmallows, I think of them. Now that is an ordinary smell, but it's an extraordinary feeling.'

'Marshmallows . . .' Veronica repeats slowly. 'Interesting. Actually, this is very interesting . . .' She sits forward in her seat, as though a fire has shot through her. 'I have been playing with something for a while but could not get the right connection. It was champagne, but what to pair it with? Strawberries would be too obvious, too . . . for the masses, not my style. But now that you remind me, my mother used to make homemade champagne marshmallows!' Her eyes light up and she claps her hands gleefully. 'Champagne marshmallow, oh my, my sister will love it! It will bring her right back to the kitchen, right before the dinner parties my mother used to throw . . .' She stalls and looks at the woman who can't remember her name. 'Olivia, thank you. You are a wonder. You really are. You don't mind if we skip dinner? I really must get back to the studio.'

She stands up, blows her a kiss and runs from the table and out of the restaurant. Max joins her. 'What did you do?'

The restaurant door opens and a very fashionable woman wearing oversized sunglasses looks around.

'Ah. That must be Madame Olivia Moreau,' Max says.

The muse. The woman who can't remember her name looks up at Max, annoyed. 'Moreau? You knew this wasn't my table. I'm not even French.'

'You could have married a Frenchman,' he shrugs, a mischievous look in his eye.

'I think you're enjoying this too much,' she replies, standing and following him back to the reservations book.

'I think you are too,' he says, smiling. He crosses a name off his reservation list. 'Muse to the perfumer, romantic advisor to a lost widower.'

'You were listening,' she hisses.

'It must be nice to forget yourself,' he studies her again, serious this time.

She frowns. 'Do you think there's something wrong with me?'

'You seem fine to me, just a little forgetful. Want to sit at table eight? I will give it away if they don't arrive.'

'But *I've* been here since eight-oh-five.'

'True.'

'Max, tell me, what name is on the final reservation?'

He blocks it with his hand, his fingers twitch as he considers moving it away. 'I can tell you, if you want. Or . . .'

'Or what?' She narrows her eyes suspiciously.

'Or, you could wait and see. See if the last person who arrives for table eight reminds you who you are.'

The woman grows nervous. 'What if they don't remind me? What if they don't even show up?'

'Well, then you go home. You remember where that is, don't you?'

The address comes to her instantly, she sees it, she smells it, she feels it. She nods.

'Up to you to take the chance.'

She sits at table eight, feeling nervous, eyes going from the clock to the centre candle glowing warmly, flickering wildly as the waiters pass by. What if she doesn't know the person? What if she never remembers her own name? Of course her husband will tell her, but she'd rather remember, there has to be a value and importance to remembering her own name.

The restaurant door opens and a woman steps inside. Elegant, pretty, flustered because she's late, shaking out an umbrella, complaining of the traffic due to the road accident. Max looks at the woman who can't remember her name hopefully, and she sees that he truly cares that she remembers her name. He's hoping that she knows. She smiles.

As soon as she sees that woman's face, everything comes to her in an instant.

Her own name comes to her immediately, but of course it would, this is the first woman to ever hold her, to comfort her, to kiss her, to say her name, to *give* her her name.

'Hi, Mom.' She stands up, opening her arms for an embrace.

11

The Woman Who Had a
Ticking Clock

The woman inherited the watch from her Aunt Crystal; a beautiful gold seashell locket containing a clock with a pearl face inside. She remembers the locket nestling in the crack of her aunt's generous boobs. As a child she would sit on her aunt's knee, captivated, opening and closing the locket, believing her aunt's story that there was magic inside.

Crystal had given it to her in the weeks before she passed away, telling her that she had no need for the timepiece now that her time was nearing its end. Her aunt lived alone all of her life, never married, never had children, and if she had ever loved a man, the woman had never met him. Crystal had always said that these were things she wanted but that the timing had never been right. It drifted away and passed her by.

The same timepiece that had hung around her aunt's neck for most of her life and had nestled itself in her bosom close to her heart, like a mussel clinging to a rock, now sits against the woman's skin, next to her heartbeat.

Thirty-seven years old, she hears the clock ticking louder now than it ever did before. It's so loud it keeps her awake as she watches her sleeping boyfriend with his head covered, wondering when things between them will change, when they can take things to the next level, how she can bring it up without sending him into another tailspin that sees him out late again and coming home smelling of booze and bumping into doorframes. He's happy as things are, and so is she, and yet . . . there is no clock around his neck, no finger prodding his ribs.

She lies awake at night, restless, seashell in her hand, feeling the vibration. Had she imagined it or had the ticking gotten louder when having coffee with her friends and their babies? All new young mothers on maternity leave, she's the only one left who hasn't had children.

Tick. Tick. Tick.

'What is that noise?' her friend had asked, looking around manically.

'I was wondering the same thing,' her other friend says, her nipple in the mouth of a chubby-cheeked babe. Fatigue-ringed eyes, both look around, then land on her.

'Is that ticking coming from *you*?'

She had tucked her seashell inside her cashmere sweater, hoping that it would absorb the sound. It had helped a little but thankfully her friends had been so distracted with their children they hadn't investigated further.

The volume of the ticking had risen again during her interview for a promotion to senior-level archivist at the library. She hadn't been the only one who heard it. They were in a grand wood-panelled room, marble floor and high ceilings, tall windows and lots of light to glaze the dark wooden surfaces, to illuminate the dust particles in its path. Hard surfaces, empty spaces, perfect acoustics for sounds to reverberate around the room.

'You know that this work will require more hours?' one interviewer behind the boardroom table had asked.

'Yes, of course.'

Tick. Tick. Tick.

'You'll be responsible for bidding for funds and managing budgets, supervising the staff. You'll be responsible for the overall strategy. More responsibility,' another had chimed in.

'Yes, of course.' She knew what they were really asking. A team of men wouldn't want to hire a woman who had to suddenly take maternity leave. But she wanted this job *and* she wanted to have a baby. She wanted both but she physically needed one thing more.

TICK. TICK. TICK.

He'd had to raise his voice to be heard over the ticking originating from around her neck, loud even when tucked under three layers of clothes; it had bounced off every hard surface. They had wrapped up the interview quickly.

She thinks of all this while lying in bed, watching her

boyfriend's pillow-covered face, opening and closing the clasp of the seashell.

'I can't do this any more!' her boyfriend suddenly yells, which startles her. He throws the pillow from his face across the room and stands up naked in front of her.

She thought he'd been asleep, but he's wide awake, pupils dilated with some kind of manic rage, chest heaving up and down as though he's been running.

'Henri,' she says, her voice low and scared. 'What are you doing?'

'I can't do this, I can't.'

'Do what? I'm not asking you to do anything?'

'No, but I can feel it. I can hear it.' He points to the clock around her neck. 'It feels like someone is standing behind me, reading over my shoulder, breathing down my neck, all of the time. I can't shake it off. I'm not ready for a baby. I'm not where you are yet. I don't know if I ever will be.'

She stares at him in surprise, though she truly shouldn't feel surprised, she should have known it was coming. He can't leave her, she thinks. They have put three years into this relationship, three long years, and if he leaves it will take another three years to find someone else, to get to this point. She works out the timing in her head. Recovering from the loss of Henri, healing her heartbreak, ready to date again, finding the right person, committing, settling down. It will all take too much time. She doesn't have time. He can't leave.

Suddenly Henri roars and she looks at him, his hands are

120

pressed hard against his ears, the ticking is so loud she can barely hear him yell but she can see the veins pulsating in his neck and his flared nostrils. He's holding his head as though he has a migraine, as though the ticking has reached inside him.

'Take the batteries out,' she lip-reads his words.

'I can't!' she shakes her head, grasping the clock even tighter.

He makes a move to grab it from her neck and she jerks back.

'I won't!' she yells. Taking the battery out would be like losing Crystal all over again. This ticking clock is like her aunt's beating heart. She can't stop it. But she can't quite explain this thinking, in the moment. The sound is too loud, he is so panicked, and she is confused.

'It was a gift, Henri!'

'It's a curse!' he yells. 'It's me or the clock,' he stares at her, deep brown eyes searing into hers.

'Both!' she replies.

'You can't have both.' He shakes his head, starting to get dressed.

She watches as he throws clothes into a bag. She is powerless to do anything, to say anything, all she can do is think about the wasted days and years, the time she has invested in him, hoping, praying that he could be the one; not in a spiritual sense but the one who will take the next step with her. The timing should be right. Three years, their ages. It should be now.

A baby. She wants a baby. Her body yearns for one, it aches. Her head is fine as things are, but something inside her yearns. It's a hunger that can be fed only by food and a thirst that can only be quenched with water . . . this emptiness in her body, in her heart, in her womb, can only be filled with another life, a life that she has created and grown. Love from her lover is not enough, she does need more.

The absence of life inside her has taken on a life of its own and is growing by the day. Time is its feeder. She can't ignore it. If she ignores it, because it's inconvenient for someone else, then it will be too late. He doesn't know what it's like to live with regret for something that hasn't yet happened. Fear, panic, that it's all slipping away.

The ticking is so loud now that Henri has left that the police stop by the house – a neighbour filed a noise complaint. As soon as the police enter her home they too cover their ears with their hands. It's unbearable.

The female police officer sits with her until the ticking quiets again. She has kind worried eyes, tired eyes. She talks in calming tones, she makes her camomile tea. They leave her sleeping on the couch with her seashell around her neck, cradled in her hand.

At work, assisting a team of students with research brings the woman to the floor of the library. Henri's belongings are all gone from the apartment, she's surrounded by gaps and spaces where he should be in both her home and her heart.

She is exhausted and has barely slept a full night since he left. It's been one month.

Tick, tick, tick.

She's showing a girl how to use the equipment when she hears a sound that stops her mid-sentence.

Ticking. And it's not from the seashell around her neck.

She looks around for the source. The prestigious grand library is quiet, low hushed voices, creaking, squeaking, coughing, throat-clearing, sneezing, nose-blowing, dragging of chair legs, footsteps, books being opened, dropped on the table, replaced on shelves.

As if in response to the faraway sound of ticking, her own seashell timepiece starts up. Her ticking and the mystery ticking are having a conversation. She holds onto it, using it as a compass to guide her. She runs her eyes over the students seated around the computers and it's obvious the sound is from elsewhere. She leaves them, winds her way through quiet aisles of dusty bookshelves, her feet echoing on the marble floor. She follows the sound, and is misled as the ticking bounces off the walls, and shelves and marble floor and deceives her. As she gets closer, it gets louder, and her own necklace responds. They don't tick in unison, they are individual, strong, getting louder.

Finally, after negotiating the labyrinth of books, she knows that the owner of the ticking clock is in the physics section, behind the shelving unit that separates them. There is nowhere left for the owner to go, this is the final corner. There is only one way in and out and the woman stands at the entrance, her heart thudding, its frenzy a contrast to her constant rhythmic ticking clock. Her clock is loud, so loud that whoever is behind the shelf must hear it too. It echoes around the quiet library.

'Hello?' she hears a man call out.

She steps out from behind the shelf and there he is. The owner of the ticking clock. She locates the watch on his wrist and then sees the book he is holding. Her breath catches in her throat. *The Unreality of Time*, Cambridge philosopher J.M.E. McTaggart's study of time and change.

'The B Theory,' she says, breathless.

'You've read it?' he asks, surprised.

B theorists argue that the flow of time is an illusion, that the past, present and future are equally real and that time is senseless. Of course it is something that she has researched, she feels time all of the time, it is at the forefront of every moment. She wants to understand it.

'You're ticking,' he says.

'So are you,' she replies.

'It freaks most people out,' he says, studying her intensely. 'Not me.'

He's the same as her. He wants the same thing.

Suddenly the rhythm of her ticking alters; she's unsure whether hers slows or his speeds but there is some shifting of time. They both feel it, hers against her chest by her beating heart, his against the pulse in his wrist, until eventually their ticking is coordinated, in unison. Second by second, moment by moment, their ticking gradually quiets.

They both witness this miraculous shifting of time together; their ticking synchronized.

As quickly as a cloud passes overhead and the sky brightens, the anxiety lessens in her, and they both breathe a long and slow sigh of relief.

Finally.

12

The Woman Who Sowed Seeds of Doubt

Prairie Rock was about community, self-reliance and sustainability. One hundred homes in the neighbourhood on fifty acres. Organized around common areas, the households were each responsible for the upkeep of their area. The village had common orchards, vineyards, meadows and extra land where residents could rent garden space for themselves. When a property owner died, it fell to their remaining descendants to take responsibility for the resale of their home and land, which had to be approved by the community. At the same time, a plot of land became available from the many wild acres as a sign of respect to the departed, a plot of land that was otherwise uncultivated, waiting to come to life to assist the community. The idea was when you put the souls of your loved ones in the ground, the ground would come to life and provide. From death comes life.

She had been a communal dweller all of her life and with a small group of people to interact with, it could sometimes feel stifling. The same old faces, the same old arguments, though of course the familiarity was comforting, too. There was rarely a new face; when somebody died, their home usually passed on to a family member. It was rare for an outsider to be welcomed, one family in ten years so far. That was until Jacob the labourer had started working with them when her father became ill and they needed assistance with his share of the work on his land. Jacob was the first fresh face she had seen in some time.

It had practically been decided who she would marry when she was fourteen years old. She and Deacon had been friends since the first day of school. Born four days apart, played together, reared together, climbed every tree together, went out of bounds together, beyond the boundaries in every way they could. Explored and learned together. Her first friend, her first kiss, her first love.

When she was eighteen she'd married him. Their celebration had taken place in August, at the harvest party. Bridesmaids wore burnt orange, the table displays were straw and corn.

Her life was going just fine, an easy, unquestioned path that she was content to skip down. No children yet, but that was okay, they weren't in any rush. Deacon had built their home on her parents' land, helped out by his father and brothers. They had moved in one year ago. And just as they were settling and it felt like their life was beginning in a new direction, her mother became ill, and passed away. Very quickly after her mother died, her father fell ill and followed her. Both of them gone so quickly. And now she was left with her grief, and a pain in her chest. Her parents' death had left a surprising hole that she never expected, and her clear head had all of a sudden clouded over.

Though she was a grown woman, she felt that she was here, in this community and on this earth, because of her parents. They were founders of the Prairie Rock community, pillars of their small but central society. Despite having her husband and the hope of building their own family, her parents were her roots, her foundation, and they'd been cut down. Without them, she felt as though she were hovering uncertainly above the ground. Even in the final few years when she cared for them, she'd still depended on them in a primal way. She had lost them within months of each other. She was relieved for her mother to be eased of her suffering, and relieved for her father to be reunited with his love, but after that came the unending sadness for herself. She knew to expect all this, but she never for a moment anticipated that she would feel so displaced without them. So wobbly, so uncertain, so filled with doubt about everything. She'd lost her backup.

The new thoughts scared her. The doubts were like stranglers wriggling around every single thought in her head, creeping in on every unrelated idea, an invader in her mind. A squatter in her head that stubbornly wouldn't leave.

Like Jacob, who'd moved to Prairie Rock to assist them with her parents' land. He lingered in her mind too. In almost every thought, like a shadow in a room. Always there, despite not being relevant. She couldn't understand why his presence was so constant in her thoughts. She tried to shake him away but he wouldn't leave. His eyes, brown and deep, seemed to see into her soul when he looked at her. She always looked away. But she always looked.

When a child of Prairie Rock community inherits the new plot of land – double acreage for her as both her parents had passed – it is up to that individual to decide what crop to sow. While it is her decision, she of course must bear in mind that it is to service the needs of the entire community. There are nightly meetings about various community issues but only one weekly gathering that everybody must attend. And it is here that she finds herself the centre of unwanted attention.

'Fruit trees?' A voice cuts into her thoughts. Barnaby, a man whose fingers are like roots to the earth.

'Mmm,' she replies, uncertain, as the faces watch her expectantly.

'The land on the north is especially good for fruit, better sun too, might do better over there.'

'We're doing okay on the south, thank you very much,' Harriet frowns.

'You're doing a fine job, Harriet, it's the sun and the soil I'm thinking about,' he reassures her.

This is an exciting moment for everybody. The woman's sad loss is the village's gain, something new to plant in honour of her parents, a real opportunity to introduce new produce to their diets.

'I've heard about these almond orchards,' Gladys suggests.

'Bobby is already growing almond trees on his allotment,' Barnaby explains softly.

'Yes, but not enough.'

'I think there's enough for the community,' Bobby says, slightly offended. 'How many more almonds do we need?'

'But there is so much more we can do – almond oil, almond butter, almond milk . . . so far we just eat almonds.' Gladys looks around the group for support. Some are interested, some not. She shrugs. 'It's her decision.'

'Mmm,' the woman replies again.

'What about prunes?' Dorothy suggests and goes on yet another lecture about the value of prunes, everything they've been hearing since her doctor seems to have put her on a prune-only diet on account of her haemorrhoids. She's like a new woman since prunes came into her life, one would think she had a new lover.

Jacob. He arrives in her mind. Standing in the corner, observing her.

Everybody starts shouting over each other as they're used to doing, the usual insults, and friendly attacks at the ready, until Barnaby silences them with a calm Jedi motion of his hand.

'It's not your decision,' he reminds them all softly.

Everyone looks at her expectantly.

'I really don't know,' she says. 'I don't know. I don't know.' She holds her head with her hands and closes her eyes.

They look at each other with concern.

'Give her time,' Barnaby says.

'But the sowing season—'

'Give her time,' he repeats.

In the car on the way home, her husband Deacon is silent. She takes a breath and goes to say something but catches herself.

'What?' he looks at her, full attention, anxious eyes. He even slows the car.

She shakes her head.

'You were about to say something.'

'It's gone,' she says, looking out her window. 'I don't know.'

The pressure from the community grew immense, despite Barnaby's efforts to calm the waters.

Every day the woman would travel to the new land in the south, the acre that she had to begin sowing. The land had been prepared, ready for sowing, ready for cultivation, but she still had no idea what to plant. She brought out a deckchair and sat watching the land, hoping for inspiration, but instead her mind would wander, over and over again, back into her own life. So many questions, so much doubt.

Her friends and neighbours from the community would take turns visiting with her with their proposals and leaflets, presentations and well-thought-out ideas for the land, information on every fruit, nut, vegetable and crop imaginable and each with his or her own personal reasons.

Arthritic Billy with the cannabis proposal, Sally who wanted to plant tea, to relive an illicit affair with a boy on a tea plantation in China from her travels as a student. They all had their ideas, good ones, valid ones, but when they'd ask her, she would invariably offer the same response:

'I don't know.'

Nothing else, there was nothing else for her to say.

And there was Jacob, whom she'd watch every chance she had. This stranger, somebody from 'outside', exotic and athletic. Handsome, brooding, often in a state of undress. While he was alive, her father had caught her staring at Jacob too many times. He'd given her that knowing look. That warning look. She'd watch Jacob from the window in her kitchen that overlooked her parents' land. Most days he'd work alongside her husband, the two of them total opposites in frame. Jacob broad and athletic, muscles rippling from his shoulders, arms, back, his narrow waist. Her husband strong and lean but tall and thin like a bean, ropey muscles in his long arms.

'What are you looking at?' her father would ask her.

'I don't know.'

It had begun back then. The questions and doubt. Before he'd passed away.

She repeated that phrase so often to everyone, all of the time. It would come out of her mouth without her even thinking of it. The doubt in her seemed alive, as if it had a life of its own, flying out of its own accord, taking over her thoughts, taking over her words. Even her actions. It came as a surprise to most people: the woman who was so self-assured, who always had a plan, who always had things figured out, who never worried even if she hadn't.

It seemed to rock the community as much as it rocked her. Her lack of certainty was contagious, and forced them to start thinking, questioning what was never previously questioned. The small everyday decisions became big questions, inspiring lively town hall debates.

The woman, it seemed, became the queen, the leader, the president of not knowing things and this made her the person everybody wanted to share their own uncertainties with. Her doubt fed theirs, and the doubts grew. And as the doubt grew in their minds, the land that she stared at daily began to grow a mystery crop.

She would sit at the plot each day staring at the soil, wondering, questioning, trying to move things around in her head, slot things together. People travelled to see her; knowing she'd be there, they'd bring with them picnics, canteens of coffee, alcohol, whatever they needed or desired, and they'd pour their hearts out about all the things they didn't know. She listened – it was all she could do, because she didn't have the answers any more than they did.

They couldn't decide whether to re-elect Mayor Alice, who had been their mayor for so many years. Under that cloud of doubt, Alice came to the woman to confess she was in doubt whether she wanted to be re-elected mayor anyway. Her daughter had just had a child, she wanted to revel in being a grandmother. And then Bizzie Brown decided that she was in doubt as to whether to continue living in the community at all. She'd been wondering about it for a while, was afraid of making the change, but it seemed so many changes were happening around her, so perhaps she should embrace the change too.

They would discuss their doubts while watching the unusual crop rising from the soil. The crop was odd, it grew in different directions as if it couldn't decide, and it grew in different colours. Some parts flowered, some looked like grain, some looked like vegetables or vines. It was so confusing, they couldn't figure out what it was and doubted whether it was anything specific at all.

'What did you sow?' they'd ask her, on their hands and knees, studying the peculiar growths.

'I don't know,' she'd reply.

Bizzie's doubts about staying reached the point that she left, after fifty years. But in order to fill her place, the community had to decide whether to follow the old entry laws for new neighbours. Doubt led them to change their minds; thus a young man and woman, newly married and under the usual age of acceptance, were invited in. The new neighbours met with the woman, who wondered whether they should use the peculiar new crop of botanicals for gin. Should they begin an artisan gin distillery, should they infuse the herbs and flowers into their gin to give it expression, something unique to the area that the rest of the world couldn't offer?

This unusual crop of doubt was like a treasure trove, a

unique biosphere harbouring a mixture of things that didn't know what it was.

After hearing the artisan gin idea, Barnaby wondered if winemaking was a logical extension of that, and then wondered why they weren't making wine with their wonderful vine-yards. So they did. And the same with the olives, which became oil, and then Bobby's tiny almond allotment became an almond orchard and so too came the almond oil and butter and milk.

And all this doubt caused so many questions and so many meetings and so many discussions about what they were unsure of doing, which led to changing their minds and their ways, which had once been so solid. All of this activity carried on around an unmoving lone woman who sat daily in a deckchair in a field watching an unidentifiable crop, musing and wondering.

'What is it?' she asked Barnaby one day, who was on his knees examining the crop stretching up through the soil.

And Barnaby, who knew everything about the soil, looked up at her. 'I don't know.'

She snorted, to her and his surprise, and her hand flew to her mouth, but she couldn't stop her laughter.

'Well if you don't know, then how can any of us know?' she laughed.

'I do know something,' he said, standing and fixing her with his knowing gaze. 'It is a field of I Don't Knows. You planted the seeds of doubt, and now you are growing an entire crop of doubt.'

She looked at the field of thriving doubt.

'I think you're wrong about not knowing, though,' he said. 'I think it is clear to see that you do know one thing. You *know* that you don't know. That is a solid certainty. You know it so well, that you have succeeded in growing an entire field of it, with your thoughts alone. However, only *you* can know exactly what it is that you don't know so very much.'

He was right.

She looked up at him as if his words had triggered an epiphany.

He nodded at her to go.

She hurries away from the crop, straight to her car. She races home, knowing exactly what it is she doesn't know about. She needs to get straight there immediately. She searches the land for Jacob, but there's no sign of him. Nor is her husband at home.

She thinks quickly. She runs across the field that her husband and Jacob have spent so many months cultivating together, straight to the guesthouse at the back of her parents' home where Jacob is staying. She rattles on the door and Jacob opens the door as if he's been expecting her.

'I need to speak with Deacon,' she says softly.

He steps aside and Deacon stands up, surprised to see her. 'Hey, honey, we were just stopping for lunch. Would you like—'

'Stop,' she says, holding a hand up. 'There's something I have to say to you. Something that you must know.'

Jacob looks downward. Deacon looks nervously from Jacob to his wife.

'You have been my loyal husband from the moment you said "I do." My best friend for as long as I can remember. My confidant. My everything.'

His eyes start to fill with tears.

'Don't do—'

'No, let me speak. You've been asking what's going on with me for long enough. It's time I told you.'

Jacob looks up. She sees the hope in his face.

'I was filled with doubt for such a long time, probably longer than I realized, but it's been brewing inside me. I wasn't even sure what I wasn't sure of, but it was there nonetheless, niggling away. I grew an entire field of doubt, and it looks mighty pretty too. It came up quick, then it grew faster, and spread. But it's not going to grow any more, Deacon, because now I know. I know what I didn't know before.'

She takes a deep breath and lets it out.

Jacob stares at her. Deacon braces himself.

'I know that you are in love with Jacob. I know that Jacob is in love with you.'

Deacon looks startled, afraid. Jacob does not.

'I can see it. I can feel it. I've been watching you both every day for a year.'

Deacon gently crumbles, covers his face.

'You alone could have cultivated fields of doubt for years, all over this mountain head. But you kept hiding it and so you cultivated what everybody else wanted instead. The time for that is over, Deacon. Now, just be together. Be good to each other.' To Jacob, 'Be good to this man,' she warns, her voice cracking.

Deacon asks, 'Where are you going?'

She smiles, suddenly filled with excitement. 'I don't know.' And she's one hundred per cent sure of that.

13

The Woman Who Returned and Exchanged Her Husband

1

The woman watches Anita stir her tea around her teacup, the spoon tinkling as it strikes the china. Twelve times and three little taps on the rim of the cup to shake off the tea before placing it in the saucer.

Her other friend, Elaine, bites into her scone; the jam and cream ooze out between the gaps in her teeth, land on her lip and a glob in the corner of her mouth. A fast lizard tongue whips it away.

'But the dress was lovely on you, why are you sending it back?' Elaine says to Anita, through her full mouth, crumbs spewing out with her words.

Anita scrunches up her face. 'The colour was the same as my skin tone, it made me look anaemic.'

'Did you hear Diane is anaemic?'

'That would make sense. She passed out twice in spin class.'

'It happened to me too, maybe I'm anaemic too,' Elaine says, taking another bite of her scone. The crumbs land on her enormous bosom.

'Are you going to get a refund or exchange it?'

'Full refund.'

'I'm returning Paddy,' the woman finally blurts out.

They both look at her in surprise, as though they'd forgotten she was there.

'You're what?' Elaine says, putting down the scone.

'I'm returning Paddy,' she repeats, less confidently now. It was easier just saying it once. 'I'm bringing him back to the shop.'

'Does the shop still exist?' Anita asks.

'*That's* your main concern?' Elaine asks.

'Well! It's been thirty years. I bought a dress online and the boutique was gone when I went to return it.'

'Husbands get a lifetime guarantee, you can return them whenever you want, and get your money back,' Elaine says.

'It's not about the money,' the woman says, feeling prickly.

'Of course not,' Elaine and Anita share a guilty look.

'It's about getting my life back, getting me back,' the woman says, feeling her confidence return again. 'I'm sixty years old on Friday; it's made me think about things, about how I want to spend the next, and final, twenty years of my life.'

'Twenty if you're lucky,' Anita says, and Elaine elbows her.

'Of course, we understand,' Elaine cooed. 'But just be prepared not to get a full refund. They don't make it easy to get full refunds on husbands. They'll probably make you exchange him.'

'That's how Valerie ended up with Earl.'

They wrinkle their noses in disgust.

'Earl is nice,' the woman defends him.

'Earl was caught sniffing the seats of women's bicycles. Three times he's been warned.'

'She must have ticked the requirement box for *lewd*.' They make a disgusted face again.

'I don't want to exchange Paddy,' she explains, trying to stay calm, wondering if they're listening to her at all and if her next step in her new life would be to rid herself of her intolerable friends too. Even her friendships have grown mildew. 'It's not about wanting somebody else, it's just about not having him.'

'You seem very sure.'

'I am very sure.'

'Have you told him yet?'

'Yes. I'm returning him tomorrow afternoon.'

They gasp.

'If you do have to exchange him, you'll have to choose somebody of the same value,' Elaine says.

'You think he's worth more now?' the woman asks, drawn into this aspect when she doesn't want to be.

'Less!' the two women say in unison.

'He's forty years older now,' Anita says. 'Not much demand for a sixty-two-year-old granddad.'

'Yes, but I always thought maturity was an asset,' the woman says, thinking of Paddy who will no longer be her Paddy.

Elaine snorts and smears more jam and cream on her second fruit scone.

'Anyway, you can add your own money to it if you see someone better.'

'I'm not exchanging him,' she says, rolling her eyes. 'I'm *returning* him, and that's all there is to it.'

'We'll see,' Anita says, hiding her smile behind her teacup.

'You know, there are women there too,' Elaine says. 'They've modernized it since the laws changed. You might want a wife.'

'I certainly do not want a wife,' the woman huffs.

'Wanda Webster bought herself a wife.'

'Well, Wanda Webster can do what she likes. I'm not buying a wife. I'm just returning Paddy.'

Silence.

'How does Paddy feel about it?' Anita asks.

Finally, the woman thinks.

Her eyes fill then, her guard down. 'He was upset.'

'Well look, he should have known this would always be a possibility. And the kids can still visit him, wherever he is, or if someone else takes him,' Anita offers gently.

The woman's throat closes up. 'I never thought of that. Of someone else buying him.'

'Ah, I wouldn't worry about that,' Elaine says, biting into her scone, and adding with a filled mouth, 'I'm sure that won't happen.'

There's cream on her nose. The woman feels defensive of Paddy. She decides not to tell her about the cream. That one's for Paddy.

2

The woman stares at the paperwork in front of her, her eyes finding it hard to focus. *Reasons for Return/Exchange.* The words blur together, she struggles to breathe in the small cubicle where even the green rubbery plant looks depressed. The ceiling is low with one panel missing, revealing the pipes, the dust, the skeleton of the warehouse.

Paddy has been taken away from her, escorted to another office to file paperwork. He'd given a gentle sad smile just before his door closed. It had hurt her heart, the gentleness in his face, the memories that came flooding with every image of that expression, the way he was still trying to tell her it was okay, he forgave her, he understood. In a way, after all the guilt, she feels relieved. She's thought about this moment for so long, lived it in her head, wondered if she would ever be able to build up the courage to make a change in her life and here she is, doing it. It's awful. The most awful thing she's ever done, but at least she's finally doing it. Amidst the tornado of terror, there's swirling exhilaration. It's happening, and she will soon be on the other side.

While they're both here in square grey offices signing forms, the Spousal Market van, black and unmarked to be discreet, has been removing Paddy's belongings. When she returns, it will be like he was never there, like their marriage never even happened. A life together wiped out.

Again that tug. Forty years, all carried away in a truck.

'Are you having difficulty deciding which box to tick?' The manager, Susan, with the bouffant and bright red lips, interrupts her thoughts. 'Between you and me, sweetheart,' she lowers her voice to a whisper, 'it doesn't really matter what box you tick.'

'Not to you perhaps.' The woman straightens up and lifts her chin. She surveys the list again. There's so much of Paddy that bothered her over the years: his disorganization, his messiness, empty toilet rolls left on the holder, empty packets going back in the cupboard. His closeness with that woman twenty-seven years ago. His snoring. His awkwardness with sensitive issues. The radio up too loud, sports always on the TV. Shoes, jackets, abandoned wherever discarded. The same long anecdotes with the same old friends. She feels like she's been picking him apart every day, unpeeling his character layer by layer to find another part of him that annoyed her.

She concentrates on the list.

- Too big
- Too small
- Fit
- Not as pictured/described

- Fabric
- Colour
- Quality
- Price
- Delivery issue
- Not for me
- Defective/faulty

Paddy wasn't defective, he wasn't faulty, there was nothing wrong with the fabric of his being, she's just grown tired of him, grown out of love. And he's grown out of love with her, she's certain of it, but Paddy would never leave. He's the type to stay. Put up with things that bother him. Much as they irritated one another, poked and prodded at each other mentally, she couldn't deny Paddy was a good man, a great father, a caring grandfather.

She ticks *Not for me* and signs her signature at the bottom.

'Great,' Susan takes the paperwork from her and gets busy with her folder and stamps, shuffling paper around. She talks as though she's said the words a thousand times but has never listened to their meaning. 'Now you're aware that you cannot get a full refund at this time, so I will—'

'No, no, I was told I could. I bought him in 1978 and the terms of the agreement still hold true today. I checked all this out with a customer service agent called Grace.' She roots in her bag for her datebook with all the information.

Susan smiles, but there's impatience beneath it.

Outside the office, people arrive and the woman listens

147

for Paddy but it's more customers buying or returning, she's not sure which. Either way, Susan is keen to press on.

'Indeed, but on closer study of your receipt, I discovered that you bought Paddy on sale. He was on special. Sale items are not eligible for total refunds.' She keeps talking and the woman is transported back to the moment she saw Paddy. It wasn't that she didn't have enough money, but he was a special offer and that seemed . . . well, special. Standing beside a giant gold star with *SPECIAL* emblazoned across the side had been a sign for her. Not just a literal one.

'We can offer you an exchange, for a husband or wife of the same value, or a credit note, which will be to the value of the original purchase.'

The woman's mouth falls open as she stares at her in shock. Susan shifts uncomfortably in her chair.

'But I don't want an exchange. I didn't come here for another husband.'

'So a credit note will do,' she says. She stamps the form loudly, ending the conversation. She opens the drawer and retrieves a small envelope. She pushes her chair back and stands, extends her hand. 'It's been a pleasure doing business with you.'

'That's it?'

The woman slowly stands.

'That's it,' Susan laughs. 'You're a free woman. The parking garage is out the green door and to the left, the market is on the right if you'd like to browse.'

'Where's Paddy?'

'He's gone,' she says, surprised.

'Gone? But—' Her heart pounds wildly, a sensation of panic engulfing her. 'I didn't get to say goodbye.'

Susan moves around the desk, gliding to the door with her hand at the woman's back, guiding her out the door, across a corridor to the green door. 'It's easier this way, believe me.'

She thinks of his sad smile. He was saying goodbye, he must have known. 'Where is he?' the woman stops at the green door.

'We'll take good care of him now, don't you worry. He'll be cleaned up, pampered, rested before he goes back on the market.' She opens the green door.

'Back on the market?' she says, aghast, feeling Susan's hand on the small of her back again, ushering her outside. 'But Paddy won't be able to handle it. He doesn't like starting new things with new people. He's sixty-two years old.'

'We wouldn't put him back on the market without his permission, he's a human being – not a piece of meat,' she chuckles. 'Paddy ticked the box for future sale. He'll be in great demand, too. There's plenty of interest for newly returned husbands. You mark my words, there are plenty of people who want an older, experienced man. It's the ones who've been on the shelf all those years that are the difficult ones to move. Plenty of women are out there who lost their spouses and want somebody who's been in a long committed relationship; Paddy has a great track record. There are plenty of people looking for adventure. Plenty of people who are lonely.'

If the woman hears the word *plenty* again, she'll scream.

Susan smiles warmly. 'Good luck. You know where we are if you choose to use your credit note.'

She closes the green door, which is steel and unpainted on the outside. The woman jumps as it clangs shut and echoes around the empty parking garage. Her car sits alone in the 'Returns' lot, while around the corner in the buying section the garage is almost full. She walks slowly towards her car, hearing her footsteps on the concrete, every step and moment and sound amplified, her feeling of aloneness overwhelming.

She drives home, hot fat tears falling down her face. An aching hollow yawns in her chest, followed by a wave of fear and loss. But by the time she reaches her home the tears have dried. The sadness has moved towards relief and the dread has become excitement. A new beginning.

3

The house is quiet. The children are long gone, married with children, working, stressing. Her own life has slowed down; watching them sweating the small stuff was a reminder to her of how enormous everything used to feel at that time of her own life. It helped her make her decision. It's time for her to live now, time for her to relax, time to truly be happy, time to feel like she doesn't owe anybody anything, time to not feel guilty about living for herself. The time for blaming other people for her own frustrations is over, she has taken her life by the horns and is taking responsibility. No more nagging at Paddy for his shortcomings – she has to make the changes herself.

She cleans the house from top to bottom until there isn't a speck of dust to be found. She marvels at the space in her wardrobe now that Paddy's clothes are gone. The guest bedroom could be a bedroom for guests again – they'd stopped sharing a bed five years earlier on account of his snoring, which had worsened with his weight, which he wouldn't do anything about.

She drinks an entire bottle of white wine and watches a trashy reality show without his sighs and tuts and grumbles of disapproval. As the days go by she dines on undercooked pasta, overcooked meat, and artichokes – just because she can. And she sheds a few pounds by eating when she's hungry rather than the times he'd demand his food. The recycling is in order, everything's where it needs to be, everything in her home has its place and nobody moves anything. She exists on her own clock, no longer has to walk on eggshells because he's in one of his moods. She can have visitors whenever she feels like it, and she's stopped going out to Friday-night drinks with his friends and their irritating wives. Her world runs according to how she likes it. She's no longer irritated.

Some nights she wakes up crying.

Some days she finds herself sitting in his bedroom, inhaling the last of his scent.

She sniffs his aftershave when out at department stores. A few of his favourite foods creep into her shopping cart. When her son and daughter come by to tell her that their father has been bought and is now off the market, she cries.

4

One day she drives to the hardware store, returning the wrong light bulbs she'd bought for her bedside lamp, and nearly crashes the car. Paddy is cutting the grass in her neighbour's garden. She is about to pull over when the front door opens and Barbara, forty-six years old, appears outside with a grin on her face, carrying a cup of coffee.

He smiles, the biggest smile she's ever seen on his face, takes it from her, and they kiss. A long, lingering kiss.

The woman turns the car around and drives home and doesn't leave her house for three days.

5

'I understand you're upset. It's difficult to move on but it has been over one month and we are following all of the correct protocol. Paddy was bought on his first day back on the market.'

'By Barbara Bollinger,' she spits.

'I can't reveal the name of the purchaser.'

'I know who she is, I saw them together. They live five doors away from me. I have to see them every day.'

'I'm confused. Are you upset about the proximity or the relationship?'

'Both!' she shouts, tears springing in her eyes.

'Perhaps it's time for you to use your credit note,' Susan's eyes sparkle mischievously.

Susan pushes the door open to the supermarket and the woman sees that it's more like a warehouse since the days she had shopped for her husband. Men of different colours, shapes and sizes, sit or stand on floor-to-ceiling shelves. Men and women browse the aisles as if doing their weekly shopping. When they see somebody they like, they read the information available on the sign, as if checking the ingredients, and then a cherry-picker rises to retrieve the man. The men pass the time by speaking cheerily to one another, texting on iPads and laptops, or reading. Some men head off on breaks or return from breaks as they follow a schedule.

Susan leads the woman to a row of computers. 'We've become more advanced since your first visit forty years ago. Here is where you input your needs, and it should find matches based on your answers. It's easier to search the database on the computer than search the shelves. We try to make every man accessible, but it's not always easy to see the top shelf. The men complain all the time and we're working on it, but it's my impression that certain women go straight to the top shelf – as if the more precious ones are up there for protection, like the shelves at a newsstand, if you know what I mean.' She winks. 'If it's just looks that people are interested in at first, they usually browse, pick a few favourites and then look up their details – but I know that's not for you. You'll want to see the details first.'

'How do you know that?'

'It was Paddy's habits that bothered you. I'm sure you're looking for character and personality traits that your previous husband didn't have. Take a scroll through the questionnaire. Any problems, Candice will assist you.'

It is detailed but entertaining. The program runs through scenarios, asking her to choose the preferred actions her prospective husband would take in a variety of situations. Susan is right, she is going for the exact opposite of how Paddy behaved.

When he'd been calm she'd wanted him to be more passionate.

When he'd lost his temper she'd wanted him to be calm.

When he'd talked too much about one subject, she'd wished he could interest her in other ways. She picked him apart, until a red alarm above the computer sounded, as if she'd won money at a slot machine. She'd found a match.

6

His name is Andrew, he is ten years younger than her. He puts his clothes away where they belong, he always lines up his shoes neatly. He cooks. He eats everything, isn't fussy about his food. He welcomes visitors to the house, he watches her soaps without irritating commentary, he joins a water-colour class with her. He is wonderfully protective of her, yet at the same time takes pride when other men pay attention to her. He is a thoughtful lover.

On paper, or in a hard drive, he is perfect for her.

And yet. And yet she is still irritated, frustrated, realizing that, no matter who she is with, *she* seems to be the same person. She can't keep changing everybody around her and expecting a difference; she is the one who is making life difficult.

One morning she is still in bed, sleeping late, which is unusual for her. The curtains are drawn. She is lying in darkness for the fourth morning in a row after being in a state ever since her children and grandchildren had spent the day in Paddy's new home, with Paddy's new wife. She'd seen the cars outside, had heard her grandchildren playing in Barbara Bollinger's garden, heard the sound of laughter and conversation drift from the open windows and down to her home. Whether real or imagined, the sounds tormented her. Andrew knocks on the bedroom door and she sits up, fixes herself. He carries a breakfast tray of huevos rancheros, something Paddy would never eat in a million years.

'Thank you, Andrew, you're so kind,' she says. Though her gratitude is genuine, she hears the strain in her voice. She summons all of her strength to give him more, more of what he deserves.

He sits on the edge of the bed, this handsome beautiful thing, and says her name. His tone catches her attention, she recognizes it as a warning. She places the napkin down, feeling a tremble growing within her, then picks it up again and grips it tight, twisting it around her finger, watching her skin go from white to purple as her flesh is squeezed and the bloodflow is constricted.

'This is our fourteenth morning together,' he begins.

She nods.

'You understand what happens on the fifteenth day?'

Her eyes widen, suddenly fearful he will ask something of her that she can't deliver. She's enjoyed being more experimental than she had been with Paddy, but perhaps not too much more.

He laughs lightly, brushing her cheekbone with his knuckles. 'Don't look so worried. It is the final day that you can return me for a full refund.'

'Oh.'

'So I have packed my bags. I'm ready to return whenever you are. First eat a good breakfast,' he smiles sadly.

'Andrew, I think there's some kind of mistake. I don't want to return you.'

'Don't you?' He studies her.

'Haven't you . . . enjoyed your stay?'

He smiles. 'Yes, of course, I think that's obvious.'

She blushes.

Taking her hands in his, he continues: 'But we are not the perfect fit and I think that you know that. And I know from your previous relationship that you stay. You stay because you think it's right, because you think it's easier, but it's not. Also, if I stay, then I am devalued.'

Though it pains her to hear him say it, she knows he is right.

'I don't want to be devalued. I am a good man. I want to be appreciated for what I am truly worth.'

She nods, understanding. Staying with Paddy for so long the way they were had devalued them both. She lifts Andrew's hand and kisses his knuckles. And with that Andrew packs his belongings into the trunk of the car and for the second time she prepares to return her husband.

7

Across the road, Paddy looks up, garden shears in hand, and watches. The woman meets his eyes for the first time in months and her heart pounds, her stomach twists. She feels alive with desire. She aches because of the longing and the sadness of what she let go, of what she willingly gave away. Being with him feels like home, but seeing him fills her with homesickness.

Andrew catches her staring.

Barbara steps outside with a mug of coffee, her long blonde hair swept back off her face, her summer dress unbuttoned up her thigh. The woman feels sick.

'It's okay to change your mind, you know,' Andrew says. 'It doesn't mean you were wrong, I know how you hate to be wrong,' he smiles.

She gets into the car and starts up the engine.

When she returns from the market she parks the car and

enters the empty house that no longer feels like a home. She takes in the hallway, the tidy hallway. She listens to the silence. She knows that these are small victories in a war she lost. She acknowledges what has been eating at her for some time now; she would gladly trade all this in to have Paddy back again.

She opens the front door and runs across the road. She knocks on Barbara's door.

Barbara opens the door, views her with surprise but is polite.

'I'm very sorry to disturb you,' she begins, 'but I want Paddy back. I need him back,' she adds breathlessly.

'Excuse me, Paddy is my husband, you can't just take him!' Barbara says, bewildered.

'With all due respect, Barbara, he's not mine. And he's not yours either. He's Paddy. I'm very sorry, Barbara, I realize this is a great encumbrance on you and your life, and I was trying very hard not to ruin anybody else's life, but I haven't changed my mind; I've made a new decision,' she says, matter-of-factly. 'I want to be with Paddy. I miss you, Paddy,' she raises her voice down the corridor. 'I love you.'

Paddy steps into the hall and gives her a soft familiar smile that grows into a grin.

'There she is,' he says, smiling. 'My knight in shining armour.'

'I didn't know you needed rescuing,' Barbara says, rightly offended.

'*We* needed rescuing,' Paddy says simply. 'She was the only one who had the gumption to do something about it. I'm sorry, Barbara.'

'I can't afford you, Paddy,' the woman says. 'I have a credit note, but it's not enough for you – I checked your price. I can go to the credit union for the rest of it.' She looks at Barbara. 'I'll give you every cent I have, Barbara, and everything I ever earn again. Will you come home? Paddy, please.'

Barbara steps aside, and looks at him, unable to argue with this show of love.

'That's all I want,' he says.

8

Back in their home, Paddy hangs his coat on the back of the chair and leaves his suitcase in the hallway. He pulls her close for a kiss. He is so strong and his movement is so sudden he topples her slightly. They misjudge the timing of their kiss and their proximity, causing their noses to squish and their teeth to crash against each other. He moves in faster than she anticipates, she feels his shoe tread on her toes, her neck aches as she stretches up to meet him.

It's clumsy and imperfect. It's real, it's honest, and it's all she wants.

14

The Woman Who Lost Her Common Sense

She was found walking down the centre of a three-lane motorway, in rush-hour traffic at eight a.m. on a Monday morning. It would have been more dangerous had a collision not occurred at the exit, meaning traffic was backed up. She walked past the cars, looking straight ahead with a determined – though others said lost – look on her face.

Drivers stared at her from behind windscreens, minds still too foggy from recent sleep to register what they were seeing, which was a thirty-something woman in a dressing gown, wearing a pair of trainers. Some thought she had been involved in the accident ahead, was wearing pyjamas for school drop-off, and in shock had wandered away from the scene. Some even tried to coax her to safety but she ignored them. Others thought she was simply mad and locked their car doors as she neared them.

Only one person called the police.

Officer LaVar and his partner Lisa were the nearest to the scene and the first to make contact with her. By then her position had become increasingly dangerous. She had reached the end of the back-up and was walking head-on towards oncoming traffic travelling at 120 km. Those who came upon her braked hard, honked loudly and flashed their hazards to alert the traffic behind, but it didn't deter her.

Only when LaVar and Lisa flew down the shoulder, sirens blaring, did she seem to snap out of her trance. She finally stopped walking. They managed to stop the cars, causing yet another traffic jam, and rushed to her, wary of her reaction.

'Thank goodness,' she said, breaking into a relieved smile. 'I'm so glad you finally came.'

LaVar and Lisa looked at one another in surprise at her lack of hostility, and Lisa left the handcuffs behind. They guided her to the side of the road, to safety.

'It's an emergency,' the woman said, serious now, 'I need to report a crime. Somebody has stolen my common sense.'

The concern fell from LaVar's face, though it rose in Lisa's. They put her gently into the car and drove her to the station. LaVar sat down with her in the station's cell, because Lisa couldn't keep a straight face. There were two steaming Styrofoam cups of milky tea before them.

'So, tell me what you were doing out there,' he said.

'I told you,' she said, politely. 'I was trying to report a crime. Somebody has stolen my common sense.'

She lifted the steaming tea to her lips.

'Careful it's very ho—' he warned, too late. She winced as the tea scalded the inside of her mouth.

'Told you,' she said finally, after she'd recovered from the immediate pain. 'Who would do *that* if they had common sense?'

'Good point,' he agreed.

'Oh, I know you think I'm crazy,' she said, cupping her hands around the heat of the drink. 'Who would *steal* common sense? And how?'

He nodded along. Good questions. Valid questions.

'How do you know it was stolen?' he asked. 'Maybe you lost it.'

'I did not,' she said quickly. 'I am very careful. I make sure not to lose things, to put everything in the correct place, and something like my common sense . . . no,' she shook her head. 'I keep my common sense with me at all times, I always check for it. It's a necessity, like my phone. I wouldn't go anywhere without it.'

'Okay, okay.'

'Someone stole it,' she repeated. 'It's the only logical explanation.'

'Fair enough,' he said, bowing to her conviction. 'So we're looking for a perpetrator.'

'Yes,' she said, relieved to be finally taken seriously.

'Any ideas who? Anybody suspicious lurking around?'

She shook her head, bit down on her lip.

LaVar thought too. 'Let's put it this way: did you have particularly strong common sense? The sort that would be envied by others?'

'I liked to think so,' she replied.

'So you may have been known to have good common sense? I'm just trying to think as the perpetrator would. Burglars target homes where they know there are valuables to steal. If somebody stole your common sense, then they knew that you had it.'

She nodded, happy with his analysis.

'So, were there any occasions in which you showed your common sense, where somebody else may have witnessed it, and decided to steal it?'

LaVar looked at her. He felt that she was withholding something, and urged her to tell him.

She sighed. 'It's just a theory. And there's no point in offering theories if it will get people in trouble.'

'No one will get in trouble until we figure it out,' he said, motioning for her to continue.

'I recently separated from my husband. He had been having an affair, for four months, with a girl at the office who walked like a duck, but I took him back and we were trying to make it work for the past year. But it wasn't working. Not for me. I told him I wanted to separate.'

'Sensible,' LaVar nodded.

'Yes,' she agreed. 'And that's the last time I recall using it.'

'People knew about this decision?'

'Pretty much everyone.'

'Hmm,' he said. 'So it doesn't narrow down our suspects. That's a show of great common sense to a large population.' He thought again, and then continued in the same line. 'And your husband, was he happy about the situation?'

'Not at all.'

'Hmm. Go on.'

'He wanted us to continue living together, but I thought that was a bad idea. Neither of us would be able to move on.'

'Another show of common sense,' he pointed out.

'Oh yes,' she realized. 'So I still had it then. Which means . . .' A thought occurred to her.

'Go on.'

'We had to sell the house. He packed his things and I packed mine and it was then that I noticed it missing. I unpacked all the boxes in my mother's house – I'm staying with her for a while, until I get on my feet again. But it wasn't there . . . I simply don't have it any more. My ex-husband must have taken it away with him, packed it in one of his boxes. Either deliberately or accidentally, I don't know, but it's my only theory. I'm certain I had it before we moved.'

LaVar thought hard. 'And what makes you say you don't have it now?'

'This morning I walked down the motorway in my dressing gown.'

'True,' he agreed. 'Yet . . .' He looked at her more closely. 'You seem to have your wits about you.'

'Well, it wasn't my wits he took! If he had, we would be back together again, living in our house. If anything, doing what he did restored my wits.'

He nodded. A sensible rationale once again.

'Tell me, what are you wearing beneath your robe?'

She seemed taken aback and clutched her robe tighter to her chest. 'My nightdress.'

'Why didn't you just go outside in that?'

'Because I would have frozen. And it's quite see-through.'

'Hmm.'

'What?'

He looked down at her feet.

'What about the trainers? Do you wear them around the house with your nightwear?'

'No! I usually wear my slipper socks, the ones with the grips on the sole, but they weren't appropriate for the motorway.'

'Indeed not.' He wrote something down in his notebook. 'And for what purpose did you walk down the motorway?'

'I told you, to report a crime. I know, it is nonsensical.'

'You *know* this.'

'Yes.'

'Well then, if you know it is nonsensical then surely it is your common sense that allows you to know that.'

She thought about it.

'And if your intention was to alert the authorities, you did exactly that.'

'Instead of walking into a *police station*,' she reminded him.

'Look,' he said gently, 'I can't file a report. I don't think your common sense has been stolen, nor do I think it is lost. I think that you still have it, on your person. You're merely using it in a different way.'

She pondered this.

LaVar explained his analysis of the case. 'You wore your dressing gown because you knew you would be cold, you wore sneakers because you knew slipper socks would not be good for the motorway, and you walked down the motorway in rush-hour traffic knowing somebody would alert the police, whose attention you needed to report your crime. It seems you achieved everything you set out to do, despite the method you utilized to achieve it.'

She sat back, and pondered that some more. 'Maybe you're right.'

'Under the circumstances, I'm going to let you go, with a firm warning. Whatever you do, do not endanger your life or the lives of others.'

She nodded, head down, feeling like a scolded child.

LaVar lost his authoritative tone. 'Your common sense is a little different, I'll give you that. It isn't linear, it is not the common sense of the majority of people, but that doesn't mean that it is wrong or that it has been lost or stolen. It is yours and it is unique.'

Her eyes filled and he reached into his pocket and retrieved a tissue. He handed it to her.

'Thank you,' she said gently.

'You've obviously been through a very stressful time. People think differently during those times, but you're not going crazy.'

'You're a very smart detective,' she smiled.

'See, you just knowing that tells me your common sense hasn't been stolen,' he said, grinning.

'Thank you.' She smiled, and breathed a long sigh of relief.

15

The Woman Who Walked in Her Husband's Shoes

She'd heard about men doing it, knew very well that sometimes it was part of a costume, sometimes for sexual gratification, sometimes because they didn't completely identify with the male gender, and other times because they were actually female but born in male bodies. Some felt themselves between male and female and so were bi-gendered, having both male and female sides to their soul. She knew all of this because she'd heard stories from women with husbands who liked wearing their panties, women whose sons were now daughters, a woman whose husband liked to go out one night a week as his feminine alter ego. She'd of course known about it all on a vague materialistic level, but then she'd researched it further. For herself.

She was a woman, not a man; she was born a woman,

felt like a woman, dressed like a woman, felt sexy as a woman while wearing women's clothes, felt sexier as a woman with no clothes at all just in her own skin. And yet.

She had an overwhelming desire to slip her feet into her husband's shoes.

It wasn't a casual yearning, it was a heart-pounding, head-thumping desire that felt so powerful that it alarmed her. It felt so strong that she knew it was wrong. And as soon as she felt it, she saw his shoes everywhere. They were all over the house, deserted wherever he had kicked them off. Dirty sweaty trainers by the door after his run, polished brogues underneath the table where he kicked them off during dinner after a long day at work, tartan slippers by the leather couch from when he'd put his feet up. It would have been easy at any stage to slip her feet in, even when he was looking. It would have been easy to walk around, make a joke of it; he wouldn't care, no one would. But she didn't want to make a joke of it. She wanted to wear those shoes for real. It felt like a big deal, not a casual joke, it felt like something she would rather do in private. She had a longing to wear her husband's shoes, not because she liked the style, or the fabric, or the shape or the size. She wanted to know what it would feel like to be him, to literally walk around in his shoes.

She had never felt so frightened by a desire, or embar-rassed, or so repulsed by herself.

But it was difficult to find the time to steal away and for this she was thankful. She wanted to hide from her longings. She worked, he worked, children, food, life, sleep. Days were filled, there was no room for secrecy, you couldn't go to the toilet without open doors and wandering bodies. But burying this secret desire only caused it to intensify. Like a volcano over time, this hot impulsive passion built and built.

They were watching television, binge-watching their favourite show, one episode after another, both exhausted and sleep-deprived but needing to get to the end of the series, sure through each slow hour that this one would be their last tonight, but then they'd get sucked in by the cliff-hanger ending and start watching the next episode. Tonight, however, she couldn't immerse herself in it as she usually did. She felt distracted, jittery. It was like the feeling she used to get back when she was still smoking; that craving for a cigarette that wouldn't let her rest until she'd smoked one. The volcano within her was active. And she exploded. Silently. She excused herself to go to the bathroom, told him not to pause the show and wait for her – which raised questions; they always paused the show when one of them left the room, not to would cause an argument.

Leaving him satisfied with her answers she went straight to his wardrobe, feeling more like a swindler than a sleuth, and she surveyed his shoe collection. She felt like a kid in a candy store, viewing the great selection on rows of shelves. She eyed the polished black brogues that he wore to work. How had his workday been, she wondered. Fine, he had said, but he seemed quiet, and she never really got the details. Then she saw his tan trendy brogues, the ones with the blue sole, the young cool vibey husband who was funny and engaged and entertaining after hours. She brought them to the toilet. She locked the door. She put her feet in her husband's shoes. She walked up and down the shag-pile rug, thinking, wondering, hoping for something – some kind of epiphany, a climax to her slow build, some kind of calm after the eruption that sent her up the stairs. But all it did was pique her curiosity. She needed more. She wanted to know what it was like to walk around like him, out in the world. She shared a house with him, some would argue a life, they had made people together, they had laughed and cried, buried parents, said goodbye to friends together. And yet.

And yet their lives were very different.

She didn't need to understand how he felt about his life; he was quite able to communicate that to her. It was what life was like for him that intrigued her. The normal stuff that he couldn't communicate because it just *was*, because it wasn't different, or didn't seem out of the ordinary. She wanted to know what it was like.

She waited impatiently to make her next move.

She actively encouraged a golfing holiday, which again raised questions, but it meant she would have three days to herself. After waving him off, she waited, just in case he'd forgotten something and came back to get it. She didn't want him catching her. Fighting the overwhelming urge to get started, she paced the kitchen, watching the clock. Finally, satisfied after twenty minutes that he wasn't returning, she raced upstairs, taking two steps at a time.

She entered their walk-in closet and went straight to his trainers. They were such an integral part of his casual look, that *I'm running out for bread, milk and bacon* look, *bringing kids to the playground* look, with faded jeans, T-shirt, a hoodie, sports watch.

Pushing her feet into the trainers, she straightened up and examined her image in the mirror. She giggled. With the house to herself, she posed, tried to stand as he did, giggled again. The shoes were six sizes too big – like clown shoes – and she kept tripping up.

The door to the bedroom opened and she froze. Ada, their cleaner, appeared at the door to the walk-in closet and she got such a fright, she jumped, swore and held her hands to her chest.

'Mr Simpson, I'm sorry, you gave me such a fright!' she squealed, trying to catch her breath.

The woman wearing her husband's shoes froze, absolutely mortified, waiting for Ada to open her eyes. She wondered if she should make an excuse for wearing his shoes, or if she should act like nothing had happened. She was in her own home, she shouldn't have to apologize or explain anything, and yet she felt compelled to do both. She was still trying to decide on the best story when Ada continued:

'I would have knocked, but I thought you were away on your golf trip. Just so you know, I let Max out to the garden to do his business and I cleaned out the ashtray beside the shed before you-know-who saw it,' she smirked.

The woman frowns. 'Ada?'

'Yes?'

'Are you trying to be funny?'

'No!'

'Why did you call me Mr Simpson?'

'Oh,' she rolled her eyes and hurried away. 'Mike. I'm sorry. I don't feel comfortable. It feels . . . whatever, why are you following me?'

The woman was following Ada as she worked, trying to look deep in her eyes to see why on earth she was calling her by her husband's name. But it was clear that Ada was not pretending. Startled, she left the cleaner alone and returned to the wardrobe, where she continued to stare at her reflection.

She took her husband's shoes off immediately, feeling dirty and ashamed, confused. She couldn't sleep that night. She lay awake analysing, wondering about how she felt in her husband's shoes. Setting the bizarreness of it all aside, she replayed in her mind exactly what happened and came to the conclusion that Ada had seemed like a different person to the one she knew, the woman she would speak to a few times a week. Ada had been more formal, jittery – she did not look Mike in the eye, she was less personable. Like she didn't want to be in the room with him for too long. If it wasn't because she felt her employer was wearing her husband's shoes, then it had to be because she didn't feel as comfortable in a room with Mike as she did with her. Something small but something different, and something new she had learned.

The following day she put on Mike's trainers again. She greeted the postman at her door.

'Mike,' he said in greeting.

She did not know the postman's name. He had been their postman for ten years.

'Hey,' she replied, certain her voice would give her away, but not so.

The postman, who never looked up to say hello to her, proceeded to talk about football. This new development was enough to spur her on. Already Mike's life was different. She changed into his stylish shoes, the trendy ones that he wouldn't wear to work, and headed out to collect the kids from school. Among the hundred-strong herd of women at the school gates, she saw three other men. She immediately felt eyes on her, yet not eyes that were willing to engage in conversation. Ordinarily, there was always somebody for her to chat with at pick-up, but the conversations went on around her as if she wasn't there. And yet their acting as though Mike wasn't there only made it more obvious how aware they were that he was there. She felt uncomfortable. She focused on the kids' classrooms. When the kids arrived, they broke into huge grins.

'Dad!'

They ran to her and hugged her tight, more effusive than any greeting she'd ever had from them. She was delighted to receive it and felt shitty about it too.

A mum at the school, who never looked at her because they didn't know each other, gave her a bright smile that transformed her face. 'Hi, Mike.'

'Hi,' she said, feeling light-headed.

Back at home, she felt too weak to walk in his shoes. She longed to interrogate the children on matters she knew she shouldn't, but to do so would be to betray them so with a sigh she took his shoes off and turned back into Mum. Her heart was heavy as the kids groaned when she entered the kitchen and declared it to be homework time.

The following day she wore his shoes again, this time to go into the city to shop. People expected her to be more physically helpful, to hold the doors, often failing to say thank you. She dropped by his office. As she approached his desk she felt her chest tightening and a headache coming on. She realized Mike hated his job, or felt immense pressure in his chest about it. She walked around the city for hours, feeling a need to avoid walking too closely behind women, drove to as many places as she could think of that they regularly went to, to see what the world was like for her husband. Her behaviour adjusted itself naturally, she felt her body kick into a different mode of societal compliance that she could never have imagined.

That night she arranged a babysitter for the kids and went out to a bar, wearing his trendy shoes. Taking a seat at the bar – something she never did by herself because she would never be left alone – she settled down to enjoy the peace and quiet. After a while, she felt a pair of eyes on her. She turned around and saw Bob Waterhouse watching her. Bob was the guy who dressed as his female alter ego one night a week; she remembered talking to his wife Melissa about it late one night when they'd had too much to drink. Melissa had arrived home to find him head to toe in women's clothes, and they weren't her clothes. He had an entire secret suitcase of women's clothes in his size. She didn't know what to do, but his love for her hadn't changed, his desires changed nothing between them, apart from her understanding him more and him going out once a week, sometimes with her, sometimes with like-minded people for a night out dressed as his female persona.

The way Bob was looking at her, at *Mike*, she wondered if there was more to his character that his wife didn't know. Perhaps he was coming on to Mike. She turned away and gulped her beer. Suddenly he was beside her, asking whether she'd mind if he joined her.

'No, that's okay, I'm just about to leave,' she said.

Bob gave Mike a sneaky wink. 'Wife at home?'

'Eh yeah,' she froze.

'Sure,' Bob snorted. 'Hello in there,' he said in a sing-song voice.

The woman frowned.

'It's me,' Bob whispered, 'Melissa.'

The woman who was wearing her husband's shoes focused hard and finally saw who was in front of her. The person she'd taken to be Bob was in fact Melissa.

She looked down and saw that, although she was wearing her own clothes, Melissa had Bob's Converse sneakers on.

'I started doing this a few months back, after I found Bob wearing the dress,' she said, grabbing the barman's attention and ordering two more beers. 'I thought, I want to get in on this action, see what the fuss is about. Bob loves women's shoes. It's his favourite part of it. So that's what I tried first. As soon as I put on Bob's shoes I realized that everybody thought I was him. He doesn't know I do it – or maybe he does but he figures he's had his secret all this time and now he's letting me have mine. When did you figure it out?' she asked.

'Just this week,' the woman whispered, wondering why she was whispering.

Melissa clapped her hands with glee. 'Isn't it great? Do you know the last time I went to a bar all by myself for a quiet drink?'

The woman shook her head.

'Exactly. Never. Women don't sit alone in bars. If they do, they're alcoholics, or they're looking for sex, or they're lonely and need company, some idiot to sit down and talk to them about nothing out of politeness, when all I want is to be alone. When you're a man, no one tries to keep you company, unless they want company. What has it been like for you?' Melissa asked, grinning as she gulped her beer.

'I learned that Mike hates his job, that he secretly smokes, it's uncomfortable to be alone with women in certain environments, that women can be unfairly exclusive, that he feels such an enormous pressure to protect and defend the family that it hurts his chest. He feels safe with his mother, there's a barrier with his dad, his male friends feel like an army of brothers and that a mom at the school, Polly Gorman, has a thing for him.'

'Polly Gorman!' Melissa threw her head back and laughed. 'Mike would never look at her.'

'No,' the woman mused, sipping her beer. 'Well, he flat out ignored her today.'

Melissa guffawed and they clinked their beers.

'But I learned more,' the woman said, more seriously now. 'It's a different world, isn't it?'

Melissa nodded, solemn too. 'When you wear those shoes, you're walking in a man's world.'

'Not exactly,' she disagreed. 'When I wear these shoes I'm in Mike's world. Mike's life. I thought I would understand life as a man, but I just understand life for *this* man. I feel how he feels when he enters a room. I know how others make him feel. Our world is the same but it's not. We share our lives together but we have our own. When I wear his shoes, things for me are suddenly tilted. I see the same things but from a different angle. Looks, tones, glances and reactions, that's all that separates us from our experiences. In the same way that you can't sum up what it's like to be a woman, you can't explain what it's like to be a man.'

Melissa pondered this. 'I think I could sum up what it's like to be a woman pretty well.'

'Only this woman,' the woman said, pointing at Melissa's chest.

'I guess,' Melissa agreed.

'I can't put his life into words. It's nothing that anybody has said or done. It's a feeling.'

'One for the road?' the barman asked suddenly.

'Why not?' Melissa replied.

'What wifey doesn't know, won't kill her,' the woman added, and they both laughed.

The two women standing at the bar beside them awaiting their order glared at them in disgust.

'Chauvinist pigs,' one muttered.

When Mike returned from his golfing holiday, the woman hugged him tighter than ever.

'What's this?' he murmured, dropping his bag and returning her hug, breathing her in.

'I love you,' she whispered. 'Thank you for everything you do; for all the things I see you doing, but even more for the things I don't.'

She felt his body relax and he wrapped himself tighter around hers.

16

The Woman Who Was a Featherbrain

She lies flat on her back, arms tight by her side as she moves deeper into the coffin-like space of the MRI machine. The headphones hugging her ears are intended to relax her, to make her forget the walls pressing in around her, the ceiling so close to her nose. If she ever wondered what being buried alive would be like, this is it.

She never knew she suffered from claustrophobia but as she becomes completely encased in the narrow tube her heart pounds and she feels the urge to shout, 'Stop!'

She wants to get up and run but knows that she can't. This is her last chance to find out what is wrong with her: every other test has proved fruitless and yet she's getting worse. At first she was tired, forgetful, muddled, flustered – but despite a blood test at her GP's office, nothing was detected. No iron deficiency, no thyroid problems, just the stresses of a busy life like all the young parents who felt equally as exhausted as she.

But then it moved on. Her speech became affected, and lately her movement. There is something happening in her brain, it's no longer sending the right signals to the rest of her body. And so now she is inside this MRI tube, hoping that there is nothing wrong with her but that something will be detected, something small, something insignificant, something easily fixed, but *something* so as to prove her behaviour is out of her control.

When they first saw Dr Khatri, his concern was the cerebellum. He told her its function is to coordinate muscle movements, maintain posture and balance. Removal of the cerebellum doesn't stop a person from being able to do anything in particular but it makes actions hesitant and clumsy. Which sounded just about right. She had been continuously knocking over her drink, and other people's, at the dinner table. It was funny at first but then became annoying over time and a real bone of contention with her husband. She knew she was being clumsy and he was patient at first, but then even when conscious of it, she couldn't stop, no matter how hard she concentrated.

Her spatial awareness was failing her too. She would attempt to place a plate on the kitchen counter but would miss, sending it smashing to the ground. This happened numerous times: once she even heaped a filled dinner plate into her husband's lap. She closed the dishwasher door on an open tray of plates, smashing them.

She'd found a chicken wrapped in clingfilm under the sink, and the roll of clingfilm in the fridge. She placed a kettle full of boiling water in the fridge and the carton of milk by the toaster. She drove to the shopping centre, parked, shopped, then got a taxi home, forgetting she had driven. She mixed up her children's school lunches. She brushed her teeth with cold-sore cream.

She was constantly having minor car accidents – she side-swiped walls, hit both wing mirrors, reversed into bumpers and lamp posts more times than she could count. Most of the time she didn't even notice; it was at the end of the evening when her husband would inspect the car for new damage that her mistakes were revealed. There are only so many times another driver can be blamed.

Her skin took on a similar appearance to the car. A cut on her hand where a kitchen knife slipped, burns where she'd caught herself on the oven or a hob, a bump where she'd slammed her hip against the corner of a table, a stubbed toe, bruised elbows from hitting doorframes, shins on the car door. When her speech became affected, her ability to tell a story or simply construct a sentence, or remember the word she wanted to say, the doctor changed his mind. Now it was the frontal lobe the doctor focused on, which was responsible for personality, behaviour, emotions, judgement, problem-solving, speech and concentration. But while she could put that down to sleep deprivation, because she was exhausted, unable to sleep due to the sheer anxiety about what was happening to her, she couldn't deny a growing obsession with the state of her brain.

It felt to her like her brain was slowly shutting down. And she couldn't afford to let that happen. Not with four children who were depending on her to keep going. They were her life, their four lives were hers. She alone was responsible for managing four schedules, getting them where they needed to be at all times. Feeding them, clothing them, loving them, chauffeuring them. It was all-consuming, exhausting but rewarding. She hadn't returned to work after her first child ten years ago. She'd been a financial analyst and, while the intention had always been to return, she'd extended her maternity leave over and over, then more babies came and she faced the fact she was never going back. She was content at home with her beautiful babies. She felt at peace, though it was more challenging and exhausting than any day in the office.

It had been difficult losing her income, when before she could spend whatever she wanted, without permission, without discussion. Now she scraped by on a carefully managed budget. Motherhood was not, as some might believe, a simpler life. She found it more challenging, constantly juggling responsibilities for four growing person-alities and the obstacles that life presents to each person and how the family reacts to that.

So now, as she closes her eyes and breathes deeply in the MRI scanner, she longs for the doctors to tell her that they can find nothing to be wrong with her, but at the same time she needs them to discover something. Catch-22. She needs it to be something fixable. Tears spring from her eyes and roll down to her ears, tickling her neck. There isn't the space to lift her hand to wipe them away. She momentarily opens her eyes and sees the cold white surface of the ceiling too close above her. She feels the panic rise and fights it, breathing, closing her eyes and listening to the classical music that drifts through the headphones. It's a familiar piece, but like so many other things, she can't remember what it's called.

She gets lost in her thoughts for a while, thinking about the kids, hoping they are okay and that Paul's mother has managed the school and Montessori pick-ups in time. Jamie has soccer and Ella has swimming. Lucy will need her bag of toys to play with while she's waiting for them both and Adam should be doing his homework while Ella swims . . .

She hears Dr Khatri's voice come through the headphones. She moved while they were taking the scan, they have to repeat it. She fights the frustration while the machine whirs loudly again and she ensures she doesn't move a muscle on her face.

Then finally they're finished. Back to high ceilings and air. The relief floods through her and then the fear prickles. What have they discovered?

They wait.

Paul looks exhausted, worried. She would have struggled to keep going as best she could, but he forced her to come here. Things had been bad between them for a while, and it's obvious her behaviour aggravates him. But, now that they're at the hospital, doing an MRI after a battery of other tests, she knows that he's sorry for losing his temper with her all those times.

'It's okay,' she says gently. 'I was frustrating myself. I was exhausted by myself. I am exhausted.'

He looks at her with pity, and she doesn't like it. It scares her. Things have gotten too serious. She wants to roll back the clocks to being an accident-prone silly wife, silly friend, silly sister, silly clumsy Mummy.

Dr Khatri enters looking quizzical. His eyes rest on her for a moment and she doubts he's seeing her as a person; it is a look similar to the one given by an engineer popping the hood to analyse the engine of a car.

'Is everything okay?' Paul jumps up from his chair.

'It's peculiar. We've never seen anything like it before.'

Paul swallows, sweat on his brow. He looks like a child. 'Please, explain.'

'I can't really . . . I'll have to show you both.'

Still wearing the hospital gown, she follows the men into a consultation room.

There are various X-rays on the screens, lit up on the wall. She looks at them but doesn't even attempt to analyse them. She wouldn't know what a normal brain looks like, or a tumour for that matter. Would she know one if she saw one? Should she know it's in there, if it's in there? But Paul obviously knows these things because he places his hands on his hips and stares at the scans, open-mouthed.

'Is that . . . ?'

'It appears so,' Dr Khatri shrugs, then rubs his face, confused.

'But how can . . . ?'

'I honestly don't know.'

'Honey,' Paul turns around, looks at her.

Her body is trembling. There is something wrong with her brain. She thinks of Jamie, Ella, Lucy and Adam, her babies who need her, who literally cannot survive without her. She can't deal with the thought of them being without her. All she can think of to ask is, 'How long do I have?' but she can't even bring herself to say this out loud.

'Do you see?' Paul prods her.

'No, I'm not a brain surgeon,' she says, confused.

'Neither am I but I can see . . .' The old familiar frustration seeps into his tone.

That same irritated tone he's used for the past year, perhaps longer. There's an uncomfortable silence in the room. A couple of other doctors have slipped in to study the results. She feels embarrassed, slapped in the face, scolded by her husband in such company but she slowly lifts her eyes and scans the X-rays.

'With all due respect,' Dr Khatri says, defending her, 'her brain can't be functioning in a normal—'

'Oh!' she says suddenly, seeing what they see.

She walks closer to the images of her brain and examines them. She doesn't know how she didn't see it earlier, it's so obvious.

There is a clearly defined skeletal feather highlighted on the X-ray, looping around her brain.

She turns to face Dr Khatri. 'There's a feather on my brain, a bird in my head?' She screws her face up in absolute disgust, feeling dizzy, feeling like she wants to slap her head, hit it so hard that it falls out one of her ears. Which is exactly what she does. Paul and Dr Khatri rush to her side to stop her.

'There is no bird in your head,' Dr Khatri says, trying to calm her.

'But how else would it get there?' she asks, her head throbbing after whacking herself so hard. 'Feathers don't just appear out of nowhere. They grow on birds. And chickens. And . . . what else has feathers?' She shudders again, wanting to shake her head so hard it will fall out. She steps closer to the X-ray. 'Is there a chicken in there, can you see it?'

The experts in their long white coats all move closer to the X-ray.

'Isn't the feather the evidence?' she asks.

Dr Khatri considers this. 'I don't know . . . but I can tell you what I do know. One side, as you can see – the left side – is mostly covered in this . . . feather . . . which affects your speech and language, mathematical calculation and fact retrieval, which explains your behaviour and the problems you've been experiencing.'

'How do we get it out of my head?'

'We can't operate, unfortunately. The position this feather is in is just too intricate, too dangerous.'

She looks at him in shock. 'I can't walk around with a feather on my brain.'

'Well, you have been.'

'But I can't live like this! I can't. You have to do something. What about medication?'

He shakes his head slowly. 'I don't know of any medication that could realistically achieve that.'

'What about blowing it out? Is there a machine that can just blow in one ear?' she asks.

'The feather would still be inside your head, it would just shift from one area to another. In a way, you're lucky that the area affected is this one – another part of the brain could cause paralysis, speech problems, serious brain damage.'

She feels utterly helpless. 'I have to do something.'

'I . . . um . . .' Dr Khatri turns to his colleagues for backup and they all look away nervously, uneager to respond. 'Well, I am afraid we're rather stumped on this one.'

One doctor breaks the silence. 'If I may?'

The woman nods; permission for him to continue.

'I'm a keen birdwatcher. And this is a long, dramatic feather. It is a rather impressive plumage of the brain,' he compliments her.

She stares at him blankly.

'What I'm saying is, it could be a peacock feather.'

'What are you suggesting?' her husband steps in.

'The peacock engages in train-rattling and wing-shaking, during breeding season—'

'I don't want another baby,' she says quickly. She looks at her husband. 'I do not,' she says firmly.

'Okay,' he says, nervously looking from her to the doctor.

'That's not what I'm suggesting. They do it to get attention – the wing-shaking.'

She studies the X-ray. 'Could it be related to brain activity?'

He thinks it through, and the other doctors again look away and look down, shuffle their feet. Nobody has a clue what is really happening.

She sighs. Up to her as usual to figure it out. 'I'm not as mentally challenged as I was before. I never get a break but I'm using my head in a different way. I earned a double degree in Finance and Economics and worked for ten years in the most prestigious financial services firm in London before falling in love with this man,' she says, smiling at Paul. 'But this week my main project is potty training. I haven't a clue what's going on in the stock markets but I can tell you every episode of every season of *Peppa Pig*. I am the only person in my family who has finished *Ulysses*, albeit on audiobook, and every night I read *The Gruffalo* four times in a row. I love my life, there's nothing unimportant about it. Raising people is vastly more important than stock markets, or bullshit sales meetings. But maybe my brain wants that *and* other information, other stimulation.'

She looks at the doctor; he is thoughtful.

'Actually,' he says, 'that's not a bad thought. I think you should do whatever you want to do to blow this feather out. And that's a doctor's order.'

She thinks about this and she smiles. She knows she never needed permission to look after herself, but it is difficult to put herself first. What she needed was an order, silly as it seems. Her feather brain's wing-shaking was a call for her attention.

She starts with slowing down, taking time out so she can read a book.

She finds an extra hour for walking along the beach where the wind is so strong she imagines it clearing the feather from her brain. She watches the wind to see if it floats away.

She goes away for a night with Paul.

She has a weekend away with friends.

She starts jogging.

She considers signing up for a course. Even reading through a college prospectus for potential courses thrills her.

She goes out one night and dances until her feet are so sore she has to kick off her shoes, and drinks so much she doesn't care about how she'll feel in the morning.

She relaxes her mind. She steps back. She jumps in. She blows the feather off until everything is clear again, and she emerges from her fog.

17

The Woman Who Wore Her Heart on Her Sleeve

A heart defect at birth, a heart that was too large for her chest, led to a colostomy-bag-type procedure, groundbreaking surgery by the brave Dr Nita Ahuja, which meant that as a child the woman's heart was removed from her chest and sat in a pouch connected, irreversibly, to her left sleeve. The theory mimicked that of Dr Nita Ahuja's conjoined twins case study, in which one twin survived though her heart was technically outside her body, though of course the heart was attached through vital veins and tubes to her conjoined sister's body. The young woman was the only person in the world to have this surgery. It had made a star of Dr Nita Ahuja, and a household name of the young woman who wore her heart on her sleeve.

The pouch was changed once every seven days when the

seal wore off. A colostomy pouch was usually the size of a hand, but her pouch was twice the size, as Dr Ahuja would say, as though it was being held safely in a pair of hands. The surgery saved her life and miraculously had few significant effects on her lifestyle or diet. Her clothes were normal, just something that would allow for the pouch on her left arm.

Her heart's beat was loud, its sounds intensified outside her body. While exercising, it caused people to stop and stare; when in a cake shop or ice-cream parlour the glucose would send it racing and pumping, beating under her sleeve as though she were hiding a pet in her arm. If she saw a boy that she had a crush on, it would be a giveaway, along with her rosy cheeks.

Her heart revealed when she got attached too quickly, it revealed when she wasn't attached at all. There were awkward moments when it revealed her excitement at inopportune moments, or her lack of enthusiasm. It revealed everything about her. She depended on it, and therefore had no choice but to follow its lead, even when she wanted to go in the opposite direction. Sometimes she did feel like a conjoined twin, living with a separate life that was part of her, on her sleeve.

She learned that wearing her heart on her sleeve often caused distrust, because of the contradiction between the mask she wore on her face, and the beat of her heart. In the same way people were afraid of clowns because of the discrepancy between the joy in their expression and the lack of joy in their demeanour, suspicions were aroused. On the other hand, if she allowed her heart to do the talking without attempting to veil her expression, then they found her openness off-putting. Most people showed their hand gradually; she went there straight away, she couldn't slow it down. Her heart would always give her away.

Wearing her heart on her sleeve made her vulnerable to emotional terrorists, those who saw the word FRAGILE emblazoned across her and did all they could to hurt her, just because they could.

Thirty years of it had led to bumps and bruises. Her most vital organ was in constant jeopardy of getting injured. Though, thankfully, there had been no serious injuries, there were the occasional unwelcome elbows. On a bus, or at the market, anytime she was in a crowd, she had to remember to protect her heart.

As she grew into her teenage years, she became more self-conscious and protective and changed her wardrobe to accommodate her heart. But even though it solved the visual, her heart on her sleeve continued to reveal her.

Her turquoise jutti tap over the marble floor of the Mumbai private hospital and research centre where Dr Nita has her private consultant's office. It's a service that neither she nor her family can afford to pay for, but from the moment that Dr Nita had set her eyes on the infant with the birth defect, she had insisted on waiving her fees, and making arrangements for the surgery and aftercare bills to be paid. It simply could not have gone ahead without Dr Nita and because of this, the young woman feels an enormous gratitude and duty to return the favour. She appears on television shows with Dr Nita when asked and attends conventions and Dr Nita's speaking engagements when requested. She knows, when speaking with important influential people and media, that she is always to mention Dr Nita Ahuja as the doctor who saved her life. They have even appeared together in *Time Magazine* under the headline 'Dr Nita Ahuja, The Heart Keeper'. The title had stuck. With a label like this, she knew she had to return the kindness that had been extended to her and her family in every way she could. Quite simply, she felt that she owed Dr Nita for saving her life.

She smiles and greets the security men and receptionists who wave her through the medical centre. Everything is familiar here, it is a place where she feels safe. She clutches a small canvas painting of a heart, which she plans to present to Dr Nita, to add to the wall of her artwork in her office. She is expecting a normal day; this weekly visit has been part of their routine for twenty-one years so why should today be any different?

However, when she steps into the office, it is a man who sits behind Dr Nita's desk. He stands when he sees her enter. After her first moment of shock, she recognizes him from the photographs displayed all over the desk: it is the doctor's son, Alok. Over the years, she has learned much about him through his mother: his studies at university, his work overseas, sometimes of his love affairs, and whether she approved or disapproved of them.

She takes in his big brown eyes, his intense gaze, his long neck and slender fingers. Alok; his name means light. Her heart starts to pound, she feels it pulsate against her upper arm, more intense than before, more intense than ever. Feeling alarmed, she watches the pouch on her arm vibrate.

'Sit, please, my child,' Dr Nita says, coming to her rescue. She seems to appear from thin air.

'She is not a child, Mother,' Alok mutters, as the woman sits in the chair before the desk.

Dr Nita fixes her with her warm eyes, and the young woman readies herself for bad news. 'As you know, this year is the twentieth anniversary of the surgery that changed both our lives.'

The young woman nods and waits for the doctor to continue.

'Discovering your case set me on a wild and wonderful path, which I fully embraced. I only wish you had come into my life when I was younger,' the doctor says. Her smile fades. 'It is now time for me to stop my work,' she says gently, and the young woman's panic soars, her heart pounds again, vibrating on her sleeve, she feels its intensity against her triceps.

'It's all right, my child. Alok has returned from the United States to take over where I have left off. He is young but capable,' she says firmly. 'And I trust him more than anybody else to continue my work.'

High praise indeed from a woman whose ego would never allow her to delegate.

'No disrespect intended, Dr Alok,' the woman says quietly, barely able to meet his intense concerned gaze. 'But *you* are my heart keeper, Dr Nita. You said as much yourself. You can't leave me,' she insists, hearing the tremble in her own voice.

Dr Nita smiles, a smile that reveals how proud she is of her role as the heart keeper.

'Oh, child . . . believe me, I understand that this is difficult for you. It is for me too.' The doctor breathes in. 'My connection with you runs deeper than you'll ever know. When you hold someone's heart in your hands, not just for one surgery but for their life, it is a profound responsibility that extends far beyond the professional, requiring constant monitoring of which bonds and valves have become twisted or combined.' She stands, with an air of finality. 'But it is for the best that I leave you in Alok's hands. He will keep me informed of everything he is doing and I will continue to advise on your care.' This, she says firmly as though it is an order and one that her son doesn't seem very happy about. He avoids her gaze.

Dr Nita comes towards her and the young woman readies herself for an embrace, but Dr Nita, to her surprise, goes directly to her left arm, to her heart. She gently places her hands around the pouch, feeling its heat, and leans over to kiss it. The young woman watches this goodbye to her heart, which is thumping at such a voracious rate she wonders if it will burst from her pouch. Then the doctor wipes her eyes and leaves the room without another word.

Her heart keeper is gone and the young woman is alone with this man, this handsome man who looks at her with big brown eyes and thick eyelashes.

'She is not your heart keeper any longer, and she never was,' Dr Alok says suddenly.

His words are cold, and hurtful. They break the silence like a hammer shattering ice.

'I'm sorry, that came out harsher than I intended,' he says, before she has the opportunity to tell him exactly what she thinks of him, though her heart is already communicating that in its own language.

Dr Alok stands and walks around the desk, thinking through what he is about to say. He perches on the edge of the desk before her, so close to her, and when he speaks his voice is gentler. 'While I intend to pick up where my mother left off, my work is not exactly the same as hers. We differ in our philosophies. Unlike my mother, I do not wish to be the keeper of your heart.'

She tries not to take offence, but how can she not? Her cheeks blaze with fury.

'It is not enough for us doctors to just look after the functioning of your heart, it is not enough to just keep you alive.'

This takes her by surprise.

'My mother is deeply respected in the worldwide medical community and what she did with you was, is, groundbreaking,

I acknowledge that,' he says, torn between loyalty to his mother and the need to voice his opinion. 'But she is of a different . . . time. What I feel she has missed is that you are walking around with your most vital organ on your sleeve, in constant jeopardy of being hurt, and that too is our responsibility. We put it there. We must be proactive, not reactive. You should not have to hide your heart under layers of clothes and worry. I have spent years working on a new pouch that will protect your heart, one that will defend it from the elements.'

Bending down, he retrieves a pouch from a bag by the desk. He hesitates, then holds it out to present it to her. 'From hereon, *you* will be the keeper of your own heart.'

She feels the pulse in her neck responding.

'I will aid you, but you will be in full control. I will be here for you for as long as time will allow, to supply the tools which will give you the power to protect and shelter your heart.' He stops then, cheeks pink, self-conscious under her gaze. His brown eyes and long lashes not sure where to look. 'What do you say to that? Do I have your permission?'

She smiles and nods. 'Yes, Dr Ahuja.'

'Alok, please,' he says gently, their eyes locked on one another.

Her heart vibrates with an intensity she has never experienced before. It is speaking for her, to him, and for once she is thankful that her heart can replace the words she cannot find, that it can express these surprising new emotions she has discovered for this man. She is grateful that her heart's response is greater and deeper than any words she could find.

She watches as, with her permission, his nervous but warm long slender fingers open the pouch and take hold of her beating heart. She understands now that it is hers, nobody but herself is its keeper. She controls it.

She will let him hold it in his hands. She will allow him to give her the tools to protect herself.

18

The Woman Who Wore Pink

1

The 7 a.m. alarm sounds from the pink iPhone on the nightstand and the woman reaches out with her manicured pink fingernails to silence it. She pushes her candy-pink eye mask up onto her forehead and lies in bed, staring at the ceiling, trying to stop her eyes from fluttering closed again. As she's starting to drift away again, another alarm sounds from her husband's nightstand and Dan's hand appears from beneath the duvet, feels around for his blue iPhone, then tosses it across the room. She laughs. He peeks his head up from the blanket sleepily, and they share an exhausted look.

'Let's cancel today, let's do today tomorrow, instead,' she says, feeling her heavy eyelids being pulled closed again.

Dan pats her head, then messes her hair and pushes her eye mask over her face. She laughs, removes the eye mask completely, and sits up, finally awake.

Dan stretches and roars mid-stretch, 'Let's grab the day by the balls!'

'The day has balls?'

'The day has balls.'

'Are you guys going to claim everything now? Even the days?'

'Especially the days. But the night . . . the night has boobs.' He sidles up to her and she laughs, and gently resists.

Laughing, she pulls herself out of bed and leaves to wake the kids.

2

In the bathroom, fresh after her shower, the woman stands in front of the mirror, wrapped in a pink towel. She reaches into a drawer and retrieves a small pink velvet pouch with a draw-string that contains a pink rubber wristband. She slides it on.

Dan is beside her, a blue towel around his waist. After shaving he reaches for his blue velvet pouch with a draw-string and slides the blue rubber wristband out and onto his wrist.

3

Dressed in their grey corporate work clothes, briefcases in hand, Dan and the woman step out of the elevator, with their six-year-old twins Jack and Jill. Jill wears a pink bow in her hair, Jack wears a blue baseball cap.

'Morning, Al,' the woman greets the apartment building doorman.

'Morning, guys,' Al says, high-fiving the kids.

The woman and Dan embrace their children and help them onto the waiting school bus. Jack and Jill walk down the centre of the aisle of the bus. Jack takes a left and sits with the boys on blue-covered seats, Jill takes a right and sits with the girls on pink-covered seats.

'Want me to call you two cabs?' Al asks, making his way to the road to hail a cab.

'Just one cab this morning thanks, Al,' Dan says.

'Penis or vagina?' Al asks.

'Vagina,' Dan replies, checking his watch. 'I've a meeting around the corner, I can walk.'

Al whistles for a cab. A blue cab nears and slows and a male driver hangs out the window.

'Vagina!' Al calls to him, and the blue cab speeds off. Instead a pink cab with a female driver pulls in.

The woman displays her pink wristband through the window to the driver, before getting into the car.

4

Around her in the queue at Starbucks she hears a chorus of 'penis', 'vagina', 'vagina', 'penis' as the customers place their orders, and from the barista as he places the orders on the counter, at the collection area.

'Cappuccino, no chocolate, penis!' he shouts, placing the cup with a blue holder down on the counter.

The barista on the till is the same young woman every morning. Seventeen years old, gothic-looking with dyed black hair and pale skin, piercings all over her ears, eyebrows, nose, lips and tattoos covering her arms. Her nametag says Olaf, which the woman doubts, since the barista shouting the orders claims to be Elsa. Olaf has taken the woman's order every single morning for the past year, and yet there is never a look of acknowledgement or any kind of greeting.

'Good morning,' the woman says perkily as she moves next in line.

Olaf doesn't even look up, her fingers hover over the buttons on the cash register as she awaits the order.

'Grande latte to go, please. Vagina,' the woman says, lifting her arm and pulling her coat sleeve up to reveal her pink wristband.

The woman steps aside and waits, among others, for her coffee.

Elsa, the barista, suddenly shouts, 'Grande latte.'

The woman and a man beside her both step forward at the same time. They look at each other and then back at the barista for more information. Elsa realizes his mistake and lifts the cup higher in the air. The cup has a pink holder.

'Vagina,' he shouts.

She takes her cup and goes to work.

5

The woman queues to enter her office building. Everyone ahead of her and around her seems to be dressed in grey, or dark muted colours in a charcoal world of grey, black, steel, cold glass buildings. It's taking longer than usual to gain entry, and she steps out of line to see what the hold up is.

A woman in a bright red coat, with matching lipstick, is holding the door open for a man, who is extremely agitated by this.

'Penis!' the man says, holding up his arm to reveal his blue wristband.

'Nice to meet you penis, I'm Mary,' the woman in red says, irritated. 'Go ahead, I can hold the door.'

'No, no, no, I won't hear of this,' the man says. He moves out of line and stands behind the woman at the door, gripping the long steel door handle just above where Mary's hand is placed. 'After you.'

'Really, it's fine. I can do it,' Mary replies. 'I was already holding the door for you. I may as well keep holding it. This is ridiculous, we're wasting time.'

'*You're* wasting time actually. After you. Go on. My

pleasure,' he says in a tone that suggests it is anything but his pleasure. He makes a gesture with his free hand and rolled-up newspaper for her to walk through, as if he's batting a cow into a pen, but she refuses with a firm shake of her head. Mary is not going lightly and so they continue to bicker. 'After you,' 'No after you,' 'I insist,' 'No *I* insist.' The rudest politest conversation ever had.

'Hey!' the first man in line calls down the street. 'Hey, thank God! Excuse me! Gender Police! Can you help us out here?'

The Gender Police are patrolling the sidewalk. The female gender cop is dressed in a candy-pink uniform and her younger male partner is dressed in baby blue. The two saccharine colours pop in an otherwise muted world. They're carrying takeout coffee cups in their hands, which the female cop dispenses in the nearest bin as soon as she senses a problem. She loves her job, she thrives on her power. She strolls authoritatively to the man and woman who are both still tightly gripping the handle of the door, both of them refusing to give in.

'Is everything okay here?' the female gender cop says, approaching.

'Yes,' Mary snaps. 'Everything is just fine. I am trying to be polite, that's all.'

'Polite, huh?' the female gender cop says, placing her hands on her generous hips and surveying the growing queue. She is enjoying the tense silence, the attentive audience. 'My assessment of the situation is that the opposite of polite is what's happening here. Polite would mean you allowing that man to be helpful to you. Polite means everyone knowing their place and making sure we don't upset the foundations of our society.'

'Oh,' Mary says. 'Because I thought that polite was me holding the door for this person.'

The cop takes out her scanner and aims it at the woman's pink wristband. 'Let's see who you are.' The machine beeps and she studies the screen. 'Mary Agronski. Four penalty points already. You've been misbehaving. Naughty, naughty vagina.'

'Oh come on . . . you're not going to charge me for *this*.'

'An offence has been committed contrary to the Gender Recognition Act of 2017 involving the Honourable Gentleman Holding the Door, Article 7, in a public place, at 09:05 hours on the first day of September of this year. You may, during the period of twenty-eight days, beginning on the date of this notice and including the twenty-eighth day from today, pay a fixed charge of eighty dollars. If you do not pay that fixed charge during the said period, you will be served with a summons in respect of the offence and you will be required to appear in court. In accordance with this notice you receive two penalty points for your Public Gender Act offence.'

The female Gender Police officer holds the scanner against the wristband and waits for the beep.

'That's a total of six penalty points on the Gender Recognition Act. If you reach the maximum number of twelve penalty points, I hereby warn you that it will result in your being summoned to appear in a court of law where your punishment will be determined.'

The woman in red stares down the police, goes to say something, then decides to hold her tongue. So angry she can barely contain it, she finally lets go of the door-bar and storms inside the building. The Gender Police monitor the gender display that follows. Satisfied that everything is proceeding regularly again, they continue their patrol.

But as the woman watches the Gender Police walk away, she thinks about it, about what it would be like to revolt, to speak up, to be the woman in red. She swallows her words, then walks through the door. But she doesn't say thank you.

6

The woman is seated at a grand conference table. Her beautiful secretary, Tyra, walks around the table handing out Biros and jotters. To receive these, each person displays their bracelet. Pink bracelet gets a pen with a pink lid and a pale pink pad, a blue bracelet receives a pen with a blue lid and pale blue pad. Tyra works her way around the table trying to catch the attention of the handsome businessman across the table. He looks like a male model. The woman smiles at her secretary as she watches her at work. Tyra finally stops at his seat and gives him flirty eyes. He nervously looks from her to the box in her hand, torn, not wanting to have to say the words expected of him.

But he does and he says them wearily, defeated.

'Vagina,' he says, revealing a quick glimpse of a pink wristband peeking out from his crisp white shirt.

Tyra's eyes widen in horror and she moves on as quickly as she can. He pulls the shirt and pinstriped suit sleeve down further to hide the bracelet completely and lowers his eyes.

The woman can tell that he's embarrassed, and feels degraded. She catches his eye and does her best to offer him a supportive smile but the damage has been done already. A beautiful woman balked at his true self. It seems such a simple thing, pink and blue gender recognition, but such simple acts as these mean so much more than she thought.

7

The woman stands at a fast-food counter with her six-year-old twins Jack and Jill. Her friend Rita has brought her twin son and daughter, Colin and Colleen, also six. Colleen is wearing a Disney princess dress, Colin is dressed as a pirate. Rita is chatting incessantly as she always does, without taking a breath.

'The two cheeseburger kids meals are for . . . ?' the server interrupts Rita.

'My two,' the woman replies. She pats each child's head as she explains. 'One penis, one vagina.'

The server places a pink princess meal and a blue dinosaur meal on the tray.

'I want a dinosaur one,' Jill moans.

Rita gasps. 'What did she say?'

The woman is surprised by her daughter, she has never heard her say anything like this before.

'I told you, Mum,' Colleen looks up at Rita.

'Okay, hush now, dear,' Rita laughs nervously.

'You told her what?' Jill demands.

'You know what,' Colleen replies with a scowl. 'All about you being all . . . you.'

'Well that makes no sense,' Jill argues. 'If I'm not me, who else am I supposed to be?'

This comment jolts the woman and she looks at her daughter, surprised that she would stand up for herself like that, and in admiration at her wisdom.

'Enough now, girls,' Rita interrupts. 'Let's get away from here – people are staring.'

The woman notices that the server and the customers around them are casting dubious looks at Jill. A mother places hands over her daughter's ears and sidesteps away from them. Jill bows her head, embarrassed by the reaction. The woman lifts the tray with one hand and places a protective arm around Jill's shoulders, and leads her to the tables.

'Four vaginas and two penii,' Rita announces loudly to the waiting staff in the restaurant.

The four females sit on pink chairs and the two boys on blue chairs. While Rita rattles on, the woman tunes out and watches her children's interaction with concern and intrigue. Jill plays with the plastic toy dinosaur from Jack's meal – the dinosaur is eating the princess alive – and Jack uses the pink plastic jewelled costume ring toy from the princess meal to fire a laser at the dinosaur.

Colleen sits turned away from them, combing her Barbie's hair. Colin torments her by stabbing at her doll with his pirate hook, trying to saw her hair off. Occasionally Colleen turns around to throw Jack and Jill looks of disgust. The woman, unable to concentrate on what Rita is saying, studies the dynamic with new eyes, learning.

8

In a bar, on their Saturday night out, the woman sits on a pink chair, at a pink table, drinking from glasses with umbrellas and straws and over the top fruit kebabs with a group of women. The woman sits back, feeling detached from the conversation, her mind replaying the same concerns over and over again, and watches her husband who is standing nearby with the group of husbands, all carrying pint glasses of beer.

Dan catches her eye and gives her a caring, questioning look to see if she's okay. She's not sure.

'There were female dinosaurs, weren't they?' she pipes up suddenly to her female friends.

They look at each other, confused.

'What are you talking about?' Rita asks.

'I'm talking about when dinosaurs walked the earth. There were male dinosaurs, big scary dinosaurs . . . and then there were female dinosaurs. Big scary dinosaurs. Because if there weren't female dinosaurs, how would they have had baby dinosaurs?'

'Of course there were female dinosaurs,' Rita says gently, concerned.

'So I could wear a dress, with a dinosaur on it. A female one?'

Her friend Ella giggles. 'A pink dinosaur dress, maybe.'

Rita places a hand on the woman's arm. 'Is everything okay? Is this about Jill and her . . . you know . . . issues?'

'No. Yes. No. I'm just saying. I mean, there were female dinosaurs too, you know, and I don't think any of them were pink.' She looks at them all, appealing for their understanding, but they stare back her wide-eyed.

'Okay,' Rita says slowly.

9

The woman and her husband are out for dinner with two of his male business colleagues. The woman is deep in conversation with one when the waitress approaches to take their order.

'Oh, I haven't even read the menu yet,' the woman says, apologetically. 'Sweetheart, why don't you go ahead while I decide quickly?' she says to Dan.

She studies the menu but their intense gazes on her force her to look up. 'I don't know about you, boys,' Bob says. 'But where I was raised we were all taught: vagina first.'

Dan winces at that.

She returns her attention to the menu, irritated, agitated, under time pressure and self-consciously speed-reads while the three men and the waitress stare at her in a long tense silence.

Finally she snaps the menu shut.

'Steak, please.'

The waitress looks at her for more. The woman knows what she is expected to say but for once she feels like she has said enough.

'I'll have the steak, please,' she repeats.

'Oh, I heard that part, but which steak? Petit filet for vagina, or T-bone for penis?'

She loses her temper and snaps.

'I had to order first, didn't I? So it's pretty obvious that I'm supposed to have the vagina steak.'

'Can I see your band, please?' the waitress asks.

The woman pulls up the sleeve of her tuxedo jacket and holds her wrist up with a tightly clenched fist.

There's a tense silence.

'And I'll have the steak. Penis. T-bone,' Bob says, shaking his wrist at her.

'I'm having the same,' Roger says. 'In fact, I think we all are, aren't we, Dan? How's about you write down three penis steaks.'

The woman watches Dan, who looks thoughtful. He closes the menu slowly.

'Actually, I'm going to have fish. John Dory.' He lifts his hand, fist clenched, just as the woman had. 'Penis.'

The woman and Dan share a look and they grin.

When the plates of food are placed before them there are toothpicks with small tags piercing the meat and fish. Blue tags for the T-bone and John Dory, and a pink tag for the petit filet. The woman lifts her glass of wine and notices that it's empty. She reaches to the ice-bucket beside her for the bottle of wine.

'Nu-uh,' Bob says, wagging a finger in her face, grinning. He grabs the wine bottle by the neck, and pulls it from the water. As he pours wine into her glass, the water from the bucket drips all over her steak.

'Thanks,' she says, through clenched teeth.

10

The woman leaves the shopping centre, weighed down by the number of bags in her hands. They are heavy and there are many, but she is perfectly capable of carrying them. Her car isn't far. Behind her, a man is in the same predicament. Two men, strangers, rush over to assist her.

'Let me take them from you,' says one man.

'No, no thanks, I've got them,' she says, and keeps walking.

'I've got them,' the second man steps in front of her, hands out to take them.

The woman steps around him and continues walking to her car. They block her again and try to assist her, so helpful that they almost trip her up by getting in her way.

'No thank you,' she says firmly. 'You're very kind but I'm

fine. I can carry them, really, no thank you. I'm fine. Please no.'

The man who had been struggling with his shopping bags drops one as the plastic handle snaps. A bag empties on the floor and nobody assists him as he attempts to pick everything up from the sidewalk. Oranges are rolling along the ground. A car crushes an orange while he watches on, exasperated.

The second man steps closer to her and his tone is aggressive. 'We're helping you. We're being kind and honourable.'

'This is not kindness!' she raises her voice. 'You're being pests!'

The nearby Gender Police overhear her. She is making a scene and they wander over to her, candy pink and blue in an otherwise grey concrete car park.

'Okay, okay, watch your tone now,' the female Gender Police officer says. 'Calm down please, madam.'

'Oh for goodness' sake!' the woman says. She tries to make a run for it, away from them all, to her nearby car.

'Whoa there,' the female Gender Police officer says and the gang all catch up with her. 'Do not evade the law unless you want penalty points.'

'Evade the law? I haven't done anything wrong! I just want to carry my own bags.'

'In accordance with the Gender Recognition Act of 2017, these honourable gentlemen have offered to carry your bags that you are about to drop any moment, and you, as far as I can see, are being aggressive—'

'I'm not!' she yells. She pauses. 'Okay, maybe I am now, because you are making this a big deal. My car is just over there. I can do this alone.'

The bags are slipping from her grasp.

'I tell you what's going to happen here. You're going to put those bags down. You're going to allow both of these kind men to assist you to your car and then you're going to thank them. Do you understand?' the male gender cop says.

The woman thinks about it. She is so frustrated but she is causing a scene and suddenly intimidated by these four people ganging up on her.

'Yes, I understand.'

'No funny business,' the female gender cop says.

'Fine.'

The woman begrudgingly places the bags on the ground. The two men take one each and walk the ten remaining paces to the car. She opens the trunk and they place them inside. She closes the trunk and walks to the driver door where she places her hand on the handle.

'Nu-uh,' the male police says.

She sighs and steps back. The first man opens the door for her. She gets into her seat and he closes it.

11

The woman is having a family day at a public park.

'I need to pee, Mum, really bad,' Jill says suddenly, dancing by her side.

'Okay, I'll take you.'

A male Gender Police officer stands outside the toilets monitoring the wristbands of each entrant. Baby-blue uniform against a grey wall. Ahead of them each person reveals their wristband and announces their gender before being granted entrance to the toilet. A beautiful woman ahead of them in the queue is stopped.

'Penis,' the beautiful woman says.

Jill's eyes widen. She soaks it all up.

The male Gender Police officer looks the woman up and down and nods in the direction of the men's bathroom with a quick flick of his head. The beautiful woman stalls.

'I understand your rules, but I wonder if I could go to the woman's toilet. If you could make this one exception, please,' the beautiful woman pleads. 'There was an incident the last time, and I'm really quite afraid to—'

'You're wearing a blue wristband, your birth cert says male, you're going in the men's,' the Gender Police officer says, avoiding her eye.

'That's not fair, Mummy!' Jill cries. 'Say something!'

She freezes.

'Please,' the beautiful woman before them pleads again.

'Don't make any trouble,' he says firmly, finally looking her in the eye. 'There are kids here. This is a family park.'

'I don't mind if she goes in the girls',' Jill speaks up.

The beautiful woman turns to look at Jill with gratitude, eyes filled, moved.

'Thank you,' she smiles.

219

Jill beams.

'Doesn't matter, rules are rules, into the men's or out of the queue,' the cop says.

The beautiful woman pulls her bag closer to her body, hugging it for comfort and protection, as she walks slowly into the men's toilets.

'I'm sorry you had to witness that,' the Gender Police officer says.

The woman opens her mouth to say something but she can't.

'I'm sorry I had to witness you being a mean bully,' Jill says to him, and storms past him into the toilets.

The woman chases her, shocked. She stands in her stall, her forehead pressed against the door. She closes her eyes, feeling weak. Her six-year-old can see what she is only seeing now. Her six-year-old can say what she cannot.

12

The woman sits with her family at the kitchen table for dinner. She toys with her food, lost in her thoughts. It has been a troubling week. Jack, Jill and Dan talk and joke while she feels detached. Dan looks at her with worry, then back to the children.

Dan finishes his dinner and stands up and stretches. 'I'm going to watch the football.' He moves towards the door.

She eyes the dirty plate left behind on the kitchen table. She looks so angry, she feels angry and dangerous. Dan senses this mood and carries his plate to the sink, beside the dishwasher. The dishwasher is bright pink in the sleek grey kitchen.

'The dishwasher is empty,' she says firmly.

He looks at the dishwasher, then back to her, in confusion.

She bangs down her cutlery noisily, pushes her chair back from the table and stands. She goes to the bin, and pulls the bin liners out. The bin liners are blue.

'What are you doing?' Dan asks.

'Taking the rubbish out.'

'But, sweetheart,' he says pointing to his crotch. 'Penis.'

The children are watching, wide-eyed. She looks at Jill, who wanted her to speak and couldn't, and suddenly feels motivated.

'This vagina is well able to take out the rubbish.'

The kids grin and they giggle. Dan is taken aback as she leaves the room. She stays by the chute until she calms and when she returns to her family she sees that the kitchen table has been cleared, the dishwasher has been filled. Dan is on the floor wearing a tiara, Jack is wearing a tutu with a Viking helmet and Jill is wearing fairy wings and pointing a sword at Dan.

She smiles at Dan.

13

The pink iPhone alarm sounds on the nightstand, and the woman knocks it off. She is already sitting up in bed, wide-awake.

'You look ready for action,' Dan says, sleepily.

'I am.'

'What's going on?'

'I'm going to grab today by the balls.' She thinks. 'And boobs.'

'Is it wrong that that turns me on?' Dan says, and she laughs and leans in to kiss him.

14

A cabbie is reading the newspaper when the door opens and slams shut. He turns around to see the woman sitting inside.

'Drive,' she says, with determination in her voice.

He sees the pink band around her wrist.

'No way, I can't drive a vagina on its own. You have to have a penis with you.'

The woman shoves money through the hatch. 'These are all the same colour aren't they?'

Looking around to make sure no one is watching, he starts the engine.

15

In Starbucks, the woman slams down a large silver takeout mug on the counter.

'Grande latte. To go.'

Olaf looks at her, bored. 'Penis or—'

'For *me*. This thirsty human being. Because if I'm not me, who else can I be?'

Olaf looks up at the woman and finally her cool exterior cracks. She grins. 'Cool. One latte for a human being coming up.'

The woman is surprised, she was anticipating an argument. 'Oh. Thank you.'

16

With her takeout coffee mug in one hand, her briefcase in another, she charges towards the office. She fully intends on holding the door for herself, to hell with the rules that do nothing but put limits on people. She doesn't care about the penalty points, she will continue to live her life as an individual regardless of society's punishments. But as she gets closer she realizes that this is not as easy as she thought. There is no one around and she attempts to get the door, she has no hands free. She struggles to tuck the coffee mug under one arm, which doesn't work, and so she tries to tuck her briefcase under the other arm. Neither are working. She hops around as she tries to hook her heeled shoe around the lowest part of the bar to pull the door open. This time she genuinely needs help.

A man rushes to hold the door open for her. 'I'll get that.'

She smiles. She is okay with being helped when she needs it.

'Thank you very much,' she says, sincerely.

19

The Woman Who Blew Away

She wakes up and reaches for her phone before her eyes
have even unstuck themselves. She checks her last Instagram
post, studies the photo of herself, zooms in and all around,
tries to imagine what others see of her, what impression she
has managed to convey. She thinks individually of her friends,
how this photo would impact each of them. She checks the
likes. Over one million. Not as many as yesterday. Her heart
skips a little when she sees the names of who has liked her
post, people she was hoping to impress have indeed been
impressed, or at least tapped the heart to show they've
acknowledged it. She checks up on a few other people, what
they're doing, with who, why they haven't liked her post.
This takes one hour, which felt like one minute.

She takes a shower, dresses in her workout gear. She spends
an hour doing her make-up, contouring her skin so that her
cheekbones are highlighted, her eyebrows are thick, lush and

smooth and her lips are bouncy. She wears an oversized pair of sunglasses and throws peace signs to the paparazzi who have been outside her house since the crack of dawn. She is mindful of her posture, her facial expression, everything about every muscle in her own body is in her mind as she climbs into the car and drives. Some follow her on motorbikes. She holds her pose, works hard not to think – thinking gives her an ugly concentrating frown.

She goes to the gym, asks her trainer to record some of her workouts, adds filters, she adds it to her app. No one is getting this for free, they'll need to subscribe; she's already done free photos from her house to the gym, photos that will be all over the internet by now. Playing around with the light, the filter, the editing, takes one hour to perfect. She grabs a protein drink, sucks on the straw with her oversized lips, and long newly manicured nails, straight from her own nail polish line. She drives home. She reads magazines, studies fashion, tweets and Instagram posts for the rest of the afternoon. She meets a friend for lunch, she catches up on gossip. Who did what to who, and how it all affects her. She plans new lip injections. She plans a new holiday and photoshoot around these new procedures. She tries on free clothes that have been sent to her. She answers emails about her various businesses. She browses the internet. She plans a new weekend getaway with friends on a yacht. She plans the bikini suitcase.

She turns off the news when it comes on, an election of some kind. She doesn't want to know, it doesn't affect her.

She finds a place in her bedroom with good lighting, moves some items around and takes a photo of herself. Plays around with the filters. Hours have passed. It's dark outside.

When she wakes she has a feeling that she's been floating. It gives her a fright and she lands on her back, wakes up in a sweat.

Wide awake, she checks her new post. One point five million likes.

Going downstairs, it takes longer for her feet to touch the floor, as though gravity has been affected, like she's on the moon.

New nails, hair extensions, exfoliation, an hour in make-up. She tries on various outfits, she can't decide. Nothing looks good, she doesn't want to go outside, feeling huffy. She reads magazines, the pages where they've circled women's flaws is her favourite; it scares her but she's drawn to it, drawn to seeing other people's flaws.

She checks her Instagram. Wonders how to shock with her next photo. The lips will help. Bum implants are almost ready to be revealed.

As she walks to her car, she feels light-headed, slower than usual, her feet don't connect properly with the ground. She wonders if it's the new thigh-high boots she is wearing with her skinny ripped black jeans, and a lacy lingerie body suit beneath.

She straps her seat belt tight, feeling that it will keep her secured in her seat.

She does an interview with a teen magazine about her

new self-plumping lipgloss. She fields the questions, there's nothing to trip her up, they never ask her about stuff she doesn't know about. She lies about the injections. Her insecurities are none of their business. It's so hard to be a teenager in this business with all eyes of the world on her. She is under extreme pressure to deliver. The interview and photoshoot are done at her new frozen yoghurt restaurant.

She instagrams a photo of her licking a cherry, wearing her new cherry-coloured lipgloss, with cherry-coloured nails. Hungry, seducing eyes. Later she checks her likes: two million.

As she walks back to her car her feet lift from the ground and she can't get down. The paparazzi surround her, taking photographs. She floats higher, they keep taking photos. Everybody clicks, she sees the flashes, she tries to maintain her calm exterior, her sucked-in cheekbones, but she is panicking. What is happening? She starts to lose her cool, she starts to kick and scream. Her feet reach the level of her car roof, her stilettos scratch the roof of her new car as she kicks furiously, trying to tread the air. She can't get back down.

Finally the photographer from the teen magazine runs from the frozen yoghurt restaurant and grabs her by the ankle. He pulls her down. Shaken, she runs back into the restaurant. The restaurant is besieged by the press. Her floating incident has gone viral. Business is out the door. She gains five million new followers. She's made all the top news stories, beating that election stuff on some channels.

When her mother, her manager, bursts in, she finds her

daughter reading news about herself on her phone, with her back flat against the ceiling.

Emergency services help peel her from the ceiling. They take her away and she watches the news report about herself on her phone. She has one million more new followers, she is now on seventy million followers. She starts to float again.

The hospital machines beep as she takes off, the tubes strain.

The specialist watches her.

Her momager shouts in panic for him to do something. He has never seen anything like it in his life.

'What is she doing on her phone?'

'I'm guessing she's on Instagram. Honey?'

'I'm on every single news report,' she says from the ceiling, unable to take her eyes from the screen. 'Mom, the lipgloss has sold out.'

They have a conversation about the lipgloss from floor to ceiling.

'Did she finish high school?'

'Yes.'

'Good interaction with others?'

'She was home-schooled.'

'College? Any further education? Part-time jobs?'

'She didn't need to. She has her own businesses.'

'She runs these businesses?'

'Her team does. She's the creative director.'

'I see. Do you like to read?' he calls up to her.

'I'm reading now,' she replies, keeping her eyes on her phone.

'Books?'

She scrunches up her face and shakes her head.

'Right. Do you watch the news? Documentaries?'

'I don't really watch TV. I have my own reality show. I make TV,' she laughs.

'I think I understand what's going on,' the specialist says, turning to the momager. 'Her brain is vacuous. It's busy, but it's filled with thoughts, predominantly about herself. Because of this there is nothing of any substance in her brain. There is nothing to root her, no weight at all.'

'That's ridiculous, she's a businesswoman. *Forbes* listed her as one of the top twenty Teens To Watch this year. She's worth hundreds of millions.'

'That's not really the issue.' He frowns. 'These brands are all about herself. And these brands are money-making schemes I'm guessing, all self-promotion.'

'Every business is the same.'

'Many people have passion for their subject. Passion brings a certain degree of intensity, a positive affinity to a certain subject, caring, drive, ambition, many things that have *weight*. Your daughter's passion is for self-adulation, self-promotion, attention, her passion is for herself. You cannot fill your mind with yourself, it carries no weight.'

She floats to the window to film the fans outside who are chanting her name. She snapchats it, but she's not careful and she drifts out the open window, away from her mother and manager who can't reach her, away from the specialist. She floats above the heads of the fans who film her instead of helping her. She drifts higher and higher into the sky until she disappears from sight completely.

She gains ten million more followers after that, and becomes the most followed person on Instagram, with over one hundred million followers, but of course she never discovers this. She has filled her thoughts and actions with too much of herself, there is no room for anything with weight or substance, or meaning.

She became so light, her head filled with too much nothing, she blew away.

20

The Woman Who Had a Strong Suit

It was the job interview, for a job that she didn't get, which began her quest.

'What would you say is your strong suit?' the interviewer had asked her.

The woman paused. 'Excuse me?'

'Your strong suit, what would you say it is?'

The woman frowned, puzzled. She had never heard of this before.

'I'm sorry but I don't believe I have one.'

'You must have one,' the interviewer sat forward, as though finally interested in the words coming out of her mouth, despite the fact they were not winning words.

'I really don't.'

'Everyone has one.'

'*Everyone?*'

'Yes, everyone.'

She cursed her older sister. Yet another thing that she should have told her.

'Even women have this . . . this suit?'

He frowned. 'Yes, even women.'

It was like being told that all of her life she has been wearing her shoes on the wrong feet. She felt off-kilter, completely disorientated. A strong suit that everybody in the world has, except for her. Why wasn't she told? She thought of her wardrobe, of all of her outfits, wondering if one of them was her strong suit and she never realized it. Nothing came to mind.

'This strong suit,' she cleared her throat, trying not to sound as stupid as she felt. 'Would it be something that I got for myself or that's given to me?'

'You would have it yourself, though some people would argue that it's passed down to you through the generations.'

'No. Not in my family,' she shook her head. 'They don't keep anything, and my mother wasn't big on wearing trouser suits.'

He laughed at first, thinking she was joking, then studied her curiously. 'Well, thank you for coming in.' He stood up, extended his hand, and she knew it was over.

She travelled home, furious that nobody had told her that she should have a strong suit. It wasn't on the job application. She had a master's degree, a PhD, the references and requisite experience for the job, but nobody had ever mentioned to her while growing up the need to wear a strong suit. Why hadn't her friends told her? Or was it like her period, she was just going to have to figure it out by herself, because her parents were too awkward and lazy to explain it themselves?

She called her sister.

'Hey, how did the interview go?'

'Terrible. Do you have a strong suit?' she fumed.

'A strong suit? Why?'

'Humour me.'

'Well, yes, I suppose I do. I—'

The woman gasped. Even her sister had one, her older sister who was supposed to tell her everything, who let her down about French kissing and everything else she should have told her.

'What about Jake and Robbie?' she asked about their brothers. 'Do they have them too?'

'Do they have what?'

'Strong suits?' she almost yelled down the phone but tried to breathe.

'You know them as well as I do, sweetheart – of course they do. Particularly Robbie. I mean, he has a couple.'

She gasps. A *couple?* 'Did Mum and Dad give them to you? Did they pass them down?' And if so, why was she left out?

'Are you kidding? Sweetie, are you okay? You sound . . . unusual.'

'I'm fine,' she snapped. 'Actually, I'm not. I'm sure I didn't get the job. He asked me about my strong suit and I didn't have an answer.'

'What? But you're the second smartest one in the entire family!'

'Smart is not enough. Apparently it's about what you wear too, I need a *strong suit* as well. I'm going to find one.' She hung up abruptly.

She threw open her wardrobe and examined her clothes. A suit suggested a two-piece. A similarly matched set consisting of a skirt and jacket, or trousers and jacket and perhaps a blouse. Again she was flummoxed, her sister never wore suits. However she was determined and removed every item of clothing, trying them all on, mixing and matching, pacing her room and trying to assess if any of them made her feel any different, made her feel *stronger*. There was a particular backless red dress that made her feel like standing up straighter, shoulders back, chest out. She wore it to her brother's wedding and never felt so good. That was the night she met James and had the best sex of her life, but she was not convinced that strong suit equalled best-dirty-sex-of-your-life suit, or that it would be something her new employer would require. And if it was, she wasn't sure if that made her want to work there more or less.

Her flatmate passed by and noticed the state of the room. She poked her head in.

'What are you doing?'

'Do you have a strong suit?'

She paused. 'My dad says I bring a lot of joy when I leave a room.' She smiled but was met with a blank stare and so she shrugged and left.

The woman frowned. The entire contents of her wardrobe lay in piles on her floor and bed. She had spent hours meticulously trying on everything, creating an algorithm on her computer which demonstrated how every single item could be worn together. And yet even after six solid hours of trying, she still did not know what her strong suit was.

She grabbed her bag and drove to a department store.

For the next month, she worked her way steadily through every single skirt and trouser suit they had. From ten a.m. until six p.m. and nine p.m. on Thursdays, breaking for an hour at lunch, she employed the services of personal shoppers to bring every available item from the department store to her changing room. There were five levels in the department store. She tried on everything. She even provided them with her phone number and email address for when new stock arrived. In the evenings she worked on a case study that she'd developed to address the problem. This consisted of an alphabetical list of the thousands of designers the department store stocked, from Acne Studios to Zac Posen. She had trawled through their collections for this season and next, made a note of strong-suit worthy outfits, and made projections of the probability of the inclusion of two-piece trouser and skirt suits in future collections based on their past designs. She had placed her name on waiting lists, and had over a dozen items on hold. At first she felt that a strong suit must be timeless, and not reflect changing fashion trends, but then realized she couldn't rely on that, and so readjusted her studies. There was so much she didn't know which caused the case study to grow. She included a mood board of fabrics she favoured, and a special pull-out section detailing which of these suits could be mixed and matched, combining and clashing textures and prints, according to changing fashion trends, in order to build the ideal strong suit which would flatter the proportions of her body.

It was the day after one of these regular days when she had visited the store and held up a changing room for hours, that the Department Store CEO was visiting to conduct inspections and meet with various departments. She overheard the sales staff discussing what to do about their problem customer. Should they ask her to leave the store? Ban her? Warn her? She was using up all of the personal shoppers' time with a brief for a strong suit that none of them could quite understand, and she had yet to spend any money. Even more troubling, they had discovered a briefcase she had left behind in a fitting room, which had scared the hell out of everyone when security had cleared the floor. The sales assistants huddled around the folder, examining the customer's private files.

'Is she a spy for another store?' one of them asked.

Let's find out, the other said, lifting the laptop. Her finger hovered over the power button.

The CEO cleared her throat.

They all jumped to attention, surprised to see her at the door and shuffled to gather themselves, stuffing the laptop back in the briefcase.

'Is this problem customer wearing the clothes before

returning them?' the CEO asked, motioning for them to hand her the briefcase.

'The clothes don't leave the shop. She's not buying anything at all,' a personal shopper replied. 'I don't mind helping somebody but she's taking time away from others who genuinely want to buy.'

The CEO flipped through a folder of charts, found the mood board, studied it. Her interest piqued, she looked some more. After a moment, she closed the briefcase. 'I'd like to speak with her,' the CEO said. 'Send her to me when she arrives.'

When the woman arrived, at 10 a.m. sharp, the head of security asked her to accompany him to the management level. The woman was startled but complied. Frightened by her treatment, she sat before the CEO and saw the briefcase on the table before them.

'I'm so sorry for leaving my bag behind, I honestly wasn't trying to cause a disturbance. I didn't realize I had forgotten it until late last night. I called the store but it was obviously too late by then, and it was closed. I did leave a message, explaining, in case you were concerned about its contents. I understand the security risks of a bag being left behind.'

'No need to apologize,' the CEO said. 'Though we didn't power up the laptop, we did have to take a look inside the bag to ensure there was no threat.'

'Of course,' the woman looks away, embarrassed.

'I understand that you've been in the store every day for a month, that you've tried everything on and haven't bought anything,' the CEO said.

'Is that a crime?'

'Actually, no. But you do understand how odd it seems to us that you're not buying anything.'

'I intend to buy. I'm not wasting your time. Look, I have money, if you don't believe me.' She dug in her bag for her wallet and produced it, revealing cash and credit cards.

'You don't have to show me that,' the CEO said gently. 'But tell me, what exactly are you looking for?'

'I can't.'

'Why not?'

'It's embarrassing.'

'I won't judge. You see, the reason I'm asking is because, as the CEO of a chain of six department stores, I worry when a client spends a month trying on everything we have in stock and still can't find what she's looking for. If it's not here then perhaps it's in New York, or Chicago. Or LA. And if it's not in any of those stores then perhaps I need to have a talk with our buyers. It bothers me that we have one hundred and fifty thousand square feet of clothes and a very keen customer that we can't cater to.'

'Oh,' the woman says, relieved. 'Well, this is embarrassing, but perhaps you *can* help me. I went for a job interview last month. I have a bachelor's degree in business – I graduated at the top of my class. I also have a PhD in finance, and excellent references. But I didn't get the job. I should have gotten the job.'

'Did they comment on your interview attire?' the CEO asks, trying to understand.

'No. He asked me what was my strong suit.' Again the embarrassment, her face flushes. 'And I told him that I didn't have one. I've never even heard of needing one, but apparently everyone has them. Like it's a fashion craze that I completely missed out on. So I've been here every day trying to find one.'

The CEO sits up, eyes wide, trying to process what she has heard. 'You have been shopping for a strong suit all this time?'

'Yes.'

'These charts and reviews, this mood board, this is all to combine every item we have in order for you to build your strong suit?'

'Yes,' she says quietly. 'I thought maybe if I put the right combination together, then I would just know as soon as it was on. But I'm not sure that's the case now.'

The CEO starts to smile. 'And tell me, now that you can't find a strong suit to wear, are you going to give up?'

'Give up? Of course not. Here, let me show you . . .' The woman reaches for the briefcase and pulls out her laptop. She boots up the detailed charts and entries she has made in the course of the past month, launching into a complex analysis of the various designers, styles and trends affecting women's suits. She points out some of the surprising facts she has gleaned about sizing and the pricing. 'I wait for new stock each week. If the incoming collections aren't right, perhaps I'll be more suited to Spring/Summer. I'll keep returning until I find my strong suit. Though

241

perhaps not as regularly . . .' She gives a sheepish smile. 'I agree my routine has been a bit obsessive. Can you help me?'

The CEO's head is swimming with ideas. 'I need you on my team.'

'Pardon?'

'I need you to work with me.'

The woman is shocked. 'You would like me to work for you even though I don't have a strong suit?'

The CEO smiles. 'You spent *every day* from ten a.m. to closing for an entire month, searching the racks for a strong suit. Your research and analysis have been more thorough than anything my own staff has ever prepared. My dear, I would say you found your strong suit.'

'I did?'

'You never give up, do you?'

'Of course not, but where do you think my strong suit is? Is it on the fourth floor in contemporary? If so, is it the navy blue with the pink threading, because that one I tried on five times, there was something about it.' The woman's eyes are bright with an inkling that she is close.

'No,' the CEO says. 'You're wearing it. It's part of you. When people use the term "strong suit" they refer to a long suit that contains high cards, the cards we hold in the palms of our hands that can help us win.'

The woman frowns. 'No, I'm sure that my job interview had nothing to do with a card game.'

The CEO smiles. 'Also known as a strong point, a personal

strength, one's most highly developed characteristic talent, skill or forte.'

The realization dawns on the woman, and the relief that the veil of strong suit secrecy has not been a conspiracy against her quickly turns to embarrassment.

'Don't be embarrassed,' the CEO says quickly. 'I'm glad you didn't get the last job you interviewed for, because then I would never have met you. You have displayed your personal strength in bucketloads. Your *tenacity* is your strong suit and it would be an honour if you joined my team.'

She extends her hand and the woman looks at it in surprise, beaming at this unexpected turnaround of events.

'Well?' the CEO urges. 'What do you think?'

'I think I'm going to play my hand,' she says, smiling, reaching out and shaking the CEO's hand.

21

The Woman Who Spoke Woman

The government's most powerful organ is a cabinet that
exercises executive authority over the country. The country's
inhabitants are comprised of both men and women; however,
the government and its cabinet are made up of men only.
Two hundred male politicians sit in the national parliament,
fifteen of whom hold ministerial positions in the cabinet.
These fifteen men meet every day to discuss the important
issues of the country and it is on one of these days that the
head of government's top advisor, Number One, enters the
cabinet meeting room carrying a survey.

'I have a survey of great importance. It appears that a
great number of women in this country are distressed about
our leadership.'

The men listen as he explains how the survey was
conducted, translated and analysed by more men in various
government offices.

'What is the women's problem?' asks the boss.

'They express disappointment that there are no women in the cabinet, or in the government as a whole, who can speak for them.'

Some of the men laugh.

'But we speak for everyone,' one says. 'We act on all of our citizens' behalf.'

'But they say we don't act on *their* behalf. And that in fact we don't listen to their concerns.'

'Don't listen to what? Who is saying something? Is there a report I missed?' the boss demands.

'This survey was drawn specifically from the country's female population. Or most of it.'

'What of the female population who don't object?'

'They object to the disgruntled women, they believe they are trying to be like men. They wish them to pipe down.'

'So it is kind of a civil war between the women?'

The cabinet laugh again.

The boss ponders this and studies the pie chart attached to the report. The numbers don't look good, the grumble percentages are up. Grumble percentages make him feel uncomfortable, especially in surveys of great importance. He's learned that such surveys are best listened to, and he trusts Number One implicitly.

'Boss, if I may . . .' a cabinet minister speaks up. 'If there is no woman in the cabinet or in the government, then there are no women issues to speak of. If we allow women to join us then there will suddenly be issues created, plucked out of the blue, willy-nilly.'

Willy-nilly, indeed. A dilemma for sure, when they have so many other more important issues to deal with without adding to their workload.

'Are we sure this isn't a trick by the opposition to create another nincompoop distraction?'

'It was our own survey, boss,' Number One admits. 'You asked us to secretly look into voter satisfaction.'

'Yes, but I didn't mean ask the *women*!' Conscious of having raised his voice, he makes an effort to calm himself. He is the boss for a reason, it is down to him to think and decide. He thinks. He decides. 'We must act. Send a woman in to us to speak on their behalf and we will listen to what the women have to say.'

An intelligent woman is found, an educated woman. A pretty woman. They all study her appearance, some discreetly, others not.

The woman speaks. For a long time. It seems to go on and on.

The boss frowns and looks around at the others. He feels uncomfortable, off-centre. He takes a sip of water. Is he hearing her correctly? He looks around at his colleagues and sees frowns, looks of concern, some smirks on the faces of his colleagues. Their reactions don't make him feel any better; he is flummoxed by her.

When the woman stops talking, they all turn to him,

creating a pregnant silence. He clears his throat, thanks the woman for her time, and she leaves.

He looks around at everybody. 'Did any of you understand that?'

They all shake their heads, mumbling and grumbling among themselves, and he can feel their relief that nobody else has understood a word she has said. He is hugely relieved too . . . it wasn't just him, which means he hasn't lost his touch.

'Why did you send in a woman who can't speak our national language?'

'We did, boss. She was speaking our national language, but she was speaking the woman's version.'

They ponder this.

'That explains it . . . I understood the individual words but not the way they were put together. And her tone . . .' He notices others shudder. 'It was unusual.'

'Shrill,' he hears someone else mutter.

'Women should be softer. It isn't constructive to use such a tone,' another says.

'A bit of a know-it-all,' another says.

'Yes, boss,' Number One chimes in, taking notes.

'So this is how women speak?' the boss asks.

'Yes, boss. We believe it's a different dialect.'

'And women of our country wish *us* to speak like this?'

'There are two things, boss. The women of this country wish you to understand their dialect, and they also wish women who speak this dialect to join the government so that they can use their own voices.'

'Why don't we just get rid of men altogether?' one man explodes.

'Settle down now. Women politicians to represent women citizens?' The boss ponders this. He can see the merits, it would be a way of delegating this extra load of unexpected issues to those who are raising them, but what if they made decisions that the men didn't agree with, or even worse, didn't understand?

'No, boss,' Number One interrupts his thoughts. 'The idea would be for women in the government to represent *all* the country's citizens, not just women.'

Some laughter and groans.

'How preposterous! How can they represent men when they are women and speak woman?' he asks.

'This is the very point that women raise regarding male politicians, boss.'

A quiet descends on the cabinet.

'And may I add,' Number One breaks the silence, 'it is not just the dialect that is different, it is also their thoughts that differ from ours.'

Grave news indeed. Different ideologies. New voices. A scary prospect for a stable government.

The boss thinks this conundrum through. 'But how can a woman politician represent a male citizen when she has a different dialect and also thinks differently? No man will fall for this,' he says, feeling sweat on his brow. 'The male electorate won't like it.'

'Boss, if you look here to this graph, you'll see that there is a large number of women that also make up the electorate.'

'Yes, but the male electorate is *louder*. And because it is louder their thoughts and issues receive larger font treatment in newspaper headlines. I learned this from the editor of our largest publication. They report on more issues relating to men on the most popular pages because they have more male readers and the reason for this is because men's hands are larger and are better at holding this particular broadsheet.'

'Boss, we believe women have become adept at holding the same size newspaper, and online media is growing. There are many other news sources now. Headlines and font sizes are not necessarily what matter any more.'

'But you've just seen a woman in this room and nobody had a damn clue what she was saying! How are we expected to work side by side?'

'The women believe that men will learn to understand them over time, just as women have learned to understand the language of men. All women speak man, they were raised bilingual. No men in this room speak woman. Surveys seem to suggest that women believe it should work *both* ways.'

The boss sighs. What a pickle indeed. And he's not sure that he likes that women have all this time had their own secret language.

'How many of this female electorate voted for me?'

'Half, boss. The other half didn't vote at all. So on the bright side, it was you, or no one.'

'If I bring in a woman, then the women will vote for her instead.' He tries to keep the whine out of his voice.

'Or they will vote for you because they see you are making changes and listening to them, that you perhaps even care about them, which could double your support.'

The boss doesn't feel like adding that he didn't need their support to get to this position in the first place. He sighs. 'Do we have a translator for us to at least learn how to speak woman?'

'This is preposterous!' the Minister for Justice and Equality says suddenly, standing up, his body trembling with anger. 'You have my immediate resignation!' He storms out of the room.

Number One senses the mood and steps in. 'Boss, we believe that there are some women who can and will fit into the dress and language of men . . . in order to get their foot in the door, so to speak. They can speak our language. They don't *distract* from the issues by the fact they're women. Their female traits have been minimized and can easily be ignored.'

'Well, I think we can all agree that this would make a big difference to us all here?'

Nods and mumbles of agreement.

'The less that we notice they are women, the better and more efficiently we can do our jobs. For the country.'

Murmurs of agreement.

'If the women were somehow de-womanized, and spoke our male dialect, we could find a way to communicate with them.'

This is a popular decision.

'Hmm. So let's find the man-speaking-women who don't harp on about the women issues.'

'That may be difficult,' Number One says, studying his checklist. 'They want you to allow them to express their women views.'

'Men have the majority in the government,' the boss explains. 'The women members would have to toe the party line.'

'The party line being the male view.'

'Indeed.'

'But what about their female views?'

'On what?'

'On female issues?'

'They will be taken into consideration by the men.'

'And what about their thoughts on male issues?'

'What about them?'

'Will these also be taken into consideration?'

'No!' he almost laughs. 'That's preposterous. How can a female have a view on a male issue?'

'Because all men on this cabinet have a view on female issues, they always have. In all thirty-five cabinets, in the entire history of the state.'

Awkward silence.

'That's because we're the majority! Honestly, one would think you're on the women's side.'

'Not at all, sir,' Number One says, feeling sweat on his upper lip, 'I just want to treat this survey with the seriousness it deserves. When this percentage of the population is unhappy for so very long it can have the effect of a shaken soda bottle.'

'I see,' the boss says, already bored. 'Let's begin by allowing these man-speaking-women to join us, to discuss the issues that we set forward, and then we'll see how we go from there.'

The cabinet members nod in approval. It's a fair compromise. Progress, but women of their choosing, to use as they wish.

'Meeting adjourned.'

As everybody trickles out the boss has a thought, he calls back Number One.

'A quiet word!'

They wait until the door closes behind the last cabinet minister and they are alone.

'It has occurred to me that women being women often distracts men from what they are actually saying.'

'Yes, that appears to be the case.'

'We can use this to our advantage.'

'We can, boss?'

'Indeed. Find some of these women-women. You know the ones I mean.'

'Yes, boss.'

'We can use them to distract people from certain issues. When the words come from their mouths, it will confuse the people, maybe veil what's actually being said. This can be helpful to us and our party agenda.'

'Indeed, boss. Just so I am clear, we need man-speaking-women in the government to discuss everyday issues, man-speaking-women to translate the women's issues, and we need women-women to distract from the more troubling male issues.'

'Yes,' the boss says, sitting back in his chair, feeling very satisfied with himself.

'And how are we to use the men in the government?'

The boss laughs as if this is ridiculous. 'Well the men are just the men – their role is to be a man, no distractions. When they speak, they speak man, and everyone hears them.'

'Of course.' Number One scribbles furiously, then gathers his notes and quickly leaves the meeting room. He places his pages on his desk outside, and goes straight to the bathroom, feeling the sweat trickling down his back. Once inside the cubicle he locks the door, loosens his tie and opens the top buttons of his shirt. He can barely breathe. It took everything in him not to scream during that meeting. Sweat trickles from his brow and he wipes it with his handkerchief. He picks at his forehead with a fingernail, then slowly peels off his bald head.

Her hair falls loosely down on her shoulders. She rubs her head in frustration, allows herself a moment of freedom. How much longer must it go on like this – to be the most respected advisor on the team, and yet have to conceal her true identity?

But still, today was progress. A victory of sorts.

She sits for a while, makes some notes, checks her phone.

Then she puts her bald head back on, ensuring that her hair isn't visible beneath the cap. She buttons up her shirt, tightens the knot in her tie, polishes her brogues, clears her throat to adjust its pitch, and exits the men's toilet.

22

The Woman Who Found the World in Her Oyster

She is going to a ladies' charity lunch, one that she has been nervous about since the invitation arrived in the mail. The gold envelope with familiar handwriting had made her stomach heave. If she was ever to pass the 'test' of being a true woman, then today is surely it. She is exfoliated, pruned, facialled, manicured, pedicured, waxed to perfection. She has chosen her outfit carefully, a sophisticated blush shift dress, nothing too brash, nothing too crude, or bright. A cashmere cardigan with pearl detail that drapes over her shoulders. Blush court shoes with a low kitten heel – she's still getting used to heels and daren't risk a fall in front of these ladies – and a box clutch to hold in one hand while holding a glass of champagne in the other. That way she will have no free hands, nothing to fidget with or wave around nervously.

And of course she's wearing a set of pearls. They were her mother's. Her sister had taken all of their mother's jewellery after her death, not knowing that the woman longed for much of it, but had presented the pearl necklace to her only days ago, knowing how nervous she was about today, knowing how she wanted to be accepted.

The pearl necklace offering had been a gesture to show that her mother would have been proud of her, of her bravery, her courage to become her true self. And though the woman appreciated it, she wasn't sure she agreed that's what her mother would have thought at all. Still. It was a nice thought. Pearls are considered by many as the most feminine and magical gems, the only ones created by a living organism, and with jewellery their family trade, her sister would have understood the link.

The charity lunch is being held at Mother of Pearl, a Michelin-starred restaurant in an affluent area, where the old fishing port has been gentrified by the arrival of a series of artisanal cafés, pricey fishmongers, and restaurants with Michelin-star celebrity chefs. The woman's ex-wife, Charlotte, is on the fundraising committee of the charity. She's the one who invited her this year, the first contact they'd had in a long time, the first civil contact they'd had in even longer. The woman feels wary of Charlotte's invitation, suspicious of her generosity.

She follows other women as they wobble in their heels on the cobblestoned fishing pier, holding each other by the elbows, heads down, concentrating. She's relieved she wore her kitten heels, nothing higher. She recognizes these women from the school, from pick-ups, drop-offs, birthday parties, but mostly she knows them from her own jewellery store in town, the family business that was handed down to her after her father's death. She hasn't met them all yet as her true self, she has stayed away from the shop over the past year, was running the business at a remove. Regardless of her ex-wife's intention, she would not allow herself to feel that this day would be a test of her womanhood. She has come too far for this.

She feels a drop of sweat trickle down her cleavage as she approaches the entrance, where two ladies sitting behind a table are marking off names on the list. She's convinced that this invitation has been designed to trip her up, to make her feel like the odd one out, as if she didn't belong. Well, she's felt like that her entire life.

She lifts her chin and follows the women, clad in their Hervé Léger, Roland Mouret and Chanel, to the door. The women at the desk don't even need to check their list when she walks in, they recognize her immediately. Bright smiles, huge welcomes. The transgender has arrived. She lifts a glass of champagne from a tray and sips as she moves further into the room. She sips again quickly, then a larger gulp when no one is looking.

'There you are!' She hears the loud sing-song cry of her ex-wife, and turns to see her coming towards her, arms out, welcoming, pulling her into a hug.

'Charlotte, hi,' she says. 'Thank you for the invitation.'

'Well, don't you look beautiful,' Charlotte says, looking down at her dress, eyes lingering on her breasts. 'What a great colour on you.'

They're both aware of the stares they're receiving and so perform appropriately, pretending they don't notice. Charlotte squeezes her arm extra tight, 'Isn't this fun?'

Charlotte is wearing the same perfume she has worn for twenty years, the one the woman bought for her every year for her birthday: Chanel No. 5. She remembers holding the sophisticated pots and smelling the luxurious silky body lotion over the years and wanting to use it herself, soured by the stabs of envy. She may have taken those feelings out on Charlotte, using the rage she felt at herself against her. She denied so much for so long; she owes it to her ex-wife not to deny that now.

Charlotte looks beautiful. She's wearing black as usual. Her toned arms are revealed by her Dolce & Gabbana shift dress. Her feet are in sky-high black pointed heels, which show off her slim, bronzed calves. The woman envies her ability to wear shoes that high and walk so effortlessly in them, not like the others tottering around in the room. She even used to wear towering heels while pushing the kids in their strollers. Her hair, her make-up, everything about Charlotte is beautiful, seemingly effortless, but the woman knows how much time and effort goes into this stylish woman's seeming simplicity.

She knows Charlotte inside out, can sense her nerves now, not that anybody else would. She knows Charlotte's tricks.

She can see her eyes are just a little too bright, the pitch of her voice is a little too high, the pace just a little too fast.

Knowing this calms the woman somewhat. They are both nervous. She takes her by the hand, she squeezes her tight, as if to say she understands. It's a familiar act from all those years as a husband, but instead of calming Charlotte, it seems to rattle her. She removes her hand instantly. Perhaps she's thinking it's easier to pretend the woman is someone new, a new friend to get to know. The woman feels embarrassed.

Charlotte looks steadily into her eyes. 'You're still in there,' she says gently.

She thinks she sees Charlotte's eyes moisten slightly, then as suddenly as the tears surface, they disappear, and she's back in organization mode, accompanying her to her table, introducing her to the other nine champagne-giddy ladies that she will be spending the afternoon with.

To her surprise, her table is not out the door, by a fire exit with the misfits. It is prominent, centrally located, and she is seated with smart, successful, interesting women. Once she's seated, she starts to enjoy herself; the champagne is taking effect, and she feels warm and buzzy, happy. The starter arrives. Oysters.

The woman smiles. There are several reasons she has an affinity with oysters. The most obvious reason is that they produce her favourite gem, the pearl. It's that Catch-22, that reminder that in nature and in life you can't have it all; the edible oysters don't produce pearls and the pearl oysters aren't edible – their flesh is fat and rank in flavour.

Natural pearls are extremely rare: only one in ten thousand wild oysters will yield a pearl and, of those, only a small percentage achieve the size, shape and colour of desirable gems. The woman knows this as a matter of business, of course; it's part of why she loves them.

The second reason is that during their first year oysters spawn as males by releasing sperm in the water. Over the next few years they develop greater energy reserves and they spawn as females by releasing eggs.

But there is a third reason, and it involves Charlotte. She looks over to see if she is remembering the same thing, but Charlotte is deep in conversation, holding court while hosting her own table, her oysters untouched.

The woman lifts her first oyster and moves it around with her fork. She pauses when something catches her eye. Something shiny and iridescent. A small ball. A pearl! But it's impossible, it's not a pearl oyster. She moves the flesh aside with her fork and examines the pearl, tuning out of the group conversation. She needs her glasses, but she didn't bring them because they wouldn't fit in her box clutch. Better yet she needs her jeweller's eyeglass so she can examine it properly. She's trying to figure out where she can put it so she can transport it home to study it when a spoon clinking against a glass directs everybody's attention to the head of the room, where Charlotte is standing.

Cool, confident Charlotte is a natural public speaker, a strong advocate for women's rights. She begins by welcoming them all, sharing with them how much money was raised last year and where it went, how much it helped those in need. She spares no details, these women are not just here to have fun, they need to hear the facts, and she doesn't gloss over them.

'As you all know, each year has a theme. We've been spending time with children and women, trying to find funding to assist, encourage and inspire them to prosper in this world. We want them and us to be in a position to seize the opportunities that life has to offer. This year's theme is "The World Is Your Oyster", which is why we chose this wonderful setting today – and thank you so much to Chef Bernard and all the staff for such a wonderful and memorable lunch so far.'

The woman's heart pounds. Charlotte keeps talking but the woman can't concentrate; she is emotional, she is perplexed. How does she have a pearl in her oyster? For a moment, she wonders whether Charlotte arranged it deliberately, and if so, why? They have been at war with each other for two years. Even longer, if you include the years they were married.

When Charlotte sits to a roaring round of applause, she looks over at the woman. She offers her a small shrug, almost playful. She summons a waiter and whispers into his ear. He looks up at the woman and walks across the room to her, jug of water in his hand, but it's not the water he offers, he leans down discreetly and says, 'She told me to tell you that she's glad you didn't choke on it.'

The woman's hand flies to her chest at hearing the phrase.

She holds onto the pearls around her neck. She thinks back to twenty years ago when she proposed to Charlotte at a restaurant, watching her nervously as she opened an oyster shell on her plate and stared at the engagement ring inside.

'I'm glad you didn't choke on it,' the woman had said to Charlotte at the time, nervously trying to fill silence as she always did then, though she doesn't do that any more. She's learned to be comfortable with silences.

She looks again at the oyster and the pearl.

Today has not been about Charlotte humiliating her, it is quite the opposite. The woman has received Charlotte's message of acceptance and proposal of friendship loud and clear.

The world is her oyster.

23

The Woman Who Guarded Gonads

'I'd like to have a vasectomy,' the man says, fingers fidgeting, playing with his wedding ring, sliding it up and down his finger.

He is sitting at a boardroom table, feeling revealed and vulnerable opposite three women in pinstriped suits. Despite his experience working in corporate environments, this visit is regarding a personal matter and he feels intimidated by their demeanours. The tense atmosphere is generating an air of an interrogation to their meeting and is not at all what he was expecting. He directs his words to the woman in the centre, because so far she has been the person doing all of the talking. He reaches for the glass of cold water before him and takes a gulp.

The woman on the right bristles at his words, the woman on the left's posture is ramrod straight; she looks down her long nose at him, but again, it's the woman in the centre who responds.

'It's normal to have mixed feelings about not wanting children, especially when they are unplanned,' she says.

Don't tell me what I want, don't tell me what I feel, he rages to himself.

'So you should always plan for them,' the stout one on the right adds.

'We are here to counsel you,' the woman in the centre continues, 'on your decision to have a vasectomy.'

'I already have two children,' he says. 'I understand the responsibilities, I love my children, but we just can't have any more. We feel that our family is complete, and financially, we couldn't cope. My wife certainly doesn't want to have another child.'

'Can I ask where you learned about vasectomies?'

'I read about it online.'

'Then you know that it is illegal in this country.'

'It is? Why can't we do it here? I hear it's a safe, quick ten-minute procedure.'

'Not in this country.'

'But I want to share the burden of contraception. I want to take control of my own fertility.'

'No,' the stout woman on the right says.

'What do you mean, no?'

'You're not allowed.'

'Says who?'

'The law.'

He feels the anger rising.

'Forgive Mary, she is very passionate about this subject,' the woman in the centre says gently. 'When you say you couldn't cope with more children, do you mean you would feel suicidal?'

'No!' he exclaims.

'Oh. Shame,' she tut-tuts. 'Well, I'm afraid that's the only circumstance under which we could have performed your vasectomy today.'

'Or if the sperm that was being ejaculated from your penis was about to kill you,' the skinny one on the left adds.

He looks at her, alarmed. 'Can that happen?'

'Thank you, Amanda,' the woman in the centre places a calming hand on her colleague's arm. 'Mr Smith, have you thought about your moral responsibilities to your sperm?'

His eyes widen. 'A sperm is not a life.'

There's a sharp intake of breath from Mary.

'The science of embryology and genetics makes clear that human life begins at fertilization,' the man says, angry now.

'Could your wife have had your two children without your sperm?' Mary asks.

'No. Of course not.'

'Well, then. Without sperm, life is not possible. With sperm, comes the creation of life. You cannot annihilate the creation of life,' Mary says.

'And what about your lack of thought for the sperm? Why deny your sperm its right to life?' Amanda, on the left, asks.

'It's my right to choose what I do with my sperm,' he answers, angry now.

'I know it's difficult to understand, but your reproductive rights are our business,' the woman in the centre replies.

'This is ridiculous,' he stands up, shouting. 'Whether you personally agree with it or not is beside the point! You can't make a decision about *my* body, based on *your* personal opinions. IT'S *MY* SEMEN! THEY ARE *MY* TESTICLES!' he roars, red in the face, the veins in his neck pulsating.

There is a pregnant pause.

'These are not our personal opinions,' the woman says softly, so as not to rile him again. 'It's the law. That makes it different.'

'But it's ridiculous,' he protests. 'It's my . . . how can you . . .' he scrambles for the words. 'You can't tell a man what he can do with his body,' he says. 'I've never heard anything like it in my life. It's . . . unprecedented.'

The woman in the centre raises her eyebrow.

'Why didn't you tell me this over the phone?' he explodes.

'I'd imagine whoever you spoke to told you to come in because it's illegal to give advice over the phone. It must be face-to-face.'

'You're supposed to counsel me, not try to talk me out of it . . . I'm going to report you. Anyway, I don't care what you say, I'm getting on a plane and I'll fly to any of the hundreds of countries of the world where it's legal to carry out the procedure safely, every day.'

Amanda, on the left, shakes her head. 'Oh dear.'

'You shouldn't have told us that,' the woman in the centre says. 'We may be obligated to alert the authorities, and they can impose a restraining order on you, preventing you from travelling.'

'What the hell?!'

'But if you do manage to go, without alerting the authorities, when you return,' she offers, 'please do contact us and we would be delighted to provide free post-vasectomy medical check-ups and counselling services.'

Mary looks over his shoulder, 'Evelyn's there again.'

He turns around.

He sees a woman with a placard, upon which is a detailed photo of a penis. *SAVE SEMEN.*

'That's disgusting,' he spits.

'So crude,' the woman in the centre agrees.

'In broad daylight,' the stout woman adds.

'And so close to a school,' the skinny one says.

'Sperm is a better word,' the woman in the centre says.

'Certainly better than cum,' the stout one replies.

'And boner milk,' the skinny one adds.

The man looks at them wide-eyed, unable to believe what he's hearing. He gives the three women a last look, and leaves the clinic, passing by the silent protestor.

'It's my body,' he shouts at her. 'It's got nothing to do with you!'

She reverses the placard. A wonderfully detailed image of a pair of testicles, and above, *Guard the Gonads.*

24

The Woman Who Was Pigeonholed

'Excuse me!' she calls to the clerk at the desk below her.

The clerk doesn't answer. She's incredibly busy sending papers flying at top speed into the cubbyholes that surround her, everything instantly categorized according to colour, subject, or topic.

'Yoohoo!' the woman sings, waving her arms.

The clerk either ignores her or cannot hear her from where she is crammed into a square on top of the bureau. She squirms and tries to move her arms and her legs, but she's jammed.

'Excuse me!' she yells at the clerk, who won't look at her. 'I don't belong in here, let me out!'

The clerk continues to file away paperwork in all of the squares around her.

She's insulted that she has been confined to the box. She is so much more than this one box – she could have been placed in plenty of boxes, she is many of those other things too.

'She won't listen to you,' a voice comes from beneath her. She looks down.

'Hi,' the woman squished into a box a few rows down says. 'Janet. Single mother. Can't finish what I start.'

'Hi, Janet,' she says.

'I play the ukulele too, but *a certain person doesn't seem to care about that,*' Janet says, raising her voice so that the clerk below can hear. There's no reaction.

'Ha! Well, I'm the wild crazy mother, nice to meet you,' says another woman from the far corner. The woman looks down diagonally to her right.

'Hi,' she says.

'I get out once a fortnight, and when I do, boy, do I drink,' she says. 'And dance, so that makes me wild, apparently. So crazy! Watch out, it's *dangerous Mary who likes too much gin!*' she shouts down to the clerk, her words dripping with sarcasm.

The clerk is still wildly sorting through paperwork, not paying the slightest notice to those who have been filed away.

'I also play tennis,' Mary adds. 'I like adult colouring books and walks on the beach, but she doesn't care about that, does she?'

The woman hears a snort and peeps into the pigeonhole beside her.

A woman, who is filing her nails, looks up. 'Hi, I'm Brooke. I'm shy.' She leans over the edge and throws her nail file at the clerk, who doesn't react. She sighs.

'Hello from the helicopter mom!' a woman shouts from somewhere in the pigeonhole.

'Hello, helicopter mom, meet soccer mom!' another voice calls from the other direction. 'One minute I'm a stupid woman who cares nothing about world issues and who is going to kill everyone in my path to make sure my child succeeds, and then I'm baking cookies!'

They all laugh.

'I'm odd.' The woman hears a new voice. She looks down and sees a hand waving from a pigeonhole.

'Hey.'

'I'm a working mum who's selfish and hates my kids!' a voice adds suddenly, and they all laugh.

A pair of hands high-five across the pigeonholes.

'I'm a fat woman. Nothing else!' a woman asserts, to groans.

'I'm an exercise buff who judges other people's lifestyles,' another says.

'I'm a fat woman who exercises,' someone says and they cheer.

'I'm the woman whose husband had an affair.'

'I'm the evil woman who had an affair with somebody else's husband!' another shouts out.

'Nicola Nagle, is that you?'

'Nope.'

'Thank God for that.'

The women laugh.

'Daddy issues!'

'Control freak.'

'Flirt!'

'Pestering mother-in-law.'

'Sly!'

'Do-gooder, but if only they knew the truth.'

They *oooh* in unison.

'Second wife.'

'Third wife.'

'Bunny-boiler.'

'Bossy.'

'Liar!'

'Victim.'

'Survivor.'

'Vain!'

'Materialistic!'

'WAG!'

'Mother Earth!'

'Wife!'

'Mother!'

'Motherless wife!'

'Husbandless woman!'

'Junkie.'

'Superiority complex.'

'Subversive!'

'Feminist man-hater!'

'Slut!'

'Lipstick lesbian!'

They all laugh and settle in silence for a moment as they take a break from shouting out their labels.

'It's just easier,' the clerk says suddenly, breaking the silence, and looking up at the enormous pigeonholes before her.

'What's easier?' the woman asks.

'It's like a headline. When you read further you see the content. When people meet you, they'll realize who you are.'

'But they won't meet us if they don't like the headline,' the woman replies, to general agreement. 'And headlines are always out of context.'

Everyone throws something at the clerk from their pigeonhole. She ducks for cover, then re-emerges with a bicycle helmet on for protection.

'Look, don't blame me, I'm just doing my job. It's easier this way, trust me.'

'Easier for whom? For you?' the woman asks.

'Well, yes. For me and for everybody else. Because then they'll know where to find you, how to think of you. I'll know where to reach for you when they come looking. It's efficient.'

'But I don't belong here! I'm a little bit of many of these boxes,' the woman explains. 'You are stopping me from reaching my highest potential.' She squirms around in the box uncomfortably.

'Exactly!' somebody else agrees. 'I'm a fat feminist man-hating slut. I should be in at least four boxes!'

They all laugh.

'So should I chop you up and separate your body parts?' the clerk asks.

'No! Don't be ridiculous. Just let us out,' the woman says. 'Don't bother putting us in these pigeonholes at all.'

'And then what? I'd just have you all in a big pile on the counter. Nobody would know what you are.'

'People could look through the pile and decide for themselves.'

The clerk snorts. 'Clarity. Everybody wants clarity. To know what they're getting before they get it. Look around!'

They look around and they're surrounded by hundreds, thousands, millions of pigeonholes just like theirs, all of them occupied, while the dedicated clerk wildly sifts through paperwork.

'How about they take the time to figure us out once they meet us?'

'Too much work. People like to be told.'

'I don't like to be told,' the woman says, hitting the ceiling above her, wishing she had more space. 'I like to discover things for myself, form my own opinion, and then I'll still know that it's only my opinion and not an actual fact.'

'You're rare.'

'Exactly. But this isn't the *rare* box.'

'It's better to just round you off to the nearest,' the clerk tries to reason with them.

'I don't want that.'

'Haven't you ever heard of the Pygmalion effect? Where higher expectations lead to higher performance and the inverse Golem effect where lower expectations lead to lower performance. You're doing everybody here a disservice by labelling us by our needs and risks, as opposed to our strengths and assets.'

'Not all the boxes are negative. There's a *funny* box.'

'But I want to be taken seriously,' a voice calls out from the funny box.

The clerk ignores them and goes back to filing.

But the woman doesn't give up. The pigeonhole is making her hot and irritated. 'If somebody is looking for me as I truly am, then they won't find me here. You're fooling people. And you're making those who would actually like me, miss out on me.'

'Perhaps. But it makes the paperwork less complicated.'

'What about what I want?'

'Stop being difficult.'

'I'm not in a *difficult* or *rare* pigeonhole,' she says, fuming. 'That's two things you've called me that my label doesn't even say that I am.' She folds her arms in a huff, sits back, and watches as the clerk files the entire world away.

'You know what you are?' someone shouts at the clerk, from above her. 'You're nothing but a pigeonholer!' she shouts.

At that, they all start laughing.

The clerk stops filing and looks up at them, her face raging. 'Who said that?'

'Me,' replies the shy one.

'Well, now you have to get out of there, because that wasn't very shy.'

'Where do I go?'

'*Difficult* pigeonhole. Third column fifth down.'

The once shy but now difficult woman swings out of her

pigeonhole and uses the ladders running up and down the cube to climb across to her new box.

A new clerk arrives to take over, dressed in the same beige trousers and shirt.

'Head office says you have to stop now and move to B1.'

'B1?' the clerk blurts out with anger.

'What's B1?' a woman calls down.

'Don't be so nosy,' the clerk replies.

'I'm not nosy. I'm *menopausal.*'

'B1 is the *pigeonholer* box,' the new clerk explains apologetically.

'But that's ridiculous. I was only being efficient!'

The new clerk shrugs. 'Sorry, just obeying orders.'

The clerk places her papers down and reluctantly makes her way to the pigeonhole. She sits inside and folds her arms. 'You know I thought that if this was ever to happen to me that I'd be in the *artist* box. I love painting.'

'Welcome to the team,' the woman says. She bangs the roof above her and suddenly it shifts. She removes the shelf and reads the label on the front. *Tenacious.* She chuckles and sits up more comfortably in her larger box, and kicks at the wall beside her. Thankfully the box is empty and the wall gives way, allowing her legs to rest in *libertine.*

25

The Woman Who Jumped on the Bandwagon

She'd been driving aimlessly along winding country roads when she first spotted the woman walking along the side of the road ahead of her. The pedestrian was holding a basket, appeared to be in her own world and didn't even look up as the car approached, despite the fact it was probably the first vehicle to pass her in hours. The woman driving, in truth, was bored and needed company. She also needed a co-pilot because, although she had her destination firmly in sight, she had absolutely no idea how to get where she wanted to go.

Pulling her car over just beyond the woman, she waits for her to catch up. As she nears the car, the woman lowers the window but the pedestrian keeps on walking, looking straight ahead, as if in a zombie state. She suspects that, if she hadn't called out, the pedestrian would have continued right on by.

'Hello!' she raises her voice, leaning out the window.

The pedestrian snaps out of her trance and stops walking. She turns and seems surprised to see the car by the road where she has just walked. 'Oh hello,' she says, taking steps back.

'Would you like a lift?' the woman asks.

'Oh thank you very much,' the pedestrian says gently, smiling. 'But I'm happy to make my own way. Thank you though, how kind.'

Her response annoys the woman in the car. It annoys her that this woman wants to be alone, and even worse, she seems so happy to be walking alone.

'Are you lost?' the pedestrian asks, concerned, and the woman in the car decides not to tell her. She knows where she wants to go, she's just having difficulty getting there, it doesn't mean that she's lost. She is aiming for the top of the mountain.

'Are you going to the top of the mountain?' the woman in the car asks.

'Oh,' the pedestrian looks up as if taken aback to see the enormously tall mountain in front of them. 'Maybe!' she laughs. 'I suppose I'll find out if I get there, I'm just enjoying each step of the journey.'

Again this response annoys the woman in the car who is so desperately trying to reach her destination, she can't understand that anybody wouldn't have the same goal. She tries to steal a glimpse of the contents of her basket but the pedestrian senses this and moves the basket away.

Irritated, the driver starts the car and they part ways with a final exchange of pleasantries.

It is the look of determination on the pedestrian's face, the confidence in her walk, the secrecy over the contents of her basket, this contradiction of blasé-ness that compels her to watch her in the wing mirror as she drives on. But she is so focused on what the pedestrian is doing that she drives off the road and into a ditch. The last thing she sees as her front left tyre dips into the rut is the pedestrian cutting into a neighbouring field and disappearing from view. This is incredibly frustrating. She wants to know where she is going, what is in her basket. She'd been hoping to keep her in sight in her rear-view, trail her from ahead, as it were.

Unable to drive the car out of the ditch, and unable to push it out, she stands stranded on a quiet country lane, miles from anyone or anything. Even worse, she has no signal on her phone. She is lost, tired, confused and rather desperate by the time she hears the sound of horses' hooves coming in her direction.

She brushes the dirt and sticks from her clothes and looks in the direction the music is coming from. It is happy trumpet music that instantly makes her smile. As it comes closer she can make out a nineteenth-century type of open wagon, with a band of musicians playing on top in the open air. Two coachmen wearing red military-style jackets with gold stitching sit out front. They pull the horses' reins and the wagon comes to a halt right beside her. The music instantly stops. The carriage is stunning: red velvet panels intricately decorated in gold, with images of triumphant angels, regal lions and harps. The horses' hair is plaited and knotted with gold ribbons woven into elegant braids. Gathered on top of the bandwagon is a six-piece band, and each musician is dressed in the same regal costume, with tall gold top hats.

'Good day!' a coachman calls down to her cheerily.

'Hi,' she replies, in awe of the spectacular sight.

The six-piece band comes complete with percussion: an enormous bass drum hangs over the side, threatening to tip the wagon over.

'Did you have a breakdown?' the trombone player asks.

'My car did. I was pretty close.'

They laugh. The drummer makes the punchline rim-shot drum sound.

'I was following a pedestrian, but I lost her when she cut across the fields.'

'There's no walkway through those fields,' the trumpet player says.

'She took her own route,' she says, feeling the burn of jealousy.

'Would you like to hop on with us?' the trumpet player on the bandwagon asks.

The band members hang over the edge, looking at her, tilting the gilded wagon.

'Where are you going?' she asks.

'We are going all the way, baby!' the drummer announces, and they burst into spontaneous celebratory song.

Her eyes widen. 'All the way? To the top?' she asks when they've settled down.

'Of course!'

'This is perfect. It's all I've ever wanted. Can you guys take me there?' she asks.

'Sure!' the trombone player exclaims. 'Jump on board!'

The woman steps up and jumps on the bandwagon, not thinking twice about leaving her car behind. The band plays continuously and she sits among the musicians, and is carried all the way along the winding road, constantly looking back to see who is behind, or following, and looking forward to see who is ahead, who they can overtake. On their journey they see the lone pedestrian she'd been following emerge from the fields. She has the same look of determination on her face, she's focused, eyes looking straight ahead. And now she is holding two baskets.

'Should we stop to offer her a ride?' the drummer asks. 'She's in the middle of nowhere here.'

She wants to say no but this bandwagon has been so generous to carry her all the way. The coachmen pull the reins and the bandwagon slows.

It's as though the woman hasn't heard the heavy clopping of hooves on the ground, and the six-piece band playing cheerful music all the way behind her.

'Hello there!' the woman calls down.

'Oh, hello again!' the pedestrian says, grinning and holding her hand over her eyes to shield the sunlight. 'What a beautiful bandwagon!' Her eyes scan the ornate gilded embellishments along the side, and the woman on the bandwagon feels a wonderful smug feeling glowing inside.

'Would you like to climb aboard?' the woman asks. 'We're going straight to the top!'

'Oh, how kind,' she says. 'But if you don't mind, I really am enjoying the walk,' she repeats. 'And I have some things to do.'

The woman is now really put out by this response; she has given her two opportunities to join her and has been refused twice. The pedestrian's boots are dirty from the walk through the field and as soon as the sun goes down there is no doubt she will be cold. While the band swap pleasantries, the woman sits down and folds her arms huffily, deciding then and there that if the pedestrian won't come with her for the journey, she'll do it herself and she'll do everything she can to slow her down.

The coachmen signal to the horses with the reins and the bandwagon moves on. She feels a deep satisfaction as they pass the pedestrian by, but it's spoiled by the fact that she doesn't seem to care about passing up on this chance for company and convenience, she is lost in her own world, doing her own thing, swinging two mysterious baskets by her side. The woman watches until she's a speck in the distance.

Finally, after a long journey the woman and the bandwagon arrive at a pretty little town. The band plays so loudly it attracts everybody's attention. The villagers run out of their shops and homes to surround the wagon on its way to the town square. The journey is bumpy as they roll over the cobblestones and children run alongside cheering while the band, in their element, play their greatest hits. They are guided by bunting which lines the street and, when they arrive at the town square, a mayor wearing his chain of office is standing on a makeshift stage, awaiting their arrival.

'Welcome!' he booms, stooping under the weight of the thick gold chain with the town crest hanging over his chest. 'You've made it,' he says. 'The second woman to reach us this hour. Do you know where you are?'

'Not exactly,' she says excitedly, and then frowns at the mention that she is the second woman. 'Is this as far as I can go?' she asks hopefully. 'The very top?'

'Not exactly . . . why don't you honour us by unveiling the plaque and you'll see.'

She pulls the cord and a little red velvet curtain opens to reveal their location: *Almost As Far As You Can Go*. Everyone cheers.

'This is a great achievement indeed,' the mayor booms and the band play along in celebration.

She gives them a tight smile, attempting to show gratitude, but in truth she is a little disappointed by the empty feeling of reaching this point. Almost is good, but not good enough. She needs to climb higher, but she isn't certain that the bandwagon is going to take her there. The horses are tired, the band need a break, the instruments need fine-tuning, the carriage needs maintenance and they all plan to stop for the night and rest. She does not want to settle here. She feels they have taken her as far as they can go.

'I'm very grateful for the welcome,' she tells the mayor. 'But unfortunately I can't stay. Can you tell me how I can get up to the top of that mountain?'

'I suggest you go in that direction,' the mayor says.

She follows the direction he is pointing and spots the same lone pedestrian walking away from the town and toward the steep mountain. She frowns, annoyed that the woman somehow managed to get here first. How?

She considers running to catch up with the woman but her two refusals of company have put her off. She could follow her though. That is her plan until she hears a new song she has never heard before, travelling away from her. She can't believe her luck when a new bandwagon exits a narrow laneway and joins the road leading from the town. This one is a blush-coloured velvet and the embellishments are silver. The two coachwomen holding the reins are dressed in blush-pink, with pretty silver embellishments on their grand uniforms. The band that stand at the top of the band-wagon wear similar uniforms with quirky silver hats.

She needs no invitation this time, she doesn't even bother calling them to stop and she races to catch up and she leaps onboard. Sitting on the back of the bandwagon, her legs swinging, she waves goodbye to Almost There.

As they drive along the country road that leaves the village and brings them to the mountain roads they pass the lone pedestrian, who is carrying two even larger baskets in her hands now, humming her own tune. She doesn't notice the woman sitting on the back, swinging her legs. The woman stiffens when she sees her, and before she even has a chance to think it through properly, she pulls the lock open on the back of the bandwagon, pushes open the door and watches as the contents tumble out. The pedestrian jumps off the road to avoid being knocked over. She drops her baskets and the contents scatter around her. The woman concentrates hard to see what has fallen out but they are moving away too quickly and she can't see. The woman is shocked by her own vindictive actions at first and her hands fly to her mouth, but as she watches the pedestrian stumbling over the obstacles and scrambling to gather her belongings, she starts laughing.

The coachwomen and musicians on the bandwagon don't notice the added load of the woman at the back, or the load they lost from storage. She eavesdrops on the musicians' lively conversations, absorbs their passion and talent, gobbles up their views, knowledge and ideologies as she is carried higher and higher up the mountainside.

As darkness falls, she is weary after a long day of travelling and so she climbs inside the storage area, curls up and is lulled to sleep by the gentle swaying of the bandwagon, and the soothing sound of the saxophone.

Banging on the roof causes her to awake with a start, feeling panicked, forgetting where she is. She sits up, looks around the pink and silver box, taking a moment to orientate herself, and suddenly notices the horses' hooves are quiet. The bandwagon has stopped. It sways gently as the footsteps above her bang as the musicians disembark from the wagon.

Very soon she will be revealed and they will be angry about the loss of their sleeping bags and equipment. She crawls quietly to the door and slowly pushes it open. It's dark outside, the band members and coachwomen are out of sight, gathered together discussing where to set up camp overnight.

She slips out and steals away in the opposite direction, disappearing into the darkness. It's a still night, balmy and calm, the sky is clear and the stars seem so low around her that she could reach out to touch them. She wraps her cashmere cardigan around her tightly, feeling cosy and content, and is long gone before the band even notice their belongings are missing. She senses that she is close to the top; it is more remote than ever, the air is thinner and she finds it harder to breathe. She can see the lights of the distant village, shining in the moonlight, and after a short walk from the bandwagon, across country, she steps out onto the road that leads to the town on the top of the mountain.

As she makes her way towards the town, a villager spots her and calls to some others. A friendly crowd excitedly welcomes her and guides her to the town square, and there she is greeted by the mountaintop mayor.

'Congratulations,' the mayor welcomes her. 'Would you like to do the honours?' he asks.

She looks to where the velvet curtain should be covering the plaque but it's already open.

'Oops,' the mayor says and quickly draws the curtain. 'Someone arrived just before you.'

The wind slightly taken out of her sails, the woman pulls the string and the small velvet curtains open to reveal *The Highest Point*. She feels tears prick her eyes with delight, *she has made it*, but she is absolutely exhausted.

'We have a wonderful community of accomplished people, their talents are extraordinary, their knowledge and focus is second to none,' the mayor explains. 'We look forward to seeing the fruits of your labour, and learning what it is that helped you to reach us here at the top. As I tell all of our new arrivals, the journey to get here was no doubt hard, but staying here will be the continuation of your immense hard work.' He lowers his voice and fixes her with a stern eye. 'Though it must be said that living among us here at the top carries a caveat; despite the natural abilities of those who have lived among us, unfortunately for some, their idleness drove them on, as in' – he turns to point out a dark metal gate in the distance, leading to a winding road – 'they embarked on the journey of the downward spiral. Saying goodbye to those is always a sad day for us, but I'm sure you won't follow their path and that your diligence can prevail.'

Very quickly the crowd disperses, returning to their homes and their workplaces to ponder and work on the things that helped them reach The Highest Point. The woman lingers, unsure, feeling out of place, but happy to look down and see everything and everyone beneath her. For the first time in a long time she thinks about her abandoned car, the place she had left behind and the traffic she had instructed the bandwagon to dangerously overtake on the journey here. She needn't worry about them, there will be no going back. There will be no meeting the same people on the way down that she overtook, tricked, tripped and ignored on the way up.

As she is recalling her journey, her eyes fall upon three baskets not far from her. She follows the baskets and sees the lone pedestrian ahead of her, at the edge of the summit, also surveying the grand view and the journey she has undertaken. Her clothes are torn and dirty. She is breathless and sweating but still smiling. The woman scowls, unable to believe that this lone independent woman, despite all the obstacles, and help she refused, got here first.

'Oh hello again,' the pedestrian calls out to her, still polite, though her eyes are hardened, wary, since they last met. 'Isn't it beautiful up here?'

She's irritated by this pedestrian, she can't help it. 'Are you planning on staying here?'

'I don't know,' the other replies, looking out to the distance. 'I'll see.'

This vague aloofness makes her snap. She can't help herself. 'Do you ever have any plans at all?'

The lone pedestrian fixes her with a firm look that rattles the woman. The vagueness is no longer there.

'You and I may have reached the same place, but we are not alike. I wasn't aiming for here,' the pedestrian replies. 'I was just enjoying what I was doing, was doing it very well, and it got me here. You, on the other hand, weren't doing anything in particular other than trying to get here. Now that I'm here, I can continue what I was doing. Now that you're here, what do you do?'

The lone pedestrian doesn't even wait for an answer before leaving her alone on the edge of the mountain. Feeling stung, the woman lifts her chin, but the air is thin and she's finding it hard to breathe.

26

The Woman Who Smiled

She was on her way to work. It was 7 a.m. – early, but she liked early and she liked her job. She was happy. But she was not smiling. Because not-smiling happens sometimes.

'Adult round-trip, please,' she said sliding her money through the gap in the glass to the ticket seller.

He looked up at her and smiled. 'Cheer up, love,' he said, taking the money.

'Excuse me?'

'Cheer up!' he laughed. 'It can't be that bad.'

She looked around to see if anybody had heard. The man behind her was wearing earphones and was focusing on his wallet, but he wasn't smiling either.

'Um . . . okay,' she said, confused. She frowned, then stopped herself, taking her ticket and stepping away. She watched as the non-smiling man who was next in line placed his money down on the counter. The ticket seller said nothing to him. They exchanged the money for the ticket without any demands as to how he should fix his non-smiling face.

She waited on the platform, feeling a little confused as to how to control her face, unsettled by the fact that she had essentially been monitored and directed to do so by a stranger. She wasn't unhappy. Why had a stranger asked her to smile? She studied her reflection in the window of the train station, and analysed herself in a thousand different ways. No, she did not look miserable. She looked normal, just like all the other men and women who stood on the platform with her.

Once off the train, she stopped at a shop on her way to the office to buy a chocolate bar for lunch. She was in the mood for a treat today.

'Smile, love, it might never happen,' the shopkeeper said with a wink.

Again she paused. 'Excuse me?'

'It might never happen!' he repeated, chuckling.

'What might never happen?'

'Ah it's just an expression!' he nodded.

'I'm not unhappy,' she told him, confused.

'Okay, okay,' he raised his hands. 'Whatever you say.' He nodded over her shoulder to the customer behind her to dismiss her, all business again, and she stepped to the side. She studied the next customer, an older man. He was not smiling either. They didn't talk. He paid for and left with his newspaper. It was a fast and uncomplicated exchange. The man was not forced to analyse himself or his face by a stranger in a shop.

'Can I help you?' the shop owner asked, noticing her staring.

'Why didn't you tell him to cheer up?'

'Who?'

'Him?'

He looked at the door, then frowned as though she was crazy. 'Look, a pretty girl like you shouldn't look so . . .' He made a cartoon grumpy face.

'But I wasn't making that face,' she said.

'Yes you were, I saw you.'

'And it bothers you because I'm pretty?'

'Me?' he got defensive. 'Makes no difference to me.'

'Do you like asking strangers to smile on demand?' she asked.

'Ah, go on,' he nodded at the door for her to leave, not liking her attitude, 'we're finished here.'

Fuming, she left the shop.

The following day she returned to the train station. She bought her ticket. The ticket seller looked up at her.

She donned her comedy glasses and moustache, and stuck a party blower in her mouth. She blew it so hard, the horn blasted, the foil uncoiled itself and smacked against the glass that separated them. She gave him jazz hands.

He sat back in his chair and folded his arms, not at all impressed.

Back at the shop, she stood in line. When she reached the till, the shopkeeper recognized her.

Red lipstick in hand, she took her time drawing an enormous

and messy clown-like smile, which reached the dimples in her cheeks. She placed a red clown nose over her own, pressed play on her iPod and circus music began. She proceeded to dance around his shop to the clown music while he and the customers watched. She picked up three oranges and began juggling.

Finally she finished with a 'Ta-da!'

There was silence.

'There, do you feel better? Am I prettier now?' she asked, breathless.

The shopkeeper didn't smile.

But she did.

27

The Woman Who Thought the Grass Was Greener on the Other Side

The woman stood at the kitchen window of her hillside home on the hot July morning. This spot gave her a wonderful bird's-eye view of the glistening, rushing Great Rift Valley River that separated the low hills of the Gorse Mountain Range. It was so named due to the rich yellow pea flowers that lit up the landscape when in full bloom. Despite their beauty, the bush was a mass of prickles and pines to protect them from the harsh winters, but their wonderful coconut aroma more than made up for their thorns. She warmed her hands on a cup of coffee and breathed out happily, contented. Then she glanced at the cottage on the hillside directly across the river and then she felt her body go rigid again and her chest tightened. It was this cottage that tainted her view and which was the true thorn in the side of the mountain.

Behind her, her family were engaged in lively morning conversation while they ate their cereal and debated how to spend their weekend. She tuned them out and reached for her pair of binoculars, which were sitting by the herb flower box on the windowsill. As she held them to her eyes the scent of rosemary wafted by her nostrils. It had the effect of calming her, which she knew she needed before feasting her eyes on her neighbour.

'Don't do it?' her husband Tony sang in a warning tone.

'She's doing it,' her daughter Tina sang in response.

'Uh oh,' her son Terry said, ducking to hide behind a cereal box.

The woman studied the cottage across the rift and sighed. Tony shoved bacon into his mouth, amused.

'What now?' he grinned, crunching on the bacon. 'New window boxes? Their apple tree has grown bigger than yours?'

The children chuckled.

'They don't have an apple tree,' she grumbled.

'Oh well then that's one up for us then,' he teased.

'We don't have an apple tree,' she said.

'Then we should get one,' he replied good-naturedly.

'He got a new car,' she said.

He stopped chewing the bacon. He stood and grabbed the binoculars from her. It was his turn to be laughed at by the kids. He looked through the lenses in silence.

'Lucky bastard,' he finally said.

'How can they afford that?' the woman asked. 'You'd swear they were in the Hollywood Hills and not some poky-sized cottage on the worst side of the mountain.'

'Miaow,' Tina teased.

'He got a promotion,' Terry said, peeking up over the cereal box. 'I heard yesterday.'

They left a respectful silence. Tony's bone of contention with his job was that he had been in the same position for the past fifteen years without a promotion. Everybody seemed to be speeding up, overtaking him, and leaving him far behind, though the fact that he didn't apply himself seemed to pass him by completely. He felt he deserved his promotions for the years of his life he spent there, and didn't recognize the need to earn it.

'Doesn't bother me,' he said, though no one believed him. He handed the binoculars back to his wife.

The woman resumed spying on the cottage across the rift.

'I think they're getting an extension,' she said suddenly.

'What makes you think that?' Tony asked, grumpy now.

'I can see the builders.'

'Let me see,' he said, taking the binoculars from her.

He watched. 'That's Bob Sanderson. He'll charge them a fortune, and then it will probably blow down in a storm.'

'Shouldn't you tell them that?' she asked, pretending she was concerned but secretly happy to take the wind out of their sails in any way possible.

The woman and Tony looked at each other, guiltily.

'It's none of our business what they do with their lives,' he replied, sitting down at the table again.

They continued eating their breakfast in silence. Tony opened the newspaper. The kids scrolled through their phones, bored.

The woman looked toward the window again and though she couldn't see the cottage from this angle she was picturing it in her head, imagining them all inside. Smug as can be. Her with her easel and paint sitting outside most days being artsy fartsy.

'Jake made the swim team,' Tina said to her brother, eyes still down on her phone.

The woman threw her daughter an angry look.

Terry sighed. 'I know, I was there remember?' He'd lost his appetite now, he swirled his cereal around with his spoon, reliving yesterday's heartbreak as they huddled around the notice board to read the names who'd made it through. 'He's probably over there running around the garden in his red Speedos just to annoy me.'

'Now that I'd like to see,' Tina said, carrying her bowl to the sink. She couldn't help herself. She picked up the binoculars. She gasped.

'Is he in his Speedos for real?' Terry asked, sitting up.

'Why the hell is Jacob Kowalski's car in Sally's drive?' she shrieked, frightening the cat, who leapt up from where he'd been lazing in the ray of sunlight.

'Tina!' her dad roared. 'What's wrong with you?'

'Sorry,' she mumbled, slamming the binoculars down.

'She has a thing for Jacob,' the woman said quietly.

Tony, surprised at first, then angry, took a moment to process his teenage daughter's human feelings.

'I'm sure this Jacob guy is a jerk,' he said, eventually.

'He's not.'

'Good morning everybody,' the woman's mother, Tabitha, said, arriving into the kitchen in her dressing gown.

'Morning Nanny Tabby,' Tina said, giving her a hug.

'She has arisen. We were just about to call the funeral parlour,' Tony said, and the woman rolled her eyes.

'I've been awake since six a.m., I was just resting my eyes,' Nanny Tabby said, annoyed. 'I'm going to finish the garden today, darling. What do you think? The rosebush needs seeing to.'

'You did that on Monday.'

'It still needs work.' She looked around the table at the miserable bunch. 'What's wrong with you lot this morning?' When she received grunts in response she narrowed her eyes suspiciously and turned to the kitchen window. Her eyes landed on the binoculars. Just as she suspected. 'Honestly, you've all got to stop this nonsense.' She turned to her daughter, 'See what you're encouraging! This spying is ridiculous! It does nothing but leave you all miserable and unappreciative of what you have.'

'It's not spying,' the woman defended herself, shifting

uncomfortably in her seat. 'Anyway, it's impossible not to look, they're always pushing everything in our face, what are we supposed to do?'

Nanny Tabby frowned. Their neighbour was hardly pushing anything in their face, across the river on the side of another mountain.

'You all need to remember how fortunate you are. To have each other. To have this wonderful home. Remember all your blessings. You need to stop comparing your lives with those of others. Especially them. It's outrageous and it's eating you all up on the inside, rotting your hearts, causing arguments and upset.'

They lowered their heads in shame.

'Mark my word, they're probably looking over here and thinking the very same thing as you are. The grass is always greener on the other side,' she said moving toward the teapot.

'Their grass does look greener,' Tina said, pouting.

Granny Tabby laughed. 'It's just an expression, dear.'

'Seriously. Have none of you noticed?' Tina asked, looking around. 'Their grass *is* greener.'

They all scrambled to their feet and hurried to the window, Granny Tabby included. Suddenly, what she had never noticed before became glaringly obvious. They didn't need the binoculars to see that the grass on the acres surrounding the cottage was far greener than any other patch on the mountain.

They bundled outside to the garden.

'Maybe we get more sun,' Tony said, squinting as he looked

up to examine the light. 'Our grass is scorched from the sun.'

'The sun rises in the east and sets in the west, we both get the same sun,' Granny Tabby snapped viciously, in a tone none of them had ever heard her use before. 'I'm out in this garden every day, tending to it. I water it every week. Their grass can't be greener. It's impossible!' her voice rose.

They began arguing among themselves and the row continued until they stormed off in different directions, taking their anger, their jealousy and rage with them until they compared themselves to everyone, until they were holding themselves up against everybody else in the world, barometers of what other people had versus what they didn't have.

Across Rift Valley, the woman noticed the entire family come out of their house and onto their lawn. She heard them bickering, even from here, the wind carrying their hateful words across to her.

She quickly ducked down behind a gorse bush and spied as they stared across the river in her direction, faces twisted with displeasure, hands on their hips and hands lifted to their foreheads like visors. She felt like a child playing hide and seek, her chest heaved up and down, as her heart pounded nervously. She giggled, then blocked her mouth with her gloved hand to stifle the sound, knowing that they couldn't possibly hear her from all the way over there, but afraid anyway.

Ever since the day she and her family had developed the

dilapidated cottage and moved in, she had seen their faces pushed up against the window, binoculars to their eyes. Her husband had discovered them when he was surveying the spectacular view with his binoculars and they knew they were being watched all through the construction, to the day they'd moved in.

Every single morning since, she'd felt their eyes on her. She'd felt uncomfortable in her new home for a long time, but she had more important things to worry about in her life; the money they'd sunk into developing the derelict cottage, her son's chronic asthma that they'd used swimming to help him overcome, her daughter's heartbreak at leaving her first love behind, hearing her daughter cry herself to sleep, up until recently when she'd met the sweet Jacob boy who'd come by that morning. Then there was her husband's recent promotion, which kept him away longer than anticipated, leaving her alone here on the side of the mountain. It was good for him, even though he was exhausted, and it meant she had more time to spend on her paintings, but they were more difficult to sell here, and half of them had been destroyed by the leak from their bath that the builders had been out to check that morning. She had borrowed her sister's car while she was away on holiday, just so she wouldn't feel so isolated, so she could come and go as she pleased.

It was painting that always helped her to escape and it was when she was painting one morning, out in the garden, captivated by the bright yellow gorse against the green that had given her the big idea. She was tired of her neighbours staring, their judgemental eyes on her and her family, startled by their irrational jealousy and constant comparison of their lives to hers. And so she'd sent out a message of her own.

The pack on her back was heavy and weighed her down. She wore a facemask, goggles, heavy gloves and protective clothing so they probably wouldn't even have recognized her if she hadn't dived behind a bush when they gathered on their front lawn. She had risen early with the birds and spent the morning walking the acres around her home, taking her time to spray her land with two coats. She had nothing to lie about to her family when they returned, she had been painting, perhaps just not the canvas as they knew it. All it had taken was Epsom salt for magnesium, fertilizer, green food colouring, water and a spray wand to make a healthy green paint.

She liked her life, she did her best to remedy her problems and count her blessings, she didn't care what went on behind her neighbours' walls, but she did enjoy this one task. No matter what they thought of her, her actions, her words, the way that she composed herself meant that her grass would always be greener on her side of the Rift.

28

The Woman Who Unravelled

It was the way she got out of bed. Still half-asleep, she wavered and had to reach out to the nightstand to stay upright. She snagged her finger on the corner, catching the skin and tearing it. A little more awake but flustered by all that was on her mind, she went from her bedroom to the bathroom, to her wardrobe, to the children's bedrooms, downstairs to the kitchen, around and around in circles making breakfast and school lunches, opening and closing the fridge thirty-five times to retrieve and replace, drawers, cupboards, schoolbags, upstairs; children's wardrobes, downstairs; coats, bags, hair, lice spray, keys and out the door. It was when her son stood staring at her in the hallway of the house, frozen, stunned, as if in a comatose state that she finally stopped.

'What's wrong, honey?' she asked.

'Mummy. You've got no arm.'

It was true. Her right arm was missing. She was holding her keys in her left hand and wondered how long it had been missing, how long she had been doing her morning chores without realizing she'd lost an arm. There was a thread of skin from her shoulder and a long line leading through the rooms of the house. Her son ran around picking it up as though playing a game. Skin bundled in his arms so high she could just see his brown eyes with giraffe-like lashes peeking out at her as she retrieved her arm from his arms.

'Thank you, sweetheart.'

'What are we going to do?' he asked.

'We don't have time to fix it, you'll be late for school and I have to go to work. I'll deal with it later.' She chose a larger coat and bundled the skin of her right arm into the coat.

'You're like a scarecrow,' her son giggled, helping her pad out the arm of the coat to make it appear normal.

But by the time she had completed the school run and arrived at work she had forgotten about the unravelling. She hung up her coat on the old-fashioned coat hook, away from her boss's dandruff covered wax jacket and went about her business. She tucked her spaghetti-like arm into her sweater, sat at her desk and powered up her computer. One-armed, she got on with the job at hand. Apart from one morning meeting in the conference room, she didn't move from her desk. By 11 a.m. when she stopped for a morning coffee and cigarette, she realized that the man beside her was staring at her, the cigarette hanging from his fat lip.

'Hello,' she smiled pleasantly.

'Are you okay? You seem to be . . . unravelling.'

'Oh that. Yes, yes I am. I snagged my finger on the night-stand, that's all. I'll have it seen to later.' She quickly inhaled the last of her cigarette and stamped it out. But it was difficult. Her right leg had unravelled without her noticing and with only one leg she had to hop on one foot to stamp out the cigarette. Still wondering when she had unravelled all the way down to her foot, she returned to the building and hopped up the stairway until she came to the source of the problem. It had gotten caught on her seat in the conference room. With both her arm and leg in a bundle clutched in her only remaining intact arm, she hopped to her desk. She sat down. And thought.

When you are a woman who has begun to unravel, it can be a confusing state. Her body was in ropy pieces around her and yet her thoughts were clear. Clearer, in fact. As though the unravelling of her was the making of her, because she suddenly knew exactly what she wanted to do. She could no longer sit at her desk in this unravelled state; it was unproductive and probably unprofessional. She grabbed her bag and her coat and bundled up her tangled body. She hopped into the lift without a word to anybody.

She called her older sister Dahlia and filled her in on the situation. Dahlia then told their youngest sister, Camellia. Safety in numbers. As she pulled over at Dahlia's house, she saw Camellia standing outside alone.

Camellia opened the door and looked her up and down. 'Oh dear. What happened?'

'I snagged my finger on the nightstand, and didn't notice until my arm was gone.'

Camellia gave this serious consideration and it was only then that the woman who had unravelled noticed that her sister was missing a piece from her head. A tiny hole above her forehead, jigsaw-puzzle shaped, a gaping hole that meant she could see straight through to the hydrangea bush behind her, like a keyhole through her head.

'Are you okay? There's a jigsaw-shaped hole in your head.'

'I just lost a piece.'

'Has this happened before?'

As she asked, another jigsaw-shaped piece of Camellia fell from her chest, near her heart, and more of the hydrangea bush behind her was visible. She bent down and picked it up, put it in her pocket.

'I'm okay,' she said absent-mindedly, 'but she's not.'

Camellia looked down at the ground and that's when the woman who unravelled noticed a pool of something gooey beside her, nestled in and around a pretty pair of shoes and handbag.

'Dahlia had a meltdown,' Camellia explained.

'Again?'

They watched the oozy mess that was their eldest sister with intrigue and concern.

'Sorry, girls,' the ooze said.

'Maybe I could scoop her up and bring her with us.'

'Good idea, we can't leave her here. The kids' buckets and spades are in the trunk, you could use those.'

Camellia went around the back of the car and retrieved the bucket and spade, while the woman who unravelled kept watch on the waxy plasma gooey remains of her sister. Moments later they were all in the car.

'Sorry, girls,' Dahlia's voice sounded from the bucket in the back seat. 'I just had one of those days. My head wouldn't stop.'

'Don't be sorry,' the woman who unravelled said, driving. 'I shouldn't have called you and worried you about me, I know you've a lot on.'

'Always call me when you need me. I'd rather be here,' Dahlia said.

The two sisters in the front seats couldn't help it, they started laughing.

'Well, not exactly *here*,' Dahlia laughed with them.

They chose a quiet cosy pub in the countryside. They moved to the snug and sat at a table before the fire, the wood crackling and spitting, warming them.

'Dammit,' Camellia said as a puzzle-sized piece of her hand fell into her gin and tonic. She fished it out and put it in her pocket.

'How are you feeling now, Dahlia?' the woman asked, looking into the bucket.

'I feel much better now, really. I think you should take me out of this bucket, I'm feeling a bit stronger, more firm, I don't want to get stuck in here.'

They gently extracted Dahlia from the bucket and placed her on the bar stool.

'Is it bad?' the goo asked.

'You've never looked better,' Camellia said, as a piece from her head fell off again, and into the goo that was her sister.

'Ow.'

'Sorry.'

The woman again observed her tucking the missing piece into her pocket.

Camellia took a sip of her drink, trying to maintain her dignity. 'Gin should always be drunk at lunchtime,' she said, closing her eyes and relaxing.

'If anyone saw me drinking at lunchtime . . .' The woman shuddered and looked around the quiet pub, thankful her colleagues didn't know where she'd disappeared to.

'I don't think it's the drinking they'd worry about,' Dahlia said.

'We do need the break,' the woman said. 'We have to listen to our bodies. They're telling us to stop.'

'They're telling us something,' Dahlia muttered.

'Would you mind helping me with my coat? I'm afraid my other arm is loose now,' the woman asked Camellia as she now only had her head, her body and one leg in one piece.

'Has it been this bad before?' Camellia asked as she removed the coat and surveyed her snagged sister. She looked like a ball of wool, all tied up in strings, difficult to know where she began and ended.

'It's never been this bad. It's happened a few times to a smaller extent but it was manageable, I just wrapped myself up again. I think it needs more attention this time.'

'That's what we're here for,' Dahlia said and suddenly she was beside them again, fully formed on the seat.

They cheered her return and embraced.

'You've sand in your hair by the way,' the woman laughed, dusting her down with her free hand.

'I stink of fish,' Dahlia sniffed the air, and reached into her bag for her perfume.

'We were collecting crabs on the beach. Sorry. Maybe I should always travel with a container for you, just in case. Maybe we all should.'

'Maybe she should stop needing to be contained,' Camellia suggested.

'Says you, the walking puzzle!' Dahlia snapped back.

Camellia and Dahlia ended their harmless bickering to turn their attention to helping their unravelled sister.

'No this bit goes over here, and this bit here,' Dahlia said. 'If you do that, her thumb will be on her arm.'

'No, no, because her elbow is in a knot,' Camellia said, carefully following a thread.

'You've tied yourself in knots, sweetie,' Dahlia said gently, untying her fingers. 'Seriously, we can't let it get this bad again.'

'Says you.'

'I know, I know.'

'So what's up with you?' the woman asked Dahlia.

'Do you really want to know?' Her face turned red, as her issues took centre stage in her mind. She looked ready to explode. But before she had the chance to explain her woes, she was gone again. In a waxy dripping mess on the floor.

'Fuck it,' the mess said.

'Just calm down, stop getting so riled up,' the woman said.

'I know, sorry, just give me a minute.' Dahlia the mush took deep breaths, quivering like a vibrating jellyfish.

Camellia continued the job at hand, gently putting her sister back together again.

'Is it sore?' Camellia asked her sister.

'No not exactly achingly painful, just . . . confusing, worrying, a distraction. What about both of you?'

'It makes me feel hot,' said Dahlia the mush.

The woman used her free hand to fan her liquidized sister.

'Ah, that feels good. Thank you.'

'You need to stop letting things build up so much,' Camellia said, carefully finding where the snag began and wrapping the spaghetti skin around gently.

A piece fell from Camellia's body again. She tucked it into her pocket. The woman glared at her.

'What do you do with all those pieces?' the woman asked.

'I'll put them back later.'

'I don't believe you,' Dahlia said.

'Me neither,' the woman backed her up.

'Oh please.'

When the woman's arm was back to one piece again she quickly reached out and pulled up Camellia's sleeve. Her arm was like a jigsaw puzzle, a faint outline of pieces in light blue veins. Some pieces were missing and she could see right through to the stone floor beneath.

'Oh my . . .' She wasn't the only one to notice.

'Turn out your pockets,' Dahlia was back in one piece and ready for action. She stood up and, against Camellia's will, turned out her pockets and dozens of pieces fell to the ground.

They gasped.

'You said it was just one or two pieces now and then,' Dahlia raised her voice.

'And you need to chill out and stop having meltdowns,' Camellia snapped back. 'If you're not careful you won't have anyone to keep scraping you off the floor. We'll put you back in the fish-stinking bucket, and we'll leave you there.'

The woman snorted and the three dissolved into laughter, glad to be able to poke fun at their situations.

'I'm just feeling . . . more unfulfilled than usual,' Camellia explained. 'A bit, empty. Like I'm missing something – I'm not sure how to put it into words.' But she couldn't say any more because her mouth fell off, into her drink, stealing her words away from her.

The woman fished it out and slotted it back into place.

'Well that's never happened before,' Camellia said, startled, licking her lips.

'Camellia,' the woman said softly to her little sister. 'You have to start taking care of yourself more. When a part of you falls off you should fix it straight away, don't let it build up like this.'

'The same goes for you,' Dahlia said, looking at the woman. 'As soon as you feel one little snag, you should get a Band-Aid straight away.'

'As for you,' Camellia turned to Dahlia. 'You need to chill out. Stop being so hot-headed.'

'I know, I know,' Dahlia agreed.

'Putting the pieces back takes longer than you think,' Camellia explained. 'You've no idea, or maybe you both do. I do try, but then who's got the time to fix themselves at the end of every day? I just want to eat, sleep and go to bed. Get the day over with.'

'You mean when you're too busy feeling unfulfilled to make yourself stop feeling unfulfilled?' the woman pointed out.

'Maybe you'd feel more fulfilled if you didn't keep hiding parts of yourself in your pockets,' Dahlia said. She lowered herself to her knees and gathered the missing pieces that had fallen from Camellia's pockets, while Camellia continued gently winding the woman's skin back together again.

Dahlia helped Camellia, Camellia helped the woman who unravelled and the woman watched her sisters and wondered why they didn't do this more often. She felt so much better already.

It took time for her toes to regain feeling. They felt numb until the blood started rushing and then, after the pins and needles, the feeling slowly came back. She placed her arms around her sisters' shoulders and, using their support, pushed herself to her feet again. They walked up and down the snug very slowly, so that her joints could move again, and feeling satisfied Camellia had done a fine job of winding all the important pieces back together, she sat by the fire and allowed the heat to do the rest of the healing.

Back to themselves, the woman and Dahlia looked at Camellia.

'What?' she asked, defensively.

'It's your turn. Take off your coat and show us the damage,' Dahlia ordered.

Knowing there was no point arguing with her older sisters, she removed her coat and her bare arms were revealed. She waited for an attack about her allowing things to go so far, but none came.

'Right,' the woman said. 'You know the rules; all the pieces face up on the table. Start at the edges first and work your way in.'

They were children again, back at the kitchen table solving a jigsaw puzzle together, but this time it was their youngest sister they were piecing back together. Camellia's eyes welled, and a tear fell, with gratitude.

'Thank you, I love you guys,' she sniffed.

'Oh sweetie!' Dahlia stopped working to wipe her sister's tear away. 'I don't know what I'd do without you two either.'

'Group hug,' the woman said, and the three sisters huddled in an embrace. 'To putting each other back together again.'

'Hear, hear,' they held each other tight.

29

The Woman Who Cherry-Picked

The woman began working on the farm when she was four-teen years old. She and her two older brothers, Yamato and Yuta, were employed to work the farm during the summer months from June to late August, on long hot heavy days during lavender season. The farm was owned by the Chiba family and had fifteen hundred trees with thirty cherry varieties. The farm owner was a quiet man who worked hard; he had a noisy wife whose gift lay in giving orders. They had one daughter, a lazy good-for-nothing whom the woman used to find either asleep and snoring under a tree with cherry juice all over her face, her basket empty of cher-ries, or sitting under a tree scoffing cherries. It was always one of the two.

She had never eaten cherries before coming here. Her first taste was on the day they arrived, when all the cherry-pickers were summoned to the foot of the family porch for a lesson on cherries: which were the best-tasting cherries, how to identify each cherry, how to pick them correctly. They picked from a nearby tree under the farmer's guidance and, if they made a mistake, the farmer would whip their fingers with a leather strap. Quiet men are not necessarily soft men.

The woman took an immediate interest in learning about the cherries. Unlike her mathematically minded brothers, this was a language she understood. Throughout the hour-long journey home on the bus and long into the night while everyone else was sleeping, she would read the pamphlets, learning the names of the cherries, learning to distinguish them by colour and shape. During the day she furthered her studies by tasting. She could quickly distinguish the high-sugar no acidity content of the Gassan-Nishiki. The popular large pink Nanyo was a textbook-perfect cherry. The Beni-Shuho had a less presentable dark blotchy outer layer, but its delicious flavour made up for its appearance, and while the hot pink heart-shaped Taisho-Nishiki was her favourite cherry to look at, she didn't like the taste, therefore concluding that exterior and interior were rarely related – a valuable lesson. The Summit was the purple variety, the Yuda-Giant started out purple but mystically changed to orange and Red Glory, despite its deep red hue, was technically a rare black cherry.

She grew to respect and care for the Hanokoma. It was a soft cherry, but the tree bore too much fruit, which in turn starved the tree of nutrition and caused the fruit to be too sweet. For the tree's sake they had to prune, but pruning caused a sharp pungent bitterness, and so it was a complex balance that needed delicate handling.

The Hinode was a black cherry, rich in anthocyanin, which was good for eyesight and relieving eye strain. She collected it for her grandmother; but while it was good for her grandmother's eyes it was bad for her clothes as the stains were impossible to remove.

Thirty different varieties of cherries on fifteen hundred trees. The quiet farmer did not need to whip her fingers many times. She learned quickly. This was a world she wanted to understand.

The trees were low to the ground, enabling younger, smaller workers to pick. Even though she knew it was her job to pluck from the lower branches, she climbed to reach the cherries higher up. She learned to recognize the best-tasting ones from afar.

Each day she would take the bus to the farm with her older brothers, tagging along with them, mostly being ignored. But as the weeks and months working on the cherry farm went by, she became choosy about everything, deciding one morning that she did not want to get on the bus that stopped for them. She wished to wait for the next one, a better one. She insisted. She fought. She told everybody who would listen that this bus was not good enough. Her brothers dragged her on kicking and screaming, against her will. Ten minutes later the bus broke down, and they were stranded, forced to sit in the searing heat while waiting for the next bus to collect them. The following day her brothers listened to her. They got on the third bus and still got to the farm before the first bus had left. The following week, everybody at the bus stop listened to her.

Learning to evaluate the cherries slowly changed her, broadening her perspective on life. She learned to analyse, inspect, and scrutinize the taste, smell, feel, shape and colour of everything.

When asked to dance by a boy at a local dance, she refused him. He asked her friend instead and trod on her toes with almost every step; the friend's feet were bruised and close to bleeding by the end of the night. The young woman waited for the perfect partner to ask her, someone with an expert sense of rhythm with whom she danced the night away. She chose not to kiss him as he wished, as she knew there was a better kisser in the room. She, like the quiet farmer, wanted the best, and everything in her life required careful judgement. She learned to evaluate her requirements precisely at any given time, and then choose. Sweetness or acidity. Kissing or dancing. Humour or conversation. Entertainment or knowledge. Safety or excitement. Always right, never wrong.

She watched the quiet farmer at work, but soon he was watching her, and learning from her. They all learned to follow the woman, allowed her to be their guide.

She helped the farm grow. The Chiba family bought new land, extended it to forty-seven thousand square yards, equipped it with rain covers, and began family all-you-can-eat days. She encouraged a side business for the noisy wife and lazy daughter of selling the cherry pies, cherry jams, cherry vinegars that they made to feed the workers on their breaks. The quiet farmer won awards for his farm, the noisy wife bought expensive dresses, the lazy daughter was gifted a car.

After four years the young woman walked into the farmer's office.

He looked up at her from his paperwork and she set down the basket.

'Mr Chiba, it's time for me to move on.'

He was a stern man, a quiet man, and he was a proud man. He didn't beg her to stay, but he offered her more money. When she refused the generous offer he would never consider offering anybody else on his farm, he knew that she had a path clear in her mind and there would be nothing he could do to change it. Witness to the tremendous gift he wished his lazy daughter had been blessed with, he recognized that the woman's trained eye could see that something better lay just ahead, up on a higher branch. She needed to climb.

When she finished school she moved to the city, where she chose to rent the fifth apartment she saw, to live with the seventh roommate she interviewed. She worked in a factory on a production line. After the first day, she was called to the office.

'You are not working as fast as the others,' her line supervisor chided her. 'You are slow. You just stand there, scanning pieces. I want to fire you now but the boss insists you get a second chance. You have one more chance to move more quickly or you are fired!'

'But, Mr Maki, I am not being lazy.'

'You could fool me,' he said, waving his hand dismissively at her.

'I'm choosing the best pieces,' she explained. 'I'm sure that there is something wrong with many of the pieces that go by.'

He snorted and sent her on her way, but to her utter satisfaction at the end of the day, she knew by the look on her line supervisor's face that, after the boss had visited the floor to carry out testing, her batch was the only one free of any defects.

After a time, she saw a higher, more tempting branch and she left the production line and took a job in human resources, choosing the best people for specific jobs. She was recognized for her attention to detail, her ability to pinpoint the desired character traits and required attributes. The company soared with the right people in the right positions and the team was rejuvenated, revitalized and enthusiastic. She was the secret to everyone's success.

She agreed to marry the third man she dated, on his second proposal, and they bought the sixth house they viewed. She loved all of her three children from the first second she saw them.

She didn't trust the two doctors who diagnosed her when she became ill, and against everybody's advice sought the opinion of the third doctor, who started her on the cancer treatment that saved her life.

To entertain herself, she learned about the Tokyo stock exchange. She watched, she analysed, she plucked. She out-performed everybody, and offers rolled in. She rose in the ranks, stock trader to chief risk officer. But then, when feeling comfortable, she remembered the Hanokoma cherry, how she had appreciated the trees' complexity and difficulty in bearing their sweet fruit. Complexity and failure made even-tual success so much more satisfying. She ultimately became the head of an international I-bank, and given that banks are largely political institutions, she discovered a new strength: she had a natural flair for politics.

She rose and rose, and when the woman found herself at a podium, at a prestigious event, being honoured for her contributions to business and culture, she looked out at the sea of faces, all looking up at her, waiting for her to say something profound. She wondered what to say. She saw her two brothers and their wives, her elderly parents, her children and their spouses, her grandchildren.

She thought back to the quiet farmer on the Chiba cherry farm when she was fourteen years old. She recalled the first day, when they were gathered by the steps of the Chiba household porch. The farmer had stood before them with a bucket of cherries in his hand, ready to begin the first task of identifying the different varieties of cherries. He had lifted the bucket of cherries in the air and instructed them all to look at it. Then he looked them all in the eye, one by one, ensuring he had their attention. After a long silence, he spoke three words that made a deep impression on her and had never left her.

She took a deep breath and moved closer to the microphone. Three words. 'Make good choices.'

30

The Woman Who Roared

She lives in a suburban coastal town, an idyllic location, a hub of busy young families and retirees. She has two children, she volunteers to be on the parent-teacher committee, volunteers for every school trip and sporting event, and is a volunteer badminton teacher at the school. She has a vibrant allotment in her garden, and in the summer she sells homemade strawberry jam covered in red-and-white gingham jam-jar cloths with white bows. She remembers everybody's names, children and parents, and is endlessly offering to host playdates. She is trusted, she is calm, she is organized, she is relaxed. She is the one they go to to ask questions, she always knows the answers. She doesn't drink alcohol but she is gregarious on evenings out, and holds back the hair of others who vomit at the annual class dinner, without mentioning a word of it later. She has never smoked. She is the epitome of style. When it rains, other mothers strain their eyes to see if she gets wet.

She loves her husband. He loves her.

But she has a secret.

When the children are at school and her husband is at work, when she has finished her errands, she goes to her walk-in closet and removes a shoebox from the shelf that conceals a secret key panel.

Inside the panel she enters a six-digit PIN code on the panel; the date of birth of her twin sister. It is of course her date of birth too, but it is her sister's date that she keys in. This is followed by a click. The shoe shelves that line the wall of the closet move back, and slide to the right behind her row of dresses, revealing a secret room.

Greeted by blush-pink velvet walls and a soft plush pink carpet, she removes her shoes and steps inside. As the wall of shoes closes automatically behind her, she allows her eyes to adjust to the gentle pink glow of a night-light.

She smiles, at peace.

Then she opens her mouth. And roars.

She is a judge of the High Court who had been called to the bar in 1970. One of the toughest, she's had a long and prosperous career, overseeing some of the country's most high-profile and brutal cases. Gruesome, horrifying acts that she promises herself she will never become immune to, in the moments when she feels she is becoming inured. Hour after hour, on a daily basis, the constant stream of the worst aspects of humanity assaults her brain, sprinkled with the rare flickers of human decency and kindness.

She has two children and five grandchildren, a holiday home by the sea that she stays in for the summer, and is an avid football fan with season tickets to every game. She is capable, stable, stoic, and most importantly she is fair. She is celebrated for this attribute, has been honoured with awards, and has even dined with the president.

She terrifies most people she works with, she doesn't have time for coddling others, or for waffling. Too many people rely on her decisions for justice: innocent incarcerated people who are rotting away, waiting to be vindicated; the murdered whose energies hang around her like dark matter until their murderers are brought to justice. There is no time for small talk.

She loves to walk barefoot in the sand. She wears perfume as her armour. Her first love had been a French ballet dancer. For some reason, she had never been able to tell him and wonders about him often. She doesn't enjoy eating; fancy restaurant dinners are a chore. Her grandson with his wicked sense of humour is secretly her favourite of all her grandchildren.

She is terribly sensitive, soft, though only her husband and grandchildren know that. She had been too hard on her children.

She has a secret.

While in her chambers on recess from a particularly gruesome case, she hangs her black robe on the coat stand by her library. She removes the largest law books that conceal a secret key panel on the wall. The code that activates the panel is the case file number of a woman who'd been brutally murdered by her husband. The case had cut through her so deeply that it had scarred her heart. *She* had been prosecuting the husband. *She* lost the case. It was the case that had defined her, overseen by a judge she told herself she would never become. Using the case number as this code is her way of telling the woman that, though she had been mistreated in life, she won't be forgotten in death.

Once the code has been entered, the library slides open to reveal a wood-panelled room. Walnut; her favourite. Beneath the walnut panelling, the walls are soundproofed.

The library closes behind her, leaving her in darkness for a moment until the night-light clicks in, glowing red. The colour of her anger.

She opens her mouth.

And roars.

She is a forty-four-year-old landscaper. She loves her fingers being rooted to the earth, toiling in the ground. She likes restructuring areas, finding the light, creating living spaces for people that are tailored to their needs, as much as the practical aspects of horticulture. While gardening, she prefers working in the rain, she feels more connected to the elements that way. She lives with her girlfriend in an eco-friendly home, miles away from anyone, which is exactly what she craves. Work is hectic, she had just completed a complex design of a rooftop garden in a city-centre penthouse apartment with an owner who had at times made her want to jump from the edge.

She loves liquorice, she can eat her own body weight in hummus. She is tone deaf, she can get into a physical altercation during Monopoly. She likes to follow red squirrels. She finds the tones of the national weather service radio announcer soothing and, when her girlfriend is away on overnight trips, the sound of the reports send her to sleep.

After a long day, she returns to her house powered by hydroelectric turbines and geothermal energy. The enormous windows maximize sunlight while showcasing the mountain views around it, and the grass planted on the roof prevents heat loss. It is her oasis, but every oasis is an escape, and every oasis kisses the borders of the place escaped.

She has a secret.

In the potting shed in the garden, behind the shelving unit of potted cannabis plants that she will soon need to transplant outside, is a secret key panel. She moves the cannabis pots aside and punches in the secret code – the date she intends on proposing to her girlfriend, which has changed three times due to her fear of rejection. She hears a click and the shelving unit disappears down into the ground beneath her.

It is a small room; grass covers the soundproofed walls and floor. As soon as she steps inside, the door of potting shelves closes automatically behind her. The green glow of the night-light warms the room.

She falls to her knees. Closes her eyes. Clenches her fists. And roars.

She is a schoolteacher. She teaches Geography to sixteen-year-olds. She loves her job, she is fond of most of her students. She has a boyfriend who has two children from his previous marriage. His ex-wife is trolling her on Facebook under a pseudonym that makes them both laugh. Her father has Parkinson's. Her mother has a ceramic bell collection. Her hobby is going to comedy festivals. She loves laughing. She loves surrounding herself with happy people, she loves her students with strong personalities, is grateful for the clowns even when they disturb the class. When she laughs, everyone hears it and knows it is her. It is loud and it is real, it comes from the depths of her belly. She is funny and she knows it. She could easily eat beef lasagne every single day for the rest of her life.

She has a secret.

While everybody is taking a mini break she closes the classroom door. She goes to the enormous map of the world on the wall and peels back Botswana, her grandparents' birthplace, to reveal a key panel. The secret code – the coordinates of Botswana – is followed by an audible click as the map of the world and the wall pushes forward an inch and slides to the left, revealing a small room inside.

The walls are lined in corkboard with maps pinned to them. The idea that there is more to life than just this room, in just this school, in just this state, in just this country, in just this continent, helps her. Behind the corkboard is soundproofing.

She waits for the wall with the map to close behind her and the room glows with a hot orange.

She takes a deep breath.

And roars.

She works in housekeeping in a five-star luxury hotel. Her supervisor has halitosis. She has a nine-month-old baby girl at home who is being cared for by her grandmother. Her mother relies too much on alcohol to get her through the days. Her mother is also the funniest person she knows and makes her laugh louder than anybody else ever could. Just out of school, she likes the freedom of going to work, doing something for herself. She loves the feeling of returning home, seeing the gummy smile and the chubby hands that reach out to her.

There is a guy who works in the butcher shop opposite her flat that she can't stop thinking about. She can see him from her bedroom window. She can't wipe the silly smile off her face every time she thinks of him. Her baby girl is the same when she sees him. A sure sign. She has eaten more meat this month than ever before.

She has three more rooms on the floor to clean and then she is finished. She sometimes takes the hotel chocolates that guests leave behind and places them on her mother's pillow, turning down her bed covers. Her mother loves it.

She has two secrets. Nobody knows who the father of her baby is. And this.

She steps into the storeroom cupboard and moves a box of hotel shampoo bottles to the side, revealing a secret key panel. She types in the secret code: her school locker combination.

This is followed by an audible click and the shelving containing the white fluffy towels slides open revealing a small room. It smells of fresh linen, a summer breeze, just-washed smell. She takes her shoes off and steps inside. The ground is soft cotton, the walls are draped in it too. Behind the draping is soundproofing.

Once the wall of towels closes behind her, encasing her in a lilac glow and the scent of lavender, she breathes in and out slowly.

She opens her mouth.

And roars.

She is a paediatric nurse. She doesn't have any children yet but she hopes to. Her desperate night shifts make it difficult for her to meet anyone, let alone synchronize a life schedule with someone. She lives for her job, her babies mean the world to her. She thinks about them all the time, even off the clock. Those who had made it, those who hadn't. At night, while sleeping, she sometimes hears the cries and giggles of those she has lost, she feels soft marshmallow skin touch against her face and her bedroom smells of baby powder. When she wakes the smell is gone.

She is a beautiful piano player. She is a terrible drinker.

For some unknown reason, she has the overwhelming need to flash her underwear at people, which her friends find hilarious. She has an enormous crush on a married man. Out of guilt, she has just followed his wife on Twitter. Every time she finishes reading a book, she gives it to the homeless man who sits on her street. He never says thank you. She doesn't care. Her favourite scent is the sweet manure on her family farm where she grew up. She finds that she adores the things that most people hate.

She has endless patience at work. The parents of her babies always call her an angel. She feels claustrophobic when standing in line. She loves when her father sings. She is almost 100 per cent sure that her brother is gay. She doesn't think his wife knows. At least five times a day she wonders if she should talk to him about it.

She has a secret.

In the nurses' sleeping quarters, once she is certain she is alone, she draws the blue curtain around her bed for privacy. Sitting on the bed, she reaches for the remote that controls the bed and presses the up and down buttons at the same time to release the top drawer of the bedside locker. Inside is a keypad and her secret code is the bracelet ID of the last little baby she lost.

The wall backing the bed slides open, revealing a small dark room. She climbs over the headboard and enters; the room smells of baby powder. The floor and walls are soft and fleece, like a teddy bear. The closing of the wall triggers a baby blue night-light to illuminate the darkness.

She lies on the floor, curled in the foetal position.

And roars.

She is a stay-at-home mother with four children under the age of three. She loves her children. She lives for bedtime, for those two hours she can sit on the couch with a bottle of wine. Her favourite sound is their conversations with one another. Nobody makes her laugh more than her children.

She is excellent at appearing to listen to people when she isn't. She loves to buy gifts for people all year round; when she sees something suitable for somebody, she is compelled to buy it. She loves driving fast. Sex with her husband is her favourite pastime. She likes watching porn. She has never hated before but is dangerously close to hating her brother's wife. She loves dancing. She avoids confrontation. She is socially very awkward. She is clumsy. She's lost five sets of house keys in one year.

Supermarket shopping makes her feel hot and angry. When she jogs she accidentally pees herself. She has given up jogging. She is never late. She is always cheerful. She is an excellent mother. She always burns toast. She doesn't know how to make poached eggs. She has a beautiful singing voice. Her hair is her best asset.

Everybody always says to her, 'I don't know how you do it.'

She has a secret.

When the four children are down for a nap, she goes to

their playroom and turns the handle of the Jack-in-the-Box. When Jack springs up, it wirelessly activates the key panel on the wall among the boys' Transformers.

She keys in the code: 6969, which she knows is immature but it makes her laugh, and the Transformer wall slides open to reveal a small room.

Inside, the walls are padded with red leather. She loves the feel of it.

No night-lights come on when the wall of Transformers closes behind her; she prefers the dark.

After feeling her way along the cool leather of the wall to the corner of the room, she slides to the floor, and stares into the darkness for a moment, settling her mind.

She opens her mouth.

And roars.

Find out more about Cecelia,
her books, competitions, events
and much more!

www.cecelia-ahern.com

Meet Cecelia

"The thread that links my work is in capturing that transitional period in people's lives. I'm drawn to writing about loss, to characters that have fallen and who feel powerless in their lives. I am fascinated and inspired by the human spirit, by the fact that no matter how hopeless we feel and how dark life can be, we do have the courage, strength and bravery to push through our challenging moments. We are the greatest warriors in our own stories. I like to catch my characters as they fall, and bring them from low to high. My characters push through and as a result evolve, become stronger and better equipped for the next challenge that life brings. I like to mix dark with light, sadness with humour, always keeping a balance, and always bringing the story to a place of hope."

Find Out More